A DEATH AT HIS MAJESTY'S

THE SIMON SAMPSON MYSTERIES

DAVID C. DAWSON

PARK CREEK PUBLISHING

ISBN: 978-1-9162573-9-9

Cover design by: Garrett Leigh @ Black Jazz Design

A DEATH AT HIS MAJESTY'S

The stage is set for murder

It's the summer of 1929 and there's a serial killer on the streets of London.

Bodies of young women are dumped at the stage door of London's theatres.

Noël Coward's assistant Florence Miles, known to her close friends as Bill, is dragged into the investigation when the body of her former secret lover is found outside His Majesty's Theatre.

Bill forms an unlikely alliance with the *Chronicle* newspaper's senior crime reporter Simon Sampson. Together they discover that the killer has friends in high places...

This is the prequel to the LAMBDA finalist *A Death in Berlin*. It explores the secret world of the 1920s, a time when your sexuality could make you a lawbreaker. When gay men and women were constantly on their guard, careful about how they presented themselves in a hostile society.

A Death At His Majesty's is the first of a series that brings together Bill and Simon and follows them as they embark on a series of sleuthing adventures.

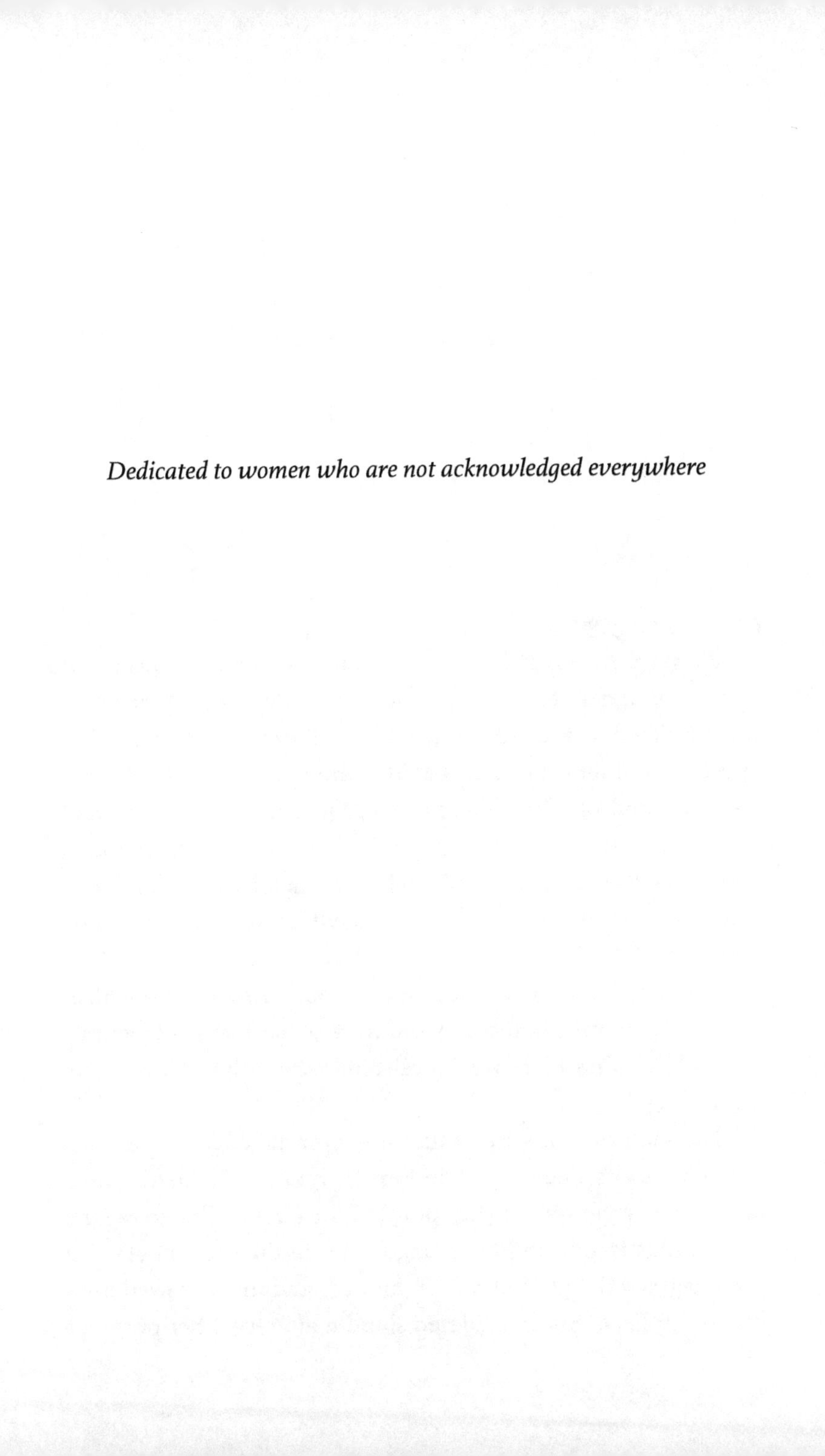

Dedicated to women who are not acknowledged everywhere

1

London, July 1929

Florence Miles, or Bill to her friends, was ready to commit murder. It wasn't for the first time in the last month she had contemplated the deed. When she reflected further on her murderous intent she realised the thought had been in her mind, on and off, for almost a year. On one occasion she had spent an entire evening on an ingenious plan involving a cocktail shaker, a mojito, and a white oleander leaf. It had been cunning. A simple death, the cause of which would be virtually undetectable.

The daydream gave her a delicious frisson of devilish delight. But it was shattered by the voice of her intended victim.

"Calling Miss Florence Miles! Bill! Where the hell are you, my darling?"

The man shouting her name stood on the edge of the stage of His Majesty's Theatre in London's Haymarket. He held a large cardboard megaphone to his mouth. It was impossible to see the detail of his face from her vantage point in the dress circle. But she imagined the glint of fury in his eyes and the furrowed lines on his forehead. She considered standing to reveal her presence but chose instead to sit back in her seat, take out a cigarette, and light it.

The fact he was currently considered the most successful and celebrated playwright in the world meant little to her. As far as she was concerned, Noël Coward had become a pompous arse.

"Bill! I need you. Stop hiding. This is a disaster, my darling." His tone changed from commanding to plaintive.

As Noël Coward's personal assistant it was Bill's duty to attend to his every demand. Now they were less than thirty-six hours away from opening night his demands were constant and ever more outrageous. She took another drag on her cigarette. Damn the man. He was impossible.

"I think I saw her go up to the dress circle."

Rhodri Williams—that bloody stage manager drafted in from the opera house in Covent Garden at Noël's insistence. Rhodri had grassed her up. The irritating Welshman hated her. And the feeling would be mutual if she gave him a moment's thought. Bill brushed cigarette ash from the lapel of her trouser suit and reluctantly hauled herself to her feet.

"Noël, darling!" She waved her cigarette in salute. "Don't be so hysterical. I'm right here. I needed somewhere quiet so I could go through the list of backstage visitors for opening night."

She checked the time on the Cartier wristwatch Noël had given her last Christmas. It was coming up to midday. Two hours into the rehearsal and they were still only on the opening number. It was going to be a very long day. Bill picked up her notebook and a sheaf of papers and headed back to the stage.

Today's technical rehearsal was for *Bitter Sweet*, Noël's first three-act operetta. The show had already opened in Manchester and run for three weeks. It had been an instant hit both with the critics and the audiences. This transfer to the stage of His

Majesty's Theatre should have been a simple process of bedding in the replacement cast and orchestra members and adapting the production to the larger space.

But nothing seemed to work as it should. Scenery and props were either missing or in the wrong place, the members of the orchestra were playing as if their music was upside down, and the lighting technicians were on an almost permanent tea break. The chaos was one of the reasons Bill had escaped to the dress circle. The other was to contemplate her future career.

It increasingly seemed that working for Noël was no longer an option.

The Master himself greeted her coldly when she arrived on stage. "So good of you to join us, my dear. We have so much time on our hands. I have simply *no* idea what to do with myself."

"Which particular disaster have you summoned me to deal with?" Bill ignored his sarcasm. "The blind follow spot operator? The deaf orchestra? Or perhaps the new chorus boys with three left feet? I'd always thought creative conundrums were your department. I'm strictly practical."

"Then kindly be 'practical' and tell me where the bloody props girl is," Noël replied icily. "My cast can't be creative when the practicals are absent. The marchioness can't express an attack of the vapours if she doesn't have her fan. And poor Claude can *hardly* be expected to serve drinks without a damn tray."

He spun on his heels and walked to the stairs at the edge of the stage. Without turning he snapped his fingers above his head. "Deal with it, Bill."

Someone chuckled behind her. It was Rhodri Williams.

"And what do you find so damned funny?" Bill asked.

The stage manager waved his clipboard at the chaotic scenes on stage.

"Maybe it's a little too ambitious, Miss Miles?" His Welsh

accent lingered on the middle syllable of 'ambitious'. "For those who've only performed cabaret and revue shows up to now this must all be a bit unnerving." Again the extended emphasis on the middle syllable. 'Un-neerv-ing'.

"Don't get all high and mighty opera house with me, Williams." Bill pointed her cigarette at him. "The Palace Theatre, Manchester has managed to stage *Bitter Sweet* perfectly well over the last three weeks without any of this palaver. And the people of Manchester loved us. As did the reviewers. They were ecstatic."

She narrowed her eyes and inhaled a lungful of smoke. "Noël insisted on bringing you in for this London run. God knows why. The only thing he knows about you is that you've been at the opera house. What did you do there? Make the tea?"

Rhodri Williams's shoulders stiffened and he turned his head to look sideways at her. "I'll have you know I stage-managed *Aida* last season. A cast of sixty-seven plus five horses and a camel."

"Did you lose any of them?"

"Certainly not."

"Then why can't you keep track of the company for *Bitter Sweet*? Where's Miss Lyon?"

"The props girl? I have absolutely no idea." He flipped over the pages on his clipboard to a sheet of paper containing a list of names. "She's one of yours who transferred from Manchester, isn't she?" He nodded. "That makes sense now. Unreliable."

"How dare you," Bill snapped. "Maureen is one of the best stage hands, property assistants, and all-round good eggs I've ever known. She's always been punctual and I will *not* have you call her unreliable."

Rhodri Williams shrugged. "Then where is she?"

It was a good question.

Bill pushed past two members of the cast who were

complaining loudly about the delays to the rehearsal and went into the wings.

"Gertie darling, have you seen Maureen this morning?"

A tiny woman wearing a smart jacket cut in the style of Coco Chanel and a pair of pince-nez perched on her nose shrugged and shook her head. "I've no idea, Miss Miles. I know she was here late last night setting all the props after they'd finished building the set. Perhaps she overslept."

"But it's nearly midday," Bill protested. "Isn't she still living in Notting Hill?"

"Yes, she shares that rather pretty mews cottage with Miss Casewell."

"Well she hasn't got far to travel then. I wonder what's happened. Sometimes I do worry about her continuing to live there. It's a nice little place but such an awfully rough neighbourhood. Have you telephoned?"

"Several times. But there's no answer."

"Such a shame Miss Casewell isn't on this production as well. She could have looked out for Maureen."

"But you remember why, don't you?" Gertie leaned in to whisper. "She can't bear Noël. Refuses to work with him ever again. They had the most awful row when she worked on *This Year of Grace* at the Pavilion last year. I think she got close to killing him at one point."

Bill nodded. "Miss Casewell's not the only one who'd like to do that." She looked around at the large number of people apparently standing idle in the wings. "Can we spare anyone to pop over to Notting Hill and find out if Maureen's still in the land of nod? Noël's getting awfully upset about the missing props."

"I heard." The diminutive Gertie reached up to tap a tall, rather emaciated youth on the shoulder. "Mr Penny. I need you to run an errand. Urgently."

She gave the young man the address in Notting Hill and a few pennies for the bus fare.

Bill watched him leave. He seemed so thin she feared he might blow away in a puff of wind. She turned back to Gertie. "Now my dear. Who do we have left with the gumption to stand in for Maureen on props stage left before Noël throws another absolute tantrum?"

Mr Penny returned almost an hour later. He reported he had spoken to Miss Casewell at the mews cottage in Notting Hill. She had not seen Maureen ever since she had left for the theatre on the morning before.

Shortly after he had delivered his message a bell rang at one o'clock and the company broke for lunch.

"I see no reason why we should stop," Noël said to Bill sulkily as she lit his cigarette. "We've not even got to the end of the first act. I know exactly what's going to happen this afternoon. They'll return with full bellies and be even more sluggish for the rest of the day. And if we do finally get going we'll only have to stop again for bloody tea."

"You can't starve them, my darling," Bill admonished him. "A hungry company is an unhappy company. I seem to remember you telling me that when we first met. You were starring in *The Constant Nymph* at the time, don't you remember? There was always a plate of something in your dressing room."

"I was very good in that play." Noël took her arm and squeezed it with what could have been either affection or control. They walked up the centre aisle of the stalls. "Now. Where are we going to eat?"

"We've no time to go out," Bill replied briskly. "I've had Fortnum's deliver sandwiches. You've got a press call, remember?" She looked at her watch and quickened their pace. "Hurry up. We're due in the dress circle bar."

Noël stopped and released her arm abruptly.

"A press call? On the day of the bloody tech run? Whose damn fool idea was that?"

"Yours." Bill turned and glowered at him. "You said there was no other time you could fit it in. I thought it was idiotic myself—"

"Then why didn't you say something?"

"I did. And you told me to stop interfering and do my bloody job."

"Do you mean I have to sit and eat oysters and crab sandwiches in front of that scurrilous lot with their poison pens and badly fitting hats? It's simply *too* terrifying."

"No oysters, my dear. It's July."

"Do you have no new good news to bring me?" Noël raised a hand to his forehead and closed his eyes. "What happened to that girl who was supposed to be looking after the properties stage left? Have you sacked her?"

"Certainly not." Bill tugged on his arm and they resumed their walk to meet the press. "And I will not have you speak ill of Maureen. Strangely there's been no sign of her. Apparently she never returned home last night."

"Probably still in bed with some chorus boy. Or girl." Noël stopped suddenly. "Oh, my dear Bill. Didn't you have a fling with her last year?"

"It was nothing of consequence." Bill pulled at his arm again. "We must keep moving. You're already late."

"If it was nothing of consequence then you'll have no qualms in dismissing her from the company," Noël replied briskly. "I really don't have time for part-timers like her. Don't let me see her again on this production."

•　•　•

Noël's fractious manner evaporated as they reached the entrance to the dress circle bar. It was as if he had stepped on stage and had instantly been caught in the follow spot. He beamed at the crowd of reporters, waved a hand above his head in greeting, and sauntered into the midst of the group. Angry as she was at his callous attitude to Maureen, Bill had to admit he was a consummate professional.

"Gentlemen." He stopped in front of Lady Banscome, the society correspondent from *Country Life* magazine. He took her hand and kissed it. "And ladies of the press," he continued. "My profound apologies for keeping you all waiting."

He swept round to face the reporters and a small clearing appeared in front of him as they stepped back. Despite her frustration with her boss Bill still felt a tingle of excitement when she saw him working a crowd. The way he could change the mood of a room and ensure all attention was focused on him. He was like a master puppeteer, knowing exactly which string to pull and when for maximum effect.

"Thank you for generously turning up here this lunchtime on the eve of the London premiere of *Bitter Sweet*. I could tell you endlessly what a brilliant, scintillating, vivacious, thoroughly entertaining production it is"—He paused to allow a ripple of polite laughter to spread through the gathering—"But you will have already read that in the glowing reviews from those who saw it in Manchester. And I can promise you our aim is to improve on perfection for its London launch tomorrow. I will say nothing more and instead invite you to ask any questions you choose to fire at me. Except about my love life. That is *never* to be discussed in public. It would be too scandalous."

Again a polite ripple of laughter. Several hands shot up.

Someone tapped Bill on the shoulder.

"Miss Miles?"

It was Samuel Raven, the box office manager. A man with a sunken chest and a permanent expression of fear on his face.

"What is it, Raven?"

"The police are here. Can you come with me immediately, please?"

"Don't be absurd." Bill indicated the crowd of press. "Can't you see we're in the middle of something far more important? Get Treadbold to see to it. He is the bloody theatre manager after all."

"Mr Treadbold is with them now." Samuel Raven's expression had changed from fear to terror, but he stood his ground as he delivered his message again. "But he specifically wants you to speak to them. You really must come."

"Why? What on earth has happened?"

"I think it's best the detective sergeant tells you himself." Raven shook his head. "It's a terrible business. Mr. Treadbold is very upset. He fears we may not be able to open tomorrow night."

2

"What's this all about, Treadbold?" Bill asked when she entered the theatre manager's office. "I'm supposed to be with Noël at the press conference right now."

Cameron Treadbold was a large man who enjoyed long lunches at the Savoy Grill accompanied by a bottle of claret and a post-prandial brandy. He shoved his chair back and stood with difficulty.

"Gentlemen," boomed Treadbold. "Allow me to introduce Miss Miles, Noël Coward's secretary—"

"Personal assistant," Bill interrupted.

"Of course." Treadbold took out a large handkerchief and blew his nose loudly. "Miss Miles, this is Detective Sergeant Daniels and Constable Smith from Scotland Yard. Bad business this. Very bad business."

"What is?" Bill asked.

"Miss Miles?" Detective Sergeant Daniels was perched on the corner of Treadbold's desk. He stood and doffed his hat to Bill. "The body of a woman has been discovered by the stage door of this theatre—"

"Good God." Bill reached into her trouser pocket for a cigarette case.

The constable pulled out a chair tucked under the front of the desk. "Would you like to sit, madam?"

"No thank you, my dear." Bill waved her cigarette at him. "But I'm in desperate need of a light."

The detective sergeant rummaged in his pocket, took out a box of matches, and lit one.

"Thank you." Bill exhaled a cloud of smoke. "Do you know who the poor lady is?"

"Sadly, they do." Treadbold blew his nose again. "It appears to be a member of the *Bitter Sweet* company."

"We believe the deceased is a Miss Maureen Lyon," added the detective sergeant.

"Good Lord." Bill reached for the chair the constable had offered and sank into it.

"Did you know her, Miss Miles?" asked the detective sergeant.

"I do." Bill took a long drag on her cigarette. "I mean, I did. She was a very reliable member of our company. And an extremely good friend."

"When did you last see her?"

Lobster paste sandwiches and caviar. That was what they had eaten, lying on Bill's bed in the Savoy Hotel last New Year. Giggling guiltily for drinking too much champagne at three o'clock in the afternoon when they both knew they had to be ready for a grand reception organised in Noël's honour in a little over two hours. The year had gone well for the theatre company and Noël had generously booked Bill into the Savoy. He had even arranged for the caviar and champagne to be delivered to her room before the festivities began. It was the time Bill had run her finger gently over the heart-shaped birthmark at the top of Maureen's thigh. When they had talked about what might have been.

"Miss Miles? Did you hear what I asked?"

The detective sergeant's question jolted Bill from her daydream.

"I'm sorry detective." She reached across to the desk, flicked the ash from the end of her cigarette into an ashtray, and raised it to her lips. "How did she…?" She paused to inhale. "What happened?"

"I'm afraid I can't tell you much at the moment," replied the detective sergeant.

"She was strangled, Miss Miles." The theatre manager's voice boomed across the desk. "Murdered by strangulation. The murderer used a sash cord of all things. Her lifeless body hidden behind the rubbish bins stored close by the stage door." Cameron Treadbold took a large cigar from a wooden box on his desk and trimmed one end with a penknife. "Gruesome. Poor Mr Cheffins the caretaker found her when he went on his regular rat inspection late this morning—"

"Thank you, Mr Treadbold," the detective sergeant interrupted. "I think Miss Miles can be spared the details."

"Are you sure it's Maureen?" Bill asked. "Has anyone identified…?"

"Not formally," replied the detective sergeant. "An opened letter addressed to Miss Lyon was found in her possession. We would be grateful if someone from the company might help us with confirming her identity."

It took Bill a moment to realise the statement was more of a question directed at her.

"Me?" She shook her head. "Isn't there anyone else?"

"You are the de facto company manager for *Bitter Sweet*." Treadbold pointed his cigar at her. "I'm sure you wouldn't want to delegate such a ghastly task to one of your junior staff."

"Thank you for your kind assistance, Mr Treadbold." Bill glowered at him. "Presumably this is why you sent for me? No intention of offering yourself to assist the police in their inquiries at your theatre?"

"But I have no idea what the dear lady looks like," protested the theatre manager. "She's a member of Mr Coward's company, not mine. Unless you intend to hand the gruesome task to him?"

"Don't be absurd," snapped Bill. "Noël has quite enough on his plate as it is. Besides, he's in the middle of a press conference at the moment."

"The press are here?" Treadbold slapped his hand to his forehead. "My God, this is a disaster."

"I told you a moment ago, if you'd been listening," Bill replied. "That's where Noël is now."

"We mustn't let the press know about this." Treadbold turned to Detective Sergeant Daniels. "You don't have any more of your chaps in uniform roaming the building as we speak?"

Daniels shook his head. "Apart from Constable Smith and myself, there's one other officer standing guard over the body by the stage door. An ambulance will be here shortly to remove it to a mortuary. I've called for more assistance but the summer season has brought out the pickpockets. The force is pretty thinly stretched at the moment."

"My dear detective sergeant." The theatre manager's voice was plaintive. "We're on the eve of opening what may prove to be Mr Coward's finest piece of work yet. We can't have the theatre swarming with police officers. If the press get wind of this there'll be scandal. Outrage. I implore you, dear man, to keep as low a profile as possible. At least until we are clear of the opening night."

The detective sergeant scratched his head. "I'm going to need to interview everyone in the building—"

"Everyone?" Treadbold wiped his hand across his glistening

brow. "Surely you don't need to interview the press? They only got here about twenty minutes ago. You told me that the poor lady's been lying out there for much longer."

"Do you mean to say you're going to interview the whole cast?" Bill asked. "With the stage crew and orchestra that's over a hundred people. You do realise we're in the middle of a vital rehearsal. We open tomorrow night."

"And I'm investigating a murder, madam." The detective sergeant took a pipe from his coat pocket and poked at the contents of the bowl with his finger. "Some things are more important than the theatre."

"There's no need to take that tone with me, my good man," Bill snapped.

"You didn't tell me when you last saw Miss Lyon." The detective sergeant replenished his pipe from a tobacco pouch and struck a match. "Perhaps you'd be good enough to answer my question."

"I left the theatre about eight o'clock yesterday evening. She was still here then, organising the props."

"And what happened when she didn't turn up for work this morning?"

"I sent a young lad round to her house." Bill stubbed out her cigarette and took another from her cigarette case. She leaned forward in anticipation of the detective sergeant lighting it for her. "Thank you. She shares a little place in Notting Hill with Miss Casewell, another member of the company."

"Why didn't Miss Casewell raise the alarm? Surely they would travel to the theatre together."

"Miss Casewell isn't working on this production," Bill replied. "They may share a house but they lead separate lives. They're not responsible for each other."

"How well did you know Miss Lyon?"

"I told you we're very good friends." Bill exhaled smoke through her nostrils. "I mean, we *were* very good friends. Why?"

"Does she have any next of kin?"

"Not in London. If there is anyone they're down in the darkest parts of the west of England. I think she lived in Bath or somewhere equally provincial. She moved to London to work in the theatre. It was her passion."

"I see." The detective sergeant drew on his pipe and the tobacco embers glowed red in the bowl. "Well. If you're ready perhaps you would accompany me to the stage door to help identify the body."

"And I shall accompany Miss Miles." Treadbold shoved his chair back against the wall and struggled to his feet. "I have decided on reflection that the lady should not be expected to do such a dreadful deed alone." His imposing figure towered over the room.

"Do sit down, Cameron." Bill waved her cigarette at him dismissively. "You're making the place untidy. This sudden spirit of gallantry is a bit late. Don't patronise me. Just because I'm a woman doesn't mean I'm incapable of identifying a corpse without getting a fit of the vapours."

She reached forward and knocked the ash from her cigarette into the ashtray. "I'm ready, detective sergeant."

"But, Miss Miles—"

"Enough, Cameron." Bill stood and grasped the back of the chair as she felt a moment of lightheadedness. Maybe it was the cigarette. Maybe she had got to her feet too quickly. "Shall we do it now? Let's get it over with."

"Miss Miles." Treadbold slumped back into his chair and wiped the sweat from his brow again. His face was ashen. "Are you sure you don't want me to accompany you?"

"Thank you but no," Bill replied. "You don't look like you'd survive the ordeal and the detective sergeant hardly wants another body to deal with."

"Mr Treadbold could help with getting the members of the company together ready for me to interview them." Detective Sergeant Daniels suggested.

"Oh God, no," Bill said before Treadbold could respond. "I'd rather he didn't. I need to talk to Noël first. Wait until he's finished with the press. He should be the person to tell the company about this. It's better coming from him."

Treadbold's face showed a man humiliated.

"Don't pout like that, Cameron darling. It doesn't become a man in your position." Bill stubbed her cigarette out in the ashtray in front of Treadbold and smiled. "I'm sure there'll be something useful for you to do. We just haven't managed to think of it yet."

Despite her show of bravado in the theatre manager's office, Bill felt a sickening sensation in her stomach as Detective Sergeant Daniels led her round the side of the theatre to the narrow alleyway beside the stage door. A uniformed constable saluted her and stood aside to reveal a blanket covering a body-shaped form on the cobblestones.

The detective sergeant squatted down and took hold of the top edges of the blanket. "Are you ready Miss Miles?"

Bill took a deep breath. "As ready as anyone could ever be for this."

Daniels gently pulled back the blanket to reveal the face of someone Bill had once been intimate with. And yet it was no longer that person. The violent death had grotesquely distorted the memory of a woman who had been gentle, slightly shy, but loving. She could clearly see the thin sash cord used as the murder weapon cutting deep into Maureen's neck. Bill looked away.

"Yes, that's Maureen." She spoke softly to keep her voice steady, not wanting to betray the emotion she felt. "I'll go and talk to Noël for you. This is going to set the rehearsal back hours you know."

At two thirty that afternoon the entire company and cast of *Bitter Sweet* sat in the stalls of His Majesty's Theatre. A loud buzz of conversation filled the auditorium. Bill leaned against a piece of scenery in the wings with her arms folded. She couldn't bring herself to join the rest of the company.

"How are you feeling, my dear?" Noël rested his hand on her shoulder. "My offer stands. If you want to go home I quite understand. After I make this announcement we may find there are few of our company who wish to stay on today."

Bill shook her head.

"Very well, my dear. Wish me luck." Noël squeezed her shoulder and strode onto the stage. The buzz of conversation in the auditorium was silenced. Noël stood centre stage but said nothing for almost a minute. His shoulders were hunched as he looked out at the sea of faces watching him expectantly. His arms hung limply at his sides.

"My dear friends," he began finally. "My very dear friends. On the eve of what should be a thrilling first night here in London for all of us I stand before you to impart the most *terrible* news." He raised his hand to wipe a tear from his eye. "I regret to tell you that one of our family, Miss Maureen Lyon has sadly...passed on."

The chatter in the auditorium began again. Noël raised his hand and the noise subsided.

"I'm afraid the news is much worse," he continued. "Miss Lyon has been murdered."

There was a loud collective gasp. A woman screamed. Voices were raised and this time it took far longer before Noël could continue.

"The police are here in the theatre. They wish to speak to all of us. That will undoubtedly play havoc with the rehearsal. But the police must do their job. And we must all help them. It is our duty as citizens and it is our duty to poor Miss Lyon."

Noël turned to the wings and beckoned Bill onto the stage.

"Miss Miles is drawing up a schedule to allow us to proceed with the rehearsal and support the police in the most efficient way we can. I understand this has come as a great shock to you. We are all shocked. Miss Lyon was a loyal and hardworking member of the company. She was a consummate professional and she will be sorely missed. If anyone of you feels unable to continue with the rehearsal and wishes to leave then you are free to do so once you have been interviewed by the police."

He looked out into the auditorium. No one said anything. Noël raised a hand again to wipe a tear.

"My dear friends," he continued. "We will be resolute in the face of this tragedy. Nothing will stand in the way of *Bitter Sweet's* triumphant arrival in London. We will dedicate the opening night to the memory of Miss Maureen Lyon. We shall never forget her."

Someone shouted "hear hear". A ripple of applause grew in intensity. Within a few moments everyone was on their feet applauding. Noël put his arm on Bill's shoulder.

"You see?" he said into her ear above the noise. "She was much loved. And I also recall just how much you once loved her."

Bill tried to speak but the words caught in her throat. All she could do was mouth "thank you" to him.

The company continued rehearsing in a sombre yet far more purposeful way. The chaos of the morning was supplanted by a resolute determination to get through the show as quickly as possible. Even with the distraction of the police interviews they managed to cover everything crucial to the opening night.

At around eight o'clock in the evening, the last few members of the cast had left. Only a few of the backstage crew remained to make final adjustments for the following day.

Bill turned down Noël's offer of cocktails at the Savoy saying she had a slight headache. She went upstairs to the circle bar where she found a quiet corner, lit a cigarette, and sobbed quietly.

Noël's almost overwhelming kindness had forced her to rethink her resolution to resign. True, he could be an absolute beast to work with. But it was at moments like this she realised how lucky she was to be working with the world's leading playwright and performer. Perhaps her next career move was not a decision to be made hastily.

"Hello?"

She looked up to see an armchair at the far end of the bar with its high back facing her. The man who had spoken leaned around the side of the chair and smiled at her.

"Are you all right?"

Bill turned away and wiped the tears from her cheeks with a handkerchief.

The man stood and walked towards her.

"Can I help in any way?"

"I'm perfectly fine. Really." Bill sniffed loudly and stuffed the handkerchief back into her trouser pocket.

"You don't seem fine." He was tall and wore a well-tailored suit and a fedora. His voice both solicitous and reassuring. He was probably in his late twenties, clean-shaven, and with unusually long eyelashes. If Bill had had any desires for a man then she would have been attracted to this one.

She brushed a spill of cigarette ash from her lapels and stood awkwardly. Her chair tipped over as her legs banged against it and she stumbled forward.

The man grasped her arms to steady her and they fell into an unintentional romantic clinch. Bill recovered her balance and pulled away.

"I'm sorry, it's—"

"No, no. I was only trying to—"

"Of course. You're most kind but—"

"I didn't intend—"

"I know. I mean, I'm sure you didn't—"

"It's only that you were—"

An excruciating silence settled between them. Bill cleared her throat.

"Oh, for God's sake." She held out her hand. "My name's, Miles. Florence Miles. But everybody calls me Bill."

"Really?" The man took her hand and squeezed it. "Then I shall call you Bill. My name's Sampson. Simon Sampson."

3

"The Salisbury?"

Bill held back on the pavement outside the Salisbury pub in Covent Garden when Simon opened the door for her.

"Anything wrong?" he asked.

"No. Nothing." Bill was confused. Somehow the Salisbury was not the sort of place she had expected this man to take her.

"Would you prefer to go somewhere else?"

"God, no." Bill had been in the pub only twice before. Both times were with men who were colloquially called 'other' by polite society. "Is this your local?"

"Sadly not," he replied. "But I took a guess that you might not be judgmental of the people in here. And I thought it might be somewhere you'd feel less judged yourself. You see, it's a place where a man like me can be himself."

Now she understood.

The Salisbury was only moderately busy and Bill was able to find a table while Simon went to the bar. As in her previous visits she was the only woman in the pub. Her short Eton crop hairstyle and navy-blue trouser suit allowed her to blend in with refreshing anonymity. In the world outside the doors of this safe haven she was frequently questioned and occasionally ridiculed about her refusal to wear a skirt. Here, no one passed comment.

Bill lit a cigarette and watched Simon chat to the barman and a handful of customers. He was at ease and clearly among friends. The fact that he had confidently brought her to this particular pub meant he must have sensed Bill was an ally. As such she was looking forward to getting to know the handsome man who had come to her rescue when grief had overwhelmed her.

"Your gin and tonic, Miss Miles." Simon put their drinks on the table and sat opposite her. "I do beg your pardon. I should say Bill, shouldn't I?" He took a sip from his beer. "You'll have to explain why."

"Do I really?" Bill raised her glass in salute. "How boring. Can't I remain a person of mystery? Rather like yourself."

"Oh, there's nothing mysterious about me." Simon laughed. "I'm awfully ordinary. Unlike you."

"Yes, I *am* extraordinary." Bill placed her hand against her cheek in the pose of a film star.

"So please explain," Simon continued. "Why adopt a man's name and wear men's clothing."

"Does it offend you?"

"Not at all." Simon shook his head. "I admire you for your courage—"

"Piffle."

"I beg your pardon?"

"I'm sorry." Bill took a packet of Senior Service from her pocket and offered it to Simon. "I can be a little direct sometimes. Cigarette?"

"I don't." Simon replied. "But please go ahead."

"I fully intend to." Bill took out a cigarette and lit it. "But as for courage. That's baloney. This is 1929 for goodness sake. Victorian puritanism is long gone. A month ago young women under the age of thirty voted in the general election for the first time—"

"Ah, the Flapper Election," Simon interjected.

"Such an insulting term." Bill dismissed his response with a wave of her hand. "Bloody newspapers and their gutter headlines. If journalists had their way, women would still be chained to the kitchen sink all day and forced to wear skirts that covered their ankles."

"That's a little harsh." Simon fanned away a cloud of smoke from Bill's cigarette. "Newspapers only reflect the majority sentiment of the population. And despite what you say about the end of Victorian puritanism, I'm afraid most people in Britain are rather attached to traditional values. They don't want change. Newspapers print what people want to read."

"And do you think that's right?" Bill leaned back and gestured to the suit she was wearing. "Do you think I'm wrong to display myself in these clothes?"

"*I* don't." Simon nodded towards the bar. "And you know full well that none of the men in this bar think you're wrong either. That's why I brought you here."

"I thought it was for your benefit," Bill replied. "A moment ago you told me it's where you can be yourself."

"It is," Simon agreed. "But I also want you to be able to relax. And given the emotional state you were in when I found you—"

"Well really," Bill protested. "I had good reason to be."

"I'm sure that you did." Simon replied. "It's in no way a criticism. But I thought you'd want to be somewhere where people wouldn't stare at you in the way they might normally do."

Bill took a lungful of smoke and exhaled slowly.

"You're a very perceptive young man." She leaned forward and tapped the ash from her cigarette into the ashtray. "It's true I often get stared at. But do you know what? Normally I don't give a fig." She leaned back again. Tell me, Mr Simon Sampson. Given that you're so confident that you've got the measure of me, let me ask you a question. Have you ever been to the Black Cat café in Soho?"

"I may have been." Simon's face flushed crimson. "I don't rightly remember."

Bill laughed so loudly she almost dropped her cigarette. "I don't believe that for a second. You'd remember if you had. I was in there only the other night with a gentleman friend. Several of the men who sat around the tables were not only wearing women's clothing but they wore make-up as well. There was a very pretty boy with bright red hair. Quentin something or other I believe he was called. Do you think those men are in the wrong?"

"I'm not sure." Simon picked up his beer and took a drink. The colour had faded from his cheeks but his knee jogged up and down in a sign of nervousness. "I'd certainly call them courageous. Maybe even foolhardy."

"But why?" Bill leaned forward and took a drink from her glass. "This evening we've come from a theatre where it's certainly been known for men to dress as women or women to dress as men. Why should that be any different?"

"Because it's the theatre I suppose." Simon set down his beer on the table and shuffled in his seat. "Look, I think we've strayed an awfully long way from the reason we came here in the first place. You were terribly upset when I met you at the theatre. Do you want to talk about it?"

Bill sat back and crossed her legs. She would far rather continue the interesting discussion they had begun. This man had an annoying manner of steering the conversation back to her.

"Maureen's death was a bit of a shock. It put me out of sorts. I'm fine now."

"Are you sure?" Simon's eyes were intense when he looked at her. She turned away. "Was it someone close?"

"No. Well, yes. Once." Bill stubbed out her cigarette and immediately lit another. "She was a sweet girl. Worked for us on *Bitter Sweet*. On props."

"'Us'?"

"I work for Mr Coward." Bill glanced back at Simon. He was still staring at her. "Noël Coward. I'm his personal assistant."

She waited for Simon to say something. But instead he raised his eyebrows as if inviting her to say more. She cleared her throat and looked away again.

"Was this woman's death unexpected?" Simon asked.

"You could say that."

The sight of Maureen lying on the cobblestones flooded back into Bill's mind. She remembered how the body lay brutally distorted, the face a ghastly colour. And the sash cord wrapped tight around her neck. Bill wished she had never agreed to go with the policeman to identify Maureen's body. Now she would be haunted by that last image. The memory of her former lover forever tainted by murder.

It surprised Bill their relationship could have left her with such a lasting sense of longing. She usually rejected any form of attachment. Independence was her watchword. That way she avoided the pain the messiness of relationships inevitably brought. Her eyes prickled with tears and she blew out a cloud of cigarette smoke to hide her display of emotion.

"I say, are you all right?" Simon leaned forward and placed a hand lightly on her arm. "What happened to this friend of yours?"

"She was killed." Bill took another lungful of smoke and exhaled it from the side of her mouth. "Strangled. With a sash cord from a window. It was all rather ghastly. I had to... identify her body."

"How terrible for you." Simon's hand remained on her arm. It was strangely reassuring. "Was that the woman who was found in the alley by the stage door? I heard people talking about it in the foyer."

Bill nodded. Her throat was tight. She dared not speak in case her voice cracked.

"The show opens tomorrow night, doesn't it?" Simon continued. "This must be an awful shock for the company. How is Mr Coward? Will he still go ahead?"

Before Bill could reply a tall woman got up clumsily and pushed her chair against Simon's. She turned to apologise, let out a cry, and leaned down from her great height to kiss him on either cheek.

"Simon, my boy. Thought it was you." The woman said. Simon hastily removed his hand from Bill's arm. "Haven't seen you in here in a while. I thought you usually went to the Fitzroy."

Simon smiled broadly. "Aunt Cynny. How good to see you."

Aunt Cynny whispered something in his ear.

"I'm terribly sorry. I meant to say Aunt Cynthia." Simon's face flushed and he gestured towards Bill. "May I introduce you to Miss Florence Miles? Miss Miles, this is my aunt, Miss Cynthia Buckingham. She's my mother's older sister and something frightfully important at the Home Office."

"Only five years older," retorted his aunt. She held out a hand to Bill who grasped it firmly. The fingers were long and slender. Everything about Miss Buckingham seemed elongated. "Very pleased to meet you Miss Miles. Do call me Cynthia."

"And please call me Bill. Everybody else does."

"Aunt Cynthia," Simon continued. "I'm surprised to find you in here. I wouldn't have thought it was your usual haunt either."

His aunt laughed. "Oh, that's this reprobate's fault." She gestured to the man who had been sat with her at the table and who was now taking his coat down from the coat hook. "We literally bumped into each other outside and decided to come in for a drink. This is John Sankey."

The man bowed his head slightly and held out his hand to Bill. "Enchanted to meet you," he said in a low voice.

Simon's aunt laughed and raised a finger to her lips. "John is also known as the new Lord Chancellor. But don't breathe a word of it just yet."

She glanced at Simon. "Oh, god. Now the cat's out the bag. Are you still writing for *The Chronicle*?"

"Um, yes." Simon turned away from Bill but she could see him shake his head vigorously at his aunt. "No need to talk about that just now."

"Why on earth not?" His aunt asked. "I thought you were so proud of working there. Aren't you senior crime reporter or something equally grand?"

"Something like that," Simon mumbled.

"You know I've been finding out more about this new wireless invention recently," his aunt continued. "Absolutely fascinating. The BBC has just written to us at the Home Office about extending its licence so it could start reporting the news. Why don't you have a go? You've always had excellent diction."

"Honestly, Aunt Cynny—I mean, Cynthia. I don't think there's a future in reading a newspaper over the ether." Bill could see the back of Simon's neck blush scarlet. "Anyway. We mustn't keep you."

"Oh, if you say so." Simon's aunt looked put out. She held out her long arms while her companion helped her on with her coat. "We'll bugger off then. We're going to the bar at the House of Lords. Safer place to meet, frankly. Especially for John."

Aunt Cynthia picked up a long silver-topped walking stick, tapped Simon lightly on the arm with it, and the couple departed.

"Well, there's a thing," Simon said. "What on earth was the new Lord Chancellor thinking having a drink in a place like this? I can understand Aunt Cynny as she's—well, 'other'. But the new Lord Chancellor? Rather indiscreet of him wouldn't you say?"

Bill picked up her packet of cigarettes from the table.

"I think it's high time I left as well."

"Oh, no," Simon protested. "We've got so much to talk about."

"You think so?" Bill took one last drag from her cigarette. "Because I don't. You failed to mention you were a reporter, didn't you? A senior crime reporter in fact. Instead you pretended to be concerned for me. Brought me in here, bought me a drink. 'An awful shock for the company' you said. 'How is Mr Coward?' you asked. 'Will he still go ahead?'" She reached across the table and stubbed out her cigarette in the ashtray.

"It's not like that at all—"

"How can I believe a word you're saying?" Bill kept focused on being angry. That way she could avoid letting slip her tears for Maureen. "What vile nonsense are we going to read in your paper tomorrow morning? *Noël Coward show hit by stage door killer*? Or are you going to really stoop to the gutter and call Maureen *a confirmed spinster*, or some other ghastly euphemism your crowd use—"

"Stop it, Bill." Simon held up his hands in supplication. "Do you seriously think I'd do something as low as that? You know what I am in my personal life. At least I've been honest with you about that." He gestured around him. "Look at where I brought you. Do you think I'd betray us? I know what the other newspapers write about people like us. That's never going to happen in *The Chronicle*."

Bill had been fully prepared to storm out of the pub. Instead, she took out a cigarette and lit it. "I don't remember seeing you with the other reporters at the press conference. Did you arrive late?"

Simon shook his head. "I try to avoid the press huddle. Everyone ends up with the same story."

"I'm sure you do something far more devious than the others." Bill sniffed. "You probably go snooping like some kind of furtive spy and hide the fact that you're really a reporter."

"It honestly wasn't like that." Simon resumed his seat at the table. "Look. I'm sorry I didn't tell you I'm a reporter. But when I met you it genuinely didn't seem important. You were upset and I simply wanted to help. Then we got talking and we were getting on so well. Somehow, I couldn't think of an easy way to tell you that I'm also with the *Chronicle* without you running off."

Bill wrinkled her nose. "Mr Sampson, that's the biggest load of balls I've ever heard. Why don't you buy me another drink and we'll start again. Except this time I'll be ready. And if you so much as breathe a word of a lie to me, I'll chop your balls off." She handed him her empty glass. "Both of them."

JOURNAL ENTRY 17 JULY 1929

I got her today. Finally. A lot easier than I expected.

It was lucky I still had that window sash cord that I picked up from the house in Sloane Square. Piece of good fortune that. Worked like a dream. It reminds me. I need to get some more to keep in readiness. I'll go down the hardware store in Marylebone next time I'm there and buy some. Cut it into lengths ready for the next ones.

At least that's one less pervert on the sin-sodden streets of London. Her breath of impurity was extinguished.

To be honest I thought it was going to be far harder than it was. She hardly put up anything like a struggle.

Not to begin with anyways.

She even seemed pleased to see me again after so long. Very chatty. If it wasn't for our family circumstances I'd almost say she was flirting with me.

Dirty little bitch.

Wearing men's trousers and cutting her hair like a young boy's.

I bet all the others I saw are going to be exactly like her.

Why doesn't anyone do anything about them? I've put in

my complaints to the relevant authorities before but they simply turn a blind eye. Tell me there's more important things for the police to be attending to.

Well, I don't agree.

And if they're not going to do anything about this abomination then maybe I will. 'Specially now I know how easy it is.

4

"Pull over here will you, please?"

The taxi was approaching the Metropolitan Railway station in St John's Wood. Bill leaned forward and tapped on the glass behind the driver's head. "Right here. I could do with a walk. I need to clear my head."

The cabbie pulled over. Bill paid him a generous tip and the cab headed off towards Finchley Road. She felt slightly guilty about the indulgence of a taxi but there was no avoiding it. She had stayed so late with Simon at the Salisbury that her last train had gone by the time she got to Baker Street.

Despite being a wealthy and generous man, Noël was very keen that company members used public transport whenever possible. "Never lose touch with our public," he had once said. "They pay for the caviar."

It was a little galling as Noël invariably took taxis, although he had once travelled by bus with her when there were no taxis to be found. He delighted the passengers with a high-speed rendition of *Maybe It's Because I'm A Londoner* before they had alighted at Leicester Square.

Bill's second-floor apartment was in a quiet, tree-lined street around the back of Lord's cricket ground. The night air was still warm and the ten-minute walk would certainly help to clear her head. It had been quite a day.

The evening with Simon had infuriated and fascinated her in equal measure. He was very charming and quite unlike other men of his age with whom she was acquainted. Those she knew who were 'other' like Simon typically worked in the theatre and had overly flamboyant personalities. It was as if they were trying to emphasise their difference. Actors on the stage of life playing a stereotype of how they thought they ought to be.

Simon was different.

There was no flamboyance. No peacock posing. He was charming and urbane. Plus, he showed a genuine interest in people. After she had got over her fury at his failure to tell her he was a journalist, she discovered his questioning was more than a simple necessity of his profession. He was genuinely interested in people. He had pointed out several patrons in the pub and described both them and their lives in detail. It contrasted with how little she knew about the people she met and worked with.

On several occasions he'd tried to ask her about Noël. She had been quick to reject his questions as strictly off-limits. He had respected her warning and had quickly changed the subject. But later in the evening he had asked once again. He wanted to know what it was like to work with someone *"as temperamental as Noël Coward"*. This time she spoke more freely about Noël and her relationship with him. She thought she had been careful to pace her drinks and was pretty certain she had remained professional. She hoped she had not said anything indiscreet.

But now as she headed along the road, her head felt full of cotton wool and her eyes had difficulty keeping focus. Perhaps the last double gin and tonic had been one too many. She stopped and peered ahead of her but could not see the turning for Scott Ellis Gardens. She must have missed it while deep in thought. She turned around to head back the way she had come.

A man stood in the shadows of a shop doorway a few yards ahead. She was sure he had not been there when she'd passed a moment ago.

Bill wondered what he was doing there. There were no buses along this road that he could be waiting for. And no one else was on the street apart from her. Fortunately, the pavement was wide enough for her to move to its outer edge as she retraced her footsteps.

As she drew alongside the man stepped out of the doorway.

"Excuse me, miss."

Bill considered running but it was pointless. Even sober she was not a fast runner. And in her present condition he would have no difficulty in catching her.

"Do you have a light?" The man held out a cigarette.

Bill fumbled in her pocket for matches and handed them over.

"Thanks, miss." He lit his cigarette and handed back the matchbox. "Beggin' yer pardon but you shouldn't be out alone this late. Respectable lady like you. Do you want me to walk with you?"

"No thank you," Bill replied. "I live around the corner. I assure you there's no need."

"No offence, miss." The man touched the brim of his hat. "Thought I could 'elp. I'm waiting for me brother. He's gone for a Jimmy Riddle round the corner."

As he spoke another man appeared a few yards ahead at the corner of Scott Ellis Gardens.

"There 'e is." The man nodded to Bill and set off along the pavement. She waited until the two men continued past the turning for Scott Ellis Gardens before she resumed walking.

Bill continued at a brisk pace despite a feeling of nausea

threatening to overwhelm her. Her hands were clammy and she felt light-headed. Only after she had reached the mansion block of her apartment, let herself in, and closed the door could she relax.

It was all too much excitement for one day. Another gin and tonic beckoned.

When Simon's copy of *The Chronicle* arrived at seven o'clock the next morning, Pethers the porter was prompt to telephone his apartment and announce its arrival.

"You're front-page, Mr Sampson," Pethers announced with pride when Simon collected the paper from the front desk five minutes later. "An' it seems to continue onto the inside pages as well. You 'ave done well."

"Thank you, Pethers." Simon took *The Chronicle* from him. "I simply got lucky. In the right place at the right time." He folded the newspaper, tucked it under his arm, and headed back to the staircase. "This will make my boiled eggs and toast taste even better."

The headline was 'The Stage Door Killer' and Simon was by-lined as the paper's senior crime reporter. He poured himself a celebratory second cup of tea. The story ran alongside the main lead about the threat of a water shortage due to the exceptionally dry weather. To Simon's disappointment there was no photograph alongside his article. He had accompanied the paper's photographer who had taken several pictures of the stage door, the alleyway where the body was found, and the front of the theatre. But none of them had been used. The only photograph on the front page showed a man in Regent's Park spraying plants with a garden hose. It was disappointing.

Pethers was correct in saying the article continued onto the inner pages. At least, there was a small continuation on page two. Not only that but the subeditor had retained Simon's quotes *"from an anonymous source"* stating that Mr Noël Coward was *"distressed by the death of a dear friend and colleague"* but that *"the show must go on and* Bitter Sweet *will open tonight as planned."*

It was a stroke of luck bumping into Coward's personal assistant like that. She had been a prickly sort of character and Simon had had to work hard to stop her running out on him once Aunt Cynny had let slip he worked for *The Chronicle*. Fortunately a substantial amount of charm coupled with the double gin and tonics had eventually mollified her. She had even agreed to meet him for supper after Friday's show, although she had failed to offer him a free ticket. Never mind, perhaps he could work on that. She was altogether a very useful contact to have made, and not only in connection with the murder.

Simon knew plenty of men in London who were 'other' but he had only ever known one woman. His Aunt Cynthia, or Cynny as he had always known her.

Despite being his mother's older sister the only time he saw her was when his parents threw grand parties at their family home in Wiltshire. Aunt Cynny would arrive wearing a long, brightly coloured gown and carrying her distinctive silver-topped walking stick. His father strongly disapproved of her but tolerated her presence because she was very well connected through her work at the Home Office.

For some reason Simon and his Aunt Cynny had developed a close friendship, made stronger by his father's disapproval of her. On several occasions he had told Simon she was *"not the sort of woman he should associate with"*.

Aunt Cynny had kept in touch with Simon when he was at boarding school and visited him far more often than his parents. She was enormous fun, very outspoken, and challenged authority at every turn. She was everything Simon's parents were not and he was fascinated by her.

After Oxford University Simon had moved to London and joined a small publishing house. His aunt would invite him for occasional lunches at Simpsons in the Strand. Despite behaving outrageously and being very witty she was secretive about her private life. She would talk about going to parties where Virginia Woolf and other members of the Bloomsbury set would appear. But when he asked her to tell him more she would change the subject.

Although Simon had risen quickly to be senior crime reporter for *The Chronicle*, crime reporting was not his main ambition. He had set out to be a novelist but had somehow got sidetracked by journalism when the job offer with *The Chronicle* had come along. Now he was soon to be in the last year of his twenties and the prospect of not having realised his goal by the time he reached his third decade panicked him. Miss Miles, or Bill as she curiously called herself, was another connection into the underworld of 'women who loved women'. He knew it was an audacious ambition, but one day he wanted to write about the secret worlds of both men and women. Perhaps Bill could help him.

He looked at the clock on the mantelpiece. He had very little time to get to Scotland Yard for the press briefing about yesterday's murder. He hastily swallowed a final mouthful of tea and got ready to leave.

It was already warming up to be a hot sunny day when Simon strode along Victoria Embankment towards the Metropolitan Police headquarters. The mournful sound of a ship's horn drew him across the road to pause and stare out at the Thames.

Sunlight glinted off foamy wavelets on the surface of the brown water. Simon could tell the tide was low from the bad smell in the air. He held a handkerchief to his nose and leaned over the railing to see upstream. As he did so he heard the unmistakable chimes of Big Ben announce ten o'clock. Listening to the famous clock was one of Simon's simple pleasures and one he never grew tired of. He turned and went back across the road to Scotland Yard.

"Mr Sampson of *The Chronicle*," announced the officer on the reception desk. "What brings you here on this fine summer morning?"

"The press briefing." Simon raised his hat. "About the woman murdered outside His Majesty's yesterday."

"Cancelled." The officer shook his head. "Didn't you get the message? They're supposed to have told all the papers first thing."

"Damn." Simon realised he should have checked with the news desk before he set off, but he had been too engrossed in his front-page story to think of it. "Why would they do that I wonder?"

"Morning, Sampson."

Simon turned to see Detective Sergeant Daniels walk past him heading for the main doors. He tipped his hat to the officer at the reception once more and hurried after Daniels.

"I hear the press briefing was cancelled."

"That's right." Daniels pushed open one of the large wooden doors and headed out into the sunshine. Simon followed back onto Victoria Embankment.

"Do you mind if I ask you a couple of questions?" Simon

asked as they walked downstream towards Whitehall Gardens. "I was going to ask them at the press conference."

"If you must." Daniels kept up a brisk pace. "I'm going to grab a cup of tea from the wagon and sit in the gardens for five minutes." He stopped abruptly and looked out at the Thames. "River's a bit whiffy this morning. Glad I'm not with the water police on days like this."

Simon pulled out his notepad and pen and was about to ask a question when Daniels strode off again. Simon hastened to catch up with him.

"Why was it cancelled this morning?"

"My chief decided there was no need for it," Daniels replied. "Why did you still come here even though it was cancelled?"

"I didn't get the message from my news desk."

They stopped by a tea wagon on the corner of Horse Guards Avenue.

"Can I get you a tea?" Simon asked.

"White with two sugars," Daniels replied. He pulled out his pipe and replenished it from a tobacco pouch while Simon bought their tea.

"Why did your chief decide there was no need for the press conference?" Simon asked. He put their two mugs on a low wall next to the tea wagon and took out his notebook again. "It was a brutal killing. Next to a major theatre in the West End. It's a big story for us."

"That's as may be." Daniels shrugged. "But the powers that be decided they didn't want your lot terrifying the public. After all, it's more than likely a one-off."

"How do you know it's a one-off?" Simon asked. "Remember Jack the Ripper started with Mary Nichols. But he didn't stop with her—"

"That's precisely what my chief means." Daniels held up a hand to silence Simon. "You start doing comparisons with Jack the Ripper and you'll create hysteria. Panic. It's not good for tourism. Especially in the summer. Business has boomed since the end of the war. They don't want visitors to London getting terrified by newspaper reporters alleging there's a new Ripper on the loose when there isn't."

Simon stopped writing and frowned at the detective sergeant. "Are you seriously telling me that Scotland Yard is muzzling this story because of tourism?"

"Not at all." Daniels picked up his mug of tea and stirred the spoon in it vigorously. "But they don't want your lot making a big song and dance about it."

"Then what can you tell me about your investigations so far?" Simon asked. "Any motive? What leads are you pursuing?"

"That's a bit tricky." Daniels drank from his mug and put it back on the wall. "The victim being the kind of woman she was."

"What do you mean?"

"Well, you know." The detective sergeant took out a match and lit his pipe.

"I'm afraid I don't," Simon replied. "What kind of woman was she?"

"She wasn't normal." Daniels picked up his mug again and drained it. "From what we can make out she mixed with perverts. She was probably one herself. It's difficult to get any answers from them when you start to make enquiries. They all clam up and won't tell you anything."

"'Perverts'?" Simon shook his head. "My understanding is she had a highly respectable job in the theatre working for Mr Noël Coward."

"Exactly. The theatre's full of them, isn't it?" Daniels looked at his watch. "Look, I've got to get back."

"Before you go." Simon put the cap back on his pen. "Can I ask you one more question, detective sergeant? Are you going to investigate this murder properly?"

Daniels took out another cigarette and lit it. "Mr Sampson. I will do everything in my power to find Miss Lyon's killer. Whatever kind of woman she was. But I can only do that with the limited resources the Metropolitan Police service is prepared to give me."

He faced Simon and jabbed a finger in his chest.

"And I won't have you accuse me of not doing my duty properly."

5

The foyer of His Majesty's Theatre was filling with people attending the London opening of *Bitter Sweet*. Gentlemen stood stiff and awkward in their dinner jackets. Their female companions shone brightly in lavish evening dresses and eyed each other haughtily. Among them were many of the capital's most influential writers and gossip columnists. It was one of Bill's vital tasks to ensure they were present, especially as the production had transferred directly from Manchester. The opening night doubled as the press night. Despite the likely presence of critics among the audience Bill found Noël to be calm and serene, his usual first night nerves almost entirely absent. They sat drinking martinis in a small dressing room reserved exclusively for them.

"Do you know I really no longer care for the dogs of the press," he mused. "I've tried hard to stop paying attention to the whole ghastly lot of them. Especially the critics. I've never understood the mentality of anyone whose sole aim is to write venom about an artist's work. If they can't create joy then they should simply take up a trade more appropriate to their abilities, such as professional mourner."

He raised a hand to his mouth and a guilty expression passed across his face.

"My dear that was a clumsy example for me to use after the tragedy of yesterday. I do apologise. How are you feeling today? I know it was the most terrible shock for you."

"Please don't worry on my account." Bill waved a hand. "I was more concerned about how it might have affected the other members of the company. But everyone seems to be in good spirits."

"They've all got the show business spirit, thank God." Noël sipped his drink. "I hope none of them saw the newspapers this morning. Salacious drivel at its worst. And such poor-quality writing. Especially that scandal sheet the *Daily Express*. Hateful rag. Run by that ghastly Beaverbrook man. I must say *The Chronicle* was surprisingly restrained in its reporting. The article was even rather flattering about me. But then I've always had a soft spot for that paper."

"Have you?" This statement failed to ring true with Bill. Noël had never had a good word to say about any newspaper as long as she had known him. "By the way, I forgot to tell you I met the man who wrote that piece in *The Chronicle*."

"Good God, Bill. Have you been fraternising with the enemy?" Noël almost spilled his drink. "When was this?"

"Yesterday." Perhaps she should have avoided telling him. "He was very charming."

"I'm sure he was, my dear." Noël drained his glass and stood. "About as charming as the cobra before it strikes at the mongoose. A word of advice. Try to avoid the snakes of Fleet Street if you want to keep your job with me."

"Ah, but you forget, my dear Noël." Bill pointed her cigarette at him. "The mongoose is invariably the victor in that fight."

The after-show party was held in the cocktail bar of the Savoy. Guests gushed their admiration for the production and assured Noël that the reviews would be equally full of praise, ensuring *Bitter Sweet* would run and run.

Bill was not in the mood for a party, especially one containing the superficial flotsam of London society. She had a headache and felt guilty she had still made no effort to contact Maureen's flatmate, Jenny Casewell. The poor girl must be distraught. After little more than an hour she made her excuses and left for the sanctuary of her apartment.

As she walked towards the turning for Scott Ellis Gardens she remembered the encounter with the man who had asked her for a light the night before. Her chest tightened and she quickened her pace.

"Oi, Miss. 'ang on a minute."

The man's voice came from behind her. She dared not turn round. Her flat was less than a hundred yards away. She strode on purposefully.

"Oi, Miss. Didn't yer 'ear me?"

The voice was harsh, aggressive. Bill began to run. She heard footsteps running behind her. The mansion block of apartments where she lived was in sight.

"Oi, Miss," the man's voice was breathless. "Don't run away. I've got yer gloves. Yer dropped them outside the station. Dontcha want 'em?"

Bill stopped abruptly and checked. She had indeed lost her gloves. The man was only being kind. She had to stop being so jumpy. Although two frights in as many nights was becoming an unwelcome regular occurrence. She turned and forced a smile at the man holding a pair of white kid gloves. The pounding in her head reminded her she was in desperate need of an aspirin. Or a gin and tonic.

Jenny Casewell's cottage was in a narrow mews off Holland Park Road. All the cottages in the row were painted different primary colours. Miss Casewell's house had pale pink walls with a red front door. Bill tugged on the bell pull and stood admiring a basket of geraniums while she waited for her ring to be answered.

"Bill. How good of you to call."

The woman who answered the door had clearly been crying. Her eyes were red and she clutched a white embroidered handkerchief. Her hair was unkempt and a lilac cardigan hung askew about her hunched frame as a result of the buttons being wrongly fastened.

"My dear Jenny, I'm terribly sorry I didn't call on you earlier." Bill so wanted to step forward and hug the sad figure peering around the open door. Instead she held back awkwardly and clasped her hands in front of her. "What with the opening of the show last night and—"

"It's all right." Jenny smiled wanly. "I'm sure you must be very busy." She opened the door wider and stepped to one side. "Won't you come in?"

The tiny living room was in virtual darkness. A single shaft of light broke through a narrow gap between the closed curtains. A plate containing the congealed remains of an unfinished meal lay on a small coffee table. Piles of magazines and papers spilled across a threadbare sofa and onto the floor.

Jenny Casewell closed the front door behind Bill. She crossed to the window, opened the curtains, and tugged on the window catch to force it ajar. The morning breeze helped to freshen the staleness of the room. Jenny moved to the sofa, scooped up a handful of the magazines, and arranged them into an untidy pile on the floor.

"Would you like to sit down? I'm afraid everything's a bit of a mess. I haven't had a chance to tidy since the police…"

She crumpled onto the sofa and turned her head away. Her body shook and she held up the handkerchief to dab at her eyes. Bill sat and tentatively reached out a hand to reassure her. To Bill's surprise Jenny turned, nestled her head into Bill's shoulder, and extended her arm in a childlike embrace.

"My dear, I'm so sorry." Bill cautiously patted Jenny's shoulder in response to the unexpected show of affection. "This is the most horrible shock for you."

Jenny sniffled. She trembled, but said nothing for several minutes. Finally, she cleared her throat and sat up. She shuffled away from Bill on the cramped sofa and looked away.

"How frightfully embarrassing." Jenny dabbed her eyes with the handkerchief. "I didn't mean to be quite so… I must apologise for… Surely this must be far worse for you. After all, you and Maureen…"

Bill stood and crossed to a glass-fronted cupboard in the corner of the room. "Let's have a drink. I'm sure you must have some gin somewhere about."

Jenny was aghast. "It's not yet eleven in the morning."

"Ah, but it's almost five o'clock in the Punjab." Bill opened the cupboard and took out a bottle of London dry gin. "Now. Where do you keep the tonic?"

Jenny curled her legs under her on the sofa and took a sip from the glass Bill had handed her. Bill sat on an uncomfortable rattan chair opposite. Noël had once rejected a similar chair as *"furniture punishment delivered from the extremes of the Empire"*. Bill was inclined to agree when she felt the narrow strips of rattan creating ridges on the back of her thighs.

"Weren't you concerned when Maureen didn't come home the night before last?"

"I wouldn't have known." Jenny shook her head. "She was often out until all hours. And you know how dedicated she was to productions. I tend to go to bed early if I'm not working on a show so we simply wouldn't have seen each other."

"But yesterday morning?"

"Her door was shut when I got up. It usually is. I wouldn't have gone snooping—"

"No of course not," Bill said quickly. "Tell me, when did you get the news? Did the police come to tell you?"

Jenny nodded. "A very young constable. Poor boy looked barely out of nappies. I almost had to comfort *him* while he told me. It was only after he left..."

"I should have come over yesterday," Bill said. "I'm so sorry you were alone."

"It's all right." Jenny smiled. "You're here now. Although it would have been nice if you'd arrived a bit earlier. Some detective sergeant turned up first thing this morning."

"That must be the one who was at the theatre," Bill replied. "Daniels was his name I think."

"That's right," Jenny nodded. "I didn't like him much. He wanted to know lots of things about Maureen's private life."

"Did you tell them about us?" Bill asked.

"Good God, no," Jenny replied. "Like I said. I didn't much warm to him. And I told him directly when he got too pushy. It's called a private life for a reason. Maureen and I might have shared the same house but we weren't privy to the ins and outs of each other's day-to-day life. He didn't like that much. Then he asked to see her room."

"The impertinence." Bill took out a cigarette and lit it. "Do you know if he found anything...?"

"It's all right, Bill." Jenny got on her hands and knees and hunted through the pile of magazines and papers on the carpet. She held up a small bundle of letters tied together with a ribbon. "I think these are the only ones you sent her."

"Oh, you darling." Bill leaned forward to take the letters with such haste she almost knocked over her drink. "What a morbid thing for you to have to do."

"It was." Jenny shrugged. "But we owe it to each other to protect ourselves. There's no need for the police to know about you and Maureen. And they certainly wouldn't care or understand even if they did."

"After me did she have any other...?" Bill paused. She regretted having started the question.

"Not that I know of." Jenny picked up a few sheets of paper from the floor and settled back on the sofa. "She was very sweet on you. I don't think she was one to jump straight into another friendship."

Bill cleared her throat and sipped from her glass. "It was foolish of me to ask. Maureen was a lovely person. It was sad when it ended. It's nearly six months now. But in my position, and with everything I'm responsible for, it didn't seem right—"

"You don't have to say any more."

They sat in meditative silence for several minutes. Even though the little house was in the heart of London, the only sound Bill could hear was the chirping of the birds in the hedge outside the window. It was remarkable how the engine of the city could be muted in this mews hidden away from the main streets.

"What about the funeral?" Bill asked eventually.

"I really don't know. I suppose it will be after the inquest. I'm not sure how long that will be. I'm not looking forward to dealing with it."

"But surely you don't have to organise it? What about her family?"

"I don't think she was in touch with them." Jenny shrugged. "I know her mum died when Maureen was very young and she was brought up by her father. I asked her about him once and she changed the subject. Did she ever talk about her family to you?"

"Hardly at all." Bill raised her cigarette. "Do you have an ashtray?"

"Use that old cough drop tin next to you." Jenny pointed at a small round tin on the floor. "I managed to drop the ashtray and break it yesterday. Going through Maureen's things last evening I was in a bit of a mess most of the time."

"It must have been terrible for you." Bill tapped the ash from her cigarette.

"It was. And in a surprising way too." Jenny held out the sheet of paper in her hand. "I found this underneath your letters. I thought it best to keep it away from prying eyes. Here. Take a look."

Bill took the paper from Jenny. It was a hand-written letter scribbled on ruled paper torn from a notebook. The sender had put neither address nor date on any part of it and the signature was indecipherable.

Have I not given you enough? I thought that the last lot of money was supposed to put an end to this sordid saga. You promised that you would hand it over, and yet you now demand more. You are a brazen young woman without an ounce of compassion. I deserve more respect from you and yet you continue to defy me in this way with your despicable blackmail. I urge you to reconsider.

Bill took out her cigarette case. Her hands shook as she lit another cigarette. The letter revealed a side to Maureen she had never known about. A darker side she would have rather not known. It tainted her memory. She handed the letter back to Jenny.

"Is it really true?" Bill asked.

"What? That Maureen was a blackmailer?" She waved the letter in the air. "What else can we conclude? Isn't it horrible?"

"Surely there's some other rational explanation for it."

"Like what?" Jenny dropped the sheet of paper onto the floor. "I've been sitting here this morning wracking my brains trying to think what that rational explanation could be. But I haven't come up with anything so far."

"Don't you think you should hand that to the police?" Bill asked.

"No."

"But the person who wrote it could well be Maureen's murderer—"

"I said no."

Bill sat and thought for a moment.

"How do you know it was sent to Maureen?"

"Because it was among her things."

"But it doesn't have *Dear Maureen* on it. Was it in an envelope addressed to her?"

"No."

"Then it could have been intended for anyone."

"That doesn't make any sense." Jenny shook her head. "Why would Maureen keep a letter like this if it wasn't hers?"

"Perhaps she was keeping it for someone else."

They both fell silent again. Bill drained her glass and stood to replenish it. "Do you want a top-up?"

"What the hell." Jenny handed up her glass. "I'm not planning on going anywhere today."

Bill took the glasses into the kitchen, refilled Jenny's, and made a half measure of gin and tonic for herself. She was due at the theatre that afternoon and needed to keep a clear head.

"You don't think it's a prop from a play?" she asked when she re-entered the living room.

"I suppose it could be." Jenny took her glass from Bill and picked up the letter once more. "But why would she bring it home with her?"

"Has she ever worked on a production about blackmail?"

Jenny shook her head. "Not for as long as she's been living here. There was that last show of Noël's. Certainly no blackmail in that. And before that she did a couple of Shakespeares down in Richmond."

"And there's no blackmail in *Bitter Sweet*." Bill pointed at the letter in Jenny's hand. "We can only conclude it was addressed to Maureen. And it was probably from her killer. You have to give it to the police."

Jenny shook her head. "You know what the police already think about people like us. And therefore what they think about Maureen. This will only make them think worse of her."

"But if you don't then you're taking away one of the few leads they might have to catch her killer."

Jenny dropped the letter to the floor again and slumped back on the sofa.

"I'll think about it."

6

Simon swore at his bowtie and tugged on one end to release the untidy knot he had created. He decided there was a certain kind of demon that possessed a bowtie whenever he tried to tie it. It must know he should have left for the theatre ten minutes ago. Try as he might the fabric would not take the intended form it should. Instead, the finished result looked like a knotted noose, the uneven ends of the tie hung crookedly around his neck as if to mock him. He smoothed down the creases in the black fabric, stared into the mirror, took a deep breath, and began the laborious process once more.

He was due at His Majesty's Theatre, Drury Lane in forty minutes time to watch *Bitter Sweet*. True it only took twenty minutes from his apartment in Marylebone to reach the theatre and also true there was more than an hour until the show started. But Simon had promised to meet Bill for a drink and he was anxious to allow time for at least one gin martini before the curtain went up.

The telephone rang.

He considered ignoring it but its insistent, continuous ring got the better of his curiosity. He went into the hallway and picked up the receiver.

"Sampson? It's Somerskill here. Sorry to bother you on a Friday evening but we need a new angle on the murder story for the Sunday edition."

Frank Somerskill was the editor of *The Chronicle*. A quietly spoken, thoughtful man with an almost deferential attitude to his staff. He was unlike any of the other newspaper editors in Fleet Street Simon had come across. Even when a deadline to roll the presses was looming, Somerskill would never put pressure on his reporters. Instead, he calmly encouraged them to write the best and most original news stories they could.

"I can go back to Scotland Yard tomorrow and try to find out how the investigation is going," Simon suggested. "But if you remember, they cancelled the press conference. Said something about not wanting to alarm the public, especially during the holiday season."

"Yes," Somerskill replied languidly. "Didn't really add up, did it? You'd have thought they'd be seeking the publicity to try to bring witnesses forward. Strange. Have another go with them would you, there's a good chap."

Somerskill cleared his throat. Simon knew this was usually a cue for a further demand, always delivered with great charm.

"The thing is," Somerskill continued, "I think we need something a bit more than that if we're to keep the story on the front page. Do you know what I mean? It is the Sunday edition after all. What about that secretary of Noël Coward's? Can't you get anything more from her? With his new show having just opened this week it gives a great show business twist to the murder."

"I'm meeting her later." Simon looked at the mantel clock through the sitting room doorway. "Actually, I'm a bit late so I need to get going."

"Oh, please don't let me hold you up." Somerskill was solicitous with no hint of sarcasm. "Have a pleasant evening. Take her for a decent meal afterwards and expense it. See what more you can glean. And get me something decent for the front page."

"It's all in hand, Mr Somerskill. Leave it to me."

Simon hung up the phone. The conversation had left him in a quandary. His duty as a journalist was to get his editor what he wanted. But he had hoped to develop a friendship with Bill. She was already wary of him concealing his profession from her. Any prying questions during the evening would more than likely drive her away.

He walked back into the sitting room. There would be time to think about the problem on the bus ride to the theatre. For the moment there was a more pressing task. He grabbed the two ends of his bowtie and squared his shoulders in readiness to do battle once more.

The show was much better than Simon had expected. He was not a fan of operetta ever since his mother had dragged him to a production of *The Merry Widow* when he was thirteen years old. He had failed to laugh at any of the feeble jokes with the rest of the audience and had found the music dull and ponderous.

Maybe it was because he was more mature but Simon thought *Bitter Sweet* was wittier and the music more interesting than *The Merry Widow*. It meant he could be entirely honest when he met Bill at the stage door after the show.

"Come along my dear." Bill grabbed his arm and ushered him towards the Haymarket. "I'm *famished*. Haven't eaten a thing all day. Where are you taking me?"

Simon looked over his shoulder at the stage door. "Is Mr Coward not...?"

"Noël's meeting a New York producer for supper this evening." Bill lengthened her stride and tugged on Simon's arm to force him to keep up. "You'll meet him one day. Possibly. But after your deceit last time I'm certainly not in a hurry to introduce you two. Who knows what you'll end up printing about him."

"I say, that's a bit unfair," Simon protested. "I made certain *The Chronicle* was very complimentary about him in my piece."

"Very obsequious of you I'm sure," Bill replied briskly. "But it's not going to buy you an interview with him. Not quite yet. I need to get to know you a bit more before I can trust you."

They reached the top of the Haymarket and Simon steered them towards Piccadilly Circus.

"Goodness darling, where are you taking me?" Bill asked. "Lyon's Cornerhouse? How delightfully downmarket. We can hang out with all your friends in that space on the first floor they reserve for men like you."

Simon stopped abruptly. "If you're going to continue to insult me this evening I'll not be taking you anywhere. I've actually reserved a table at a new place near the Ambassador's Theatre. I've been told that all the theatre people go there now."

"Please don't take offence my darling." Bill patted his shoulder. "It's simply my little way. It sounds divine. What's it called?"

"The Ivy."

"But the Ivy Café's been around for years," Bill replied. "That lovely Italian boy runs it."

"I know." Simon resumed walking towards Piccadilly Circus. "But they relaunched it a couple of months ago. They've made it bigger and refurbished it. Apparently anyone who's anyone in theatre likes to eat there now."

"Well Noël hasn't been there so your source is exaggerating when they say that. I'll see what it's like and then perhaps I'll recommend it." This time it was Bill who brought them to a halt. "But if the Ivy's near the Ambassador's my darling, then we're going in the wrong direction."

Despite the indignation Simon had demonstrated when Bill had suggested they were eating at Lyon's Corner House, he *had* originally reserved a table there. But when Somerskill had told him he could expense the meal, Simon had cancelled the booking and secured the last remaining table at the Ivy.

He was glad he had. Both the food and the service were excellent and Bill's barbed comments diminished markedly after her third glass of champagne.

"That meal was really rather wonderful, my darling." Bill dropped her napkin onto the table and lit a cigarette. "The vongole were exquisite. I *must* recommend this place to Noël. He needs to put in an appearance." She nodded her head to the left. "There's lovely John Gielgud over there. I wonder who that boy is who's with him? And there's that ghastly American actress Tallulah Bankhead. I don't know what she's still doing in London. She hasn't been in a West End show for years. I thought she was going to Hollywood. But then perhaps the cocaine's cheaper here."

"Do you know them?" Simon asked.

Bill nodded. "John's lovely. Noël's done several plays with him. I won't introduce you this evening. He seem to be having a rather intimate supper with his young companion."

She drained her cup of espresso coffee and stubbed out her cigarette. "You know you've been awfully good this evening."

"In what way?"

"Not a single question about Maureen. Or Noël for that matter. Have you been taken off the story?"

"Far from it." Simon shook his head. "In fact my editor called shortly before I left home this evening. He asked me to get something juicy from you that he could use for this Sunday's edition of the paper."

"Goodness." Bill seemed lost for words. "Then why haven't you been giving me a grilling?"

"Because," Simon smiled. "Despite your prickly personality and occasionally sharp tongue I rather like you. And I'd like to continue our friendship, fledgling though it might be."

Bill took time to light her cigarette. "I don't know what to say."

"There's no need to say anything. Enjoy the compliment as it was intended."

"I will." She leaned forward and rested her elbows on the table, her head cradled on her hands. Their faces were only a few inches apart.

"You know, Mr Sampson. If I liked men in the same way that I like women I could easily fall for you."

"Now it's my turn to be speechless."

"Then it's also your turn to enjoy the compliment."

Simon decided that, if they had been a conventional couple they would have kissed at this point.

"I know what we can do." Bill smiled cheekily. "I'll take you to a club in Soho."

"Oh no." Simon leaned back and shook his head. "We're not going to the Black Cat this evening."

"I don't mean there." She waggled a finger to beckon him forward again. "I was thinking about what you told me about your Aunt Cynny."

"Cynthia," Simon corrected. "'Cynny' is only reserved for family use."

"No matter." Bill waved her cigarette to dismiss his correction. "I think the point you were trying to make is that you're curious about 'women like us'."

"Don't say it like that. You make me sound vulgarly prurient."

"Would you let me finish?"

The waiter arrived with their bill and they both leaned back to allow him to place a silver plate containing the folded sheet of crisp vellum on the table.

"So where do you propose we go?" Simon held back from picking up the bill. He was certain it would be expensive.

"There's a little place in Gerrard Street I know. Exclusively for 'women like us'."

"Then surely they won't let me in."

Bill sighed. "For 'women like us' *and their guests*." She pointed her cigarette at the bill still lying on the silver plate. "I thought this was on you?"

Simon picked up the piece of paper and unfolded it. It came to nearly two pounds. He hoped his editor would be ready for the shock.

The steep flight of stone stairs led them down from street level to a metal door with a small pane of glass set into it. A gas light flickered above the door.

"Welcome to the Paradise Regained Club." Bill knocked loudly on the glass and stood back. After a few moments the door swung inwards to reveal a woman wearing a navy blue workman's overall topped off with a beret set jauntily askew on her head.

"Bill my darling." A broad grin spread across the woman's

face. "How lovely to see you again. And so soon. Twice in two days. We thought you'd be gadding about with Noël tonight."

"Sylvia my dear." Bill stepped across the threshold and embraced the woman. "I've brought a friend if that's all right. He's of the male persuasion. But fully housetrained."

Simon held back in the narrow space between the foot of the stairs and the doorway and smiled optimistically at Sylvia. With slow deliberation she tilted her head to survey the length of his body from his shoes to his hat. It reminded Simon of the way his mother would examine the animals at a cattle auction.

"You're responsible for him," Sylvia said to Bill. "If he upsets any of the customers then you're both out, I'm afraid."

"He'll be as good as gold." Bill beckoned to Simon. "Come on you. You've passed the first test."

Simon stepped over the threshold. "Thank you," he said politely to Sylvia but she was more concerned with securing the bolt on the door.

"Don't worry about her," Bill whispered in his ear. "Underneath that gruff exterior she's got a heart of tarnished gold. Follow me. And don't stare. This isn't a zoo."

The décor on the inside of the club was in sharp contrast to the gloomy, austere entrance. The walls were painted flamingo pink, and it was lit by electric wall-lights fitted with multi-coloured Tiffany glass shades. The furniture was a mix of red velvet chaise longues and leather Chesterfield sofas. In the middle of the club was a small dance floor. Several women slow-danced together to music played by a woman pianist who wore dark glasses and a matador-cut jacket studded with rhinestones.

Half a dozen couples were sprawled across the sofas either in casual embraces or demonstrating more intimate affection. Apart from the chintzy décor it was like any number of the men-only clubs Simon had visited. Except in here he was the only man.

As they walked towards the bar at the back of the club Simon stopped when he realised there was a chance he might meet his Aunt Cynny. He had no wish to embarrass her by his sudden appearance.

"What's the matter?" Bill walked back to where he stood on the edge of the dance floor. "You look like you've seen a ghost."

"Don't worry, I'm fine."

"What is it?"

"I had a sudden thought I might run into my aunt here." Now that he said it out loud it sounded faintly ridiculous.

"What if you do?" Bill laughed. "I'm sure she'd be delighted to see you."

"Are you certain I'm welcome here?" Simon looked around him nervously. "You told me not to stare but I'm getting some very odd looks."

"Don't be so sensitive. They're just curious." Bill headed for the bar. "Champagne, darling?" she called over her shoulder. "May as well continue as we started."

"Can I get these?" Simon stood alongside her while she ordered their drinks.

"Don't be silly," Bill replied. "You paid for that outrageously expensive meal." She glanced over his shoulder. "Oh my God, it's Jenny Casewell."

"The woman who shared a house with the victim?"

"Yes." Bill turned back to him. "Now, I'm about to introduce you to her. Be a good boy, won't you and don't ask about Miss Lyon? I won't have you exploiting my friendship with her. After all, you already said you wanted to keep *our* friendship."

"Don't you trust me?"

"I'm not saying that," Bill replied. "But there's no harm in me being careful."

7

No harm in me being careful. Simon understood Bill's suspicions of journalists but he had hoped to reassure her of his honourable intentions with the story he had written in *The Chronicle.*

It was clear she was yet to be convinced.

"My darling it's wonderful to see you out and about." Bill took Jenny's hand, pulled her close, and kissed her on either cheek. "You've made exactly the right decision, my dear. You can't mope about the house all day."

"That's what I decided in the end," Jenny replied. "There are so many reminders of Maureen in that place. Although I'm not sure coming here was such a good idea. She used to love this club."

"It's true she did," Bill replied. "But you know you're among friends in here. What you need is a drink. I'm getting them in now. And that reminds me." She slapped Simon's shoulder as if they were colleagues at a gentleman's club. "This is Mr Sampson. He was terribly sweet and looked after me the other night when I got the dreadful news about Maureen. Simon, this is Jenny Casewell."

"Miss Casewell, I'm delighted to meet you."

"Please, call me Jenny."

"And you must call me Simon."

Jenny Casewell had strong, angular features as though a sculptor had laboured to chisel her face from granite. She was almost skeletally thin and her lime-green trouser suit hung from her frame as if on a coat hanger. Simon wondered when she had last eaten a decent meal.

"Gin and tonic, Jenny darling?" Bill asked. "That's what we're having."

"That's very kind." Jenny turned to Simon. "Doesn't it feel strange for you to be in here? You being a man? The only one among all these women?"

"Strange maybe," Simon replied. "But not unpleasant. Anyway I think Bill may have brought me here because I took her to the Salisbury on the night your friend was murdered. She's sort of returning the favour."

"Oh, I see. And was the Salisbury your choice or did it happen to be the nearest pub to where you were at the time?"

"Both." Simon smiled. "My usual haunt is the Fitzroy Tavern over in Bloomsbury. But in a crisis the Salisbury will do."

"Now I do see." A knowing smile softened the stern lines of Jenny's face and her eyes lit up. "How kind of you to be there for Miss Miles at a moment like that."

"Oh, it was nothing. I just happened to be at the theatre at the right time. How did you get to hear the dreadful news?"

"Oh no, has he started already?" Bill turned back from the bar clutching three tall glasses. She handed one to Jenny and another to Simon. "Don't let him badger you, Jenny. He'll end up writing something scurrilous about your depraved lifestyle."

"Bill, that's grossly unfair—" Simon began.

"Don't listen to him," Bill interrupted. "I presume he hasn't told you he works for *The Chronicle*?"

"Oh, but that sounds terribly exciting." Jenny's eyes widened. She clinked her glass against Simon's. "Are you a reporter? Do tell me everything."

"He's not only a reporter," Bill began before Simon could reply. "But he's *the* reporter. The one who wrote the piece about poor Maureen in *The Chronicle*." She wagged a finger at Jenny. "Don't say I didn't warn you."

"But I always read *The Chronicle*." Jenny moved closer to Simon and rested a hand on his lapel. "How simply thrilling. Are you going to help us find Maureen's killer? You must. I don't think the police are in the least bit interested. I got the strong feeling that the officer who came round yesterday took against her when he found out we lived together. I felt thoroughly disapproved of."

"Why? What did he say?" asked Simon.

"Oh, he didn't have to *say* anything," Jenny replied. "It was his whole manner. I think the mere fact that we're women was bad enough. And when I told him we shared our little cottage together it was as if I'd said we took our holidays in Gomorrah. Or Sodom."

"Jenny darling." Bill lit a cigarette and exhaled a plume of smoke above their heads. "Aren't you reading a lot into such a short visit by the police? I'm sure they're doing everything in their power to investigate poor Maureen's death. Detective Daniels was pleasant enough when I met him at the theatre. And he was surprisingly sympathetic when he asked me to identify Maureen's—"

"Well good for you, Bill."

The icy tone in Jenny's voice was not something Simon had expected. She withdrew her hand from his lapel and glowered at Bill.

"All I can say is he wasn't sympathetic to me. I told you yesterday how he asked me all those personal questions about

Maureen. And I thought you were grateful I'd cleared her room of all your letters before they—"

"Yes, of course." Bill interrupted. She glanced nervously at Simon. "There's no need to go into that again."

"'Letters'?" Simon asked. "What letters would those be?"

"I really don't think there's any need…" Bill began.

But Jenny interrupted her. "Hasn't Bill told you?" she asked Simon. "She hasn't, has she?"

"He knows enough," Bill snapped. "Remember he's a reporter. Anything you say is more than likely to end up in the pages of *The Chronicle*."

Simon sipped his drink and watched while Bill stared angrily at Jenny and Jenny pouted back in return. This was turning into an extremely interesting evening.

It was Jenny who broke the awkward silence. "You do know that Bill and Maureen were lovers for nearly two years, don't you?" Jenny looked up at Simon and once more her stern features softened with a smile. "Do you think you can understand that? I've never met a man who would even think that such a thing is possible. But I believe you might, Mr Sampson. Did Bill not say?"

Bill inhaled deeply on her cigarette and arched an eyebrow at him.

"Sometimes these things don't need to be said," Simon replied. "They're simply understood. I do know that Bill was very upset by Miss Lyon's death. And her pain was more than that of a mere friend."

He smiled at Jenny. "Not that I'm in any way diminishing the grief of friends."

Jenny rested her hand on his lapel once more. "I'm sure you aren't, Mr Sampson."

"I would also like to add," Simon continued. "That I've never had the slightest intention of embellishing my newspaper reports with conjecture about other people's personal relationships. Especially when I know the editor would never accept that such a relationship could even exist."

"Hmm," Bill snorted and spilled her drink. "I wish you'd bloody said that before."

"You wouldn't have believed me even if I did," Simon replied. "You've made it very clear what you thought of me from the moment we first met."

"So tell me, Mr Sampson." Jenny stared up at him. Did she actually flutter her eyelashes at him? "Is there a special person in your life?"

"I don't have time for any of that." Simon avoided her eyes and took a sip of his drink. When he lowered the glass Jenny was still watching him. He felt his cheeks flush, and it wasn't just from the alcohol. "I'm very busy you know. And I can work very irregular hours if there's a flap on."

"Not even a single beau?" Jenny shook her head. "I can't believe that. A handsome man like you. I would have thought men would be falling at your feet."

"You know this is most awfully embarrassing—"

"Nobody?" Jenny turned her head slightly and her eyes widened. Was she flirting or was it simply a mischievous look in her eye?

"There was someone once," Simon began. "But it was a long time ago. As I said, my work takes up most of my time—"

"See what it's like when someone pries into your personal life?" Bill inhaled on her cigarette and blew a smoke ring in Simon's face. "Now perhaps you understand why I was so upset when I discovered you're from the press. Noël's always warned me to beware the dogs of Fleet Street."

"Did he?" Simon set his empty glass down on the bar. "I see. Well, I may not be a 'dog of Fleet Street' as Noël so indelicately puts it for much longer."

"Why's that?" Bill stubbed out her cigarette and lit another.

"You heard Aunt Cynny talk about the BBC at the Salisbury the other night," Simon replied. "I rather fancy a crack at this new wireless invention. I've been talking to a couple of people about it. She's right. The BBC is expanding its news operation since it made such an impact in the General Strike. Maybe I should think about putting my name forward. It would be an adventure."

"You certainly have a wonderful voice." Jenny gazed up at him, her eyes wide and admiring. "Bill used to work at the BBC."

"Did you, Bill?" Simon asked. "You haven't told me."

"It was hardly worth mentioning."

"But when Aunt Cynny was talking about the BBC you didn't—"

"At the time I was more concerned with what you'd been concealing from me."

Please don't start on that again," Simon replied. "You're beginning to sound like a stuck gramophone record. Why did you leave the BBC? It must have been very exciting. The wireless is the way of the future."

"She worked for the head man," Jenny interjected. "Sir John Reith. It was a very important position. I think she might have stayed if Noël hadn't come along."

"I'm perfectly capable of telling my own story." Bill half turned her back to Jenny. "The man's a pompous oaf. Unbearable to work with."

"Who?" Simon asked. "Reith or Mr Coward?"

"Ha!" Bill pointed her cigarette at Simon. "For a reporter, and a mere man, you're really quite perceptive. Now you come to ask, the pair of them. Why is it that men automatically get the top jobs? It's patently absurd. They don't have the monopoly on intelligence or ability. Far from it. And yet women are forced to work in junior positions and put up with men's bullying and fragile egos."

"Then why did you leave one pompous oaf only to work for another?" Simon asked.

"I'm asking myself that very question right now," Bill replied. "I suppose because Noël has far more charm than Sir John will ever have. And because he works in the theatre, which can be a wonderfully creative place."

"I'm sure the BBC could be a creative place as well." Simon signalled to one of the women working behind the bar. "I'm ready for another. How about you girls?"

"'Girls'?" Bill turned to Jenny. "Did you hear that? Just when we thought he was a Renaissance man, different to the rest, he goes and says a patronising thing like that."

Before Simon could protest someone called out.

"Help! Quickly. She needs help."

The voice came from near the front of the club. The bar woman turned away from Simon and hurried towards the main entrance. The band continued to play but the dancing had stopped and the hubbub of talking subsided to low whispers.

Simon turned to head towards the front of the club but Bill grabbed his arm.

"Where do you think you're going?"

"To see what's happening."

"Do you think that's the smartest move?" Bill asked. "You're the only man in here. Sounds like something pretty awful has happened. You're not going to be the most popular person they're going to want to see right now."

"Then come with me." Simon eased himself away from Bill's grasp. "I know you're not going to like me saying this, but I am still a reporter."

"Oh, for God's sake." Bill slammed her glass down on the countertop and followed Simon towards a growing throng of women who had gathered near the club entrance. Simon pushed his way through the group until he reached the front.

"Stand back please. Make room."

Sylvia at the entrance door stood with her arms held out wide to hold people back. On the floor in front of her lay a woman curled in a foetal position. Another woman dressed in the same navy blue uniform as Sylvia was on her knees next to her. She laid two fingers on the woman's neck to check her pulse.

"What happened?" Simon asked.

"Did you have to bring him?" Sylvia asked Bill. "He's making the place untidy."

"Please shut up and let me handle this," Bill whispered to Simon. She turned to the woman kneeling on the floor. "Can I help? I've read a few books on first aid."

"I'm a doctor," the woman replied without looking up. "And to answer your gentleman friend's question: someone tried to strangle her."

"Oh, my goodness." Jenny appeared at Simon's side. "Just like what happened to Maureen. Is she going to be all right?"

"She will if you'd move back and give her some air," the doctor replied.

They all shuffled back a few steps.

"Has anyone called the police?" Simon asked.

"Good God, no," Sylvia replied. "We don't want to draw attention to the club. They'd only shut us down again."

"But this woman's been brutally attacked," Simon protested.

The woman lying on the floor coughed and stretched out her hand. The doctor leaned close and whispered. The woman nodded, coughed again, and struggled into a sitting position. Lying on the floor behind her was a thin piece of cord.

"Look." Bill nudged Simon in the ribs. "That looks like the same type of cord that was used to strangle Maureen."

8

Her name was Grace Lucas. She sat at a table in the corner of the club with Simon, Bill, and Jenny, and sipped tea from a china cup. The doctor had urged her to go to the hospital to be examined but she had vehemently refused. She had also refused to go to the police despite Simon's protestations.

"It'll get the club into trouble and that's the last thing they need," Grace said. "They've been so good to me. To all of us who come here. I can't betray them just because of this. After all, I'm fine now."

"Darling, I understand your loyalty to the club," Bill said. "But some bastard's tried to strangle you with a sash cord. And it's only two days since our friend was murdered in the exact same way. It looks like this is the same killer."

"You say it was a man," Simon began. "Can you describe what he looked like?"

"It all happened so quickly." Grace set down her teacup and furrowed her brow. "I was heading off home because I've got an early start tomorrow. I'm a nurse at Paddington hospital. I stopped to light a cigarette. I couldn't find my matches so I was searching in my bag. Then I felt this cord around my neck and I was being dragged into the alleyway on the corner. I tried to get hold of the cord but it went tight so quickly. It was horrible."

She put her hand to her neck and delicately touched the surface. Simon could see a red line on the skin beneath her fingers.

"Do you think you can describe this man?" Simon asked again.

To be honest I didn't see who was behind me at all. I suppose I just assumed it was a man. It could have easily been a woman."

"A woman is just as capable of murder," Bill observed. "We shouldn't rule out the possibility. How on earth did you escape? Did someone come to your rescue?"

"No." Grace smiled. "I can handle myself, thank you very much."

"But, forgive me saying," Bill replied."You're somewhat shorter than me. And I'm not considered tall. How did you manage to fend off your attacker?"

"Ju-jitsu." Grace dropped her hand from her neck and leaned forward. "Have you got a cigarette? I could really do with one."

"Of course." Bill took out her cigarette case. "Did you learn with the suffragettes? I know a lot of them were trained in it before the war. No, how silly of me. You're far too young for that, surely?"

"You're very kind." Grace took a cigarette from Bill and accepted a light from her with a smile. "Actually I was a nurse in the war. Afterwards, when I came back home, I found the suffragettes were still running courses in ju-jitsu for women down at Golden Square. It seemed like a good idea at the time."

"It certainly proved its worth tonight," Simon observed. "Did this man, or maybe woman, run off after you tackled them?"

"I suppose so," Grace replied. "I was too busy catching my breath."

"Are you sure you won't report this to the police?" Simon asked.

"Definitely."

"Then we're going to have to do some investigating ourselves." He stood. "Would you come and show me where this all happened?"

"Of course." Grace inhaled on her cigarette.

"Well, you're not going without me." Bill also got to her feet. "This is far too thrilling. I've never been a crime investigator before."

"What do you think this is, a party?" Simon asked in frustration. "I'm about to go and examine the scene of an attempted murder. It won't help if half a dozen people's shoes trample all over it."

"Don't be so dull," Bill replied. "Extra pairs of eyes are always useful. Especially if they belong to a woman. We're far more observant." She looked down at Jenny. "Are you going to join us as well?"

Jenny shook her head. "This has been too much for one evening. I'm going home."

"On your own?" Simon asked. "After what happened to Miss Lucas?"

"I'll be fine," Jenny replied.

"No, you won't." Bill rested a hand on her shoulder. "I'll go with you. Especially as I've now been deemed surplus to requirements."

Simon took Bill's arm and pulled her to one side.

"Please don't concern yourself," she whispered sharply. "I'm not going to stay here if—"

"You don't have to be so huffy with me," Simon interrupted. "I was simply going to say thank you for going back with Miss Casewell. Make sure you look after yourself as well."

"Oh." Bill was taken aback by his concern. "Thank you. But you really don't have to worry—"

"I think we do," Simon continued. "And I still think Miss Lucas should report this to the police."

"And you know full well she won't. The police don't care about women like us. No more than they care about men like you I would imagine. We're on our own."

"But we've got to do *something*," Simon insisted. "The next person might not be as fortunate as Miss Lucas. Look, I'm going to Scotland Yard in the morning. My editor wants me to get a new angle for the Sunday edition of the paper."

"You're not going to tell them about Grace," Bill hissed. "You can't betray us just because—"

"I'm not going to betray anybody," Simon said firmly. "But they need to know that Miss Lyon's murder wasn't an isolated incident. This is surely going to force them to pay more attention."

"If you so much as breathe Grace's name or the location of the club..." Bill pointed to the bulky figure of Sylvia in her uniform and beret standing by the door. She said no more but the implication was clear.

"Mr Sampson?"

Grace Lucas stood behind them. Simon wondered how long she had been there and how much she had heard.

"I'm sorry to interrupt you both, but why don't I show you where I was attacked and then take Miss Casewell home? It means you can continue your investigations and we can both get some sleep. I for one could do with it."

"Capital idea," Bill said with enthusiasm. "With your ju-jitsu skills I'm the first to admit that you're far better qualified to protect Miss Casewell from mystery assailants. And Mr Sampson needs a close eye kept on him. Don't you, Simon my dear?"

Simon struck another match. He held it close to the pavement and scanned the area. The usual detritus of city life had collected in the unswept alleyway next to the club. Dirt, discarded cigarette ends, desiccated leaves from the previous winter, and shards of glass from broken bottles. Apart from an unused prophylactic still in its wrapper there was nothing that might give a clue to Grace Lucas's attacker.

"Over here." Bill had been searching the ground close to the club. "I think I may have found something."

She held up a tie clip. It was made of gold metal with a small black cross in the centre of the cross-bar. Simon took it to the club entrance and examined it in the gaslight. It was unlikely the metal was true gold because there were clear signs of tarnishing. He squeezed open the clip and saw a row of letters engraved beneath. Bill leaned over his shoulder and peered at it.

"What does it say?"

"I'm not sure," Simon replied. "Let's take it back into the club. The light's better in there."

"Good idea. We can ask if one of the members has lost it."

"Surely it belongs to a man. What's a woman doing with a tie clip?'

Bill shook her head. "You're really not very observant, are you? Apart from me, at least half a dozen other women were wearing ties in the club this evening."

"But you've got a waistcoat on," Simon protested. "So you don't need a tie clip."

"Come with me." Bill banged on the glass panel in the entrance door. "You've had a very sheltered upbringing when it comes to women's attire, haven't you?"

·   ·   ·

Simon held the tie clip under the lamp on Sylvia's desk and peered at the letters on the back of it.

"Well?" Bill asked impatiently. "What's it say?"

"It's still really difficult to make it out," Simon replied. "Even in this light. I think it says *'From Father to...'* someone. But I can't work out the name. It begins with a 'C' and an 'a'. Then perhaps a 't' and then there's a gap where the letters have rubbed away. And the last letter could be a 'y'." "He looked up. "Cathy?"

"Oh really, Simon." Bill grabbed the clip from him and examined it herself. "You're actually saying a father had a daughter called Cathy and he gave her a tie clip? What dream world do you live in? I know I said there were several women in this club who wear ties. But I've yet to hear of an enlightened father who accepts his Sapphic daughter for what she is and gives her a bloody tie clip."

"Well I can't think of a man's name that fits those letters," Simon retorted. "Can you?"

"That's because you're reading it wrong." Bill replied. "That's an 'l' not a 't' in the middle. I think the name's Charley."

"It could still be a woman's name," Simon commented. "Charley is short for both Charles and Charlotte."

"Don't be absurd, Simon darling." Bill dropped the tie clip onto the desk and lit a cigarette. "It's really not much of a haul after nearly an hour of crawling around on our hands and knees, is it?" She picked up the prophylactic wrapper from the desktop using the open jaws of the tie clip.

"Don't do that," Simon admonished. "They could be vital evidence."

"I really don't think so." Bill replied. "All this shows is that some bugger has an unsecured tie and he won't be getting his end away tonight. That's if they even belong to the same person."

She dropped the tie clip with the prophylactic wrapper clamped in its jaws back onto the desk.

"Perhaps Sylvia can ask around to see if it belongs to anyone who comes to the club," she continued. "The tie clip I mean. Not the other thing. Another gin and tonic? I think we've earned it."

Simon shook his head. "I've got an appointment at Scotland Yard in the morning." He stood and picked up his hat. "I'll need a clear head to deal with Sergeant Daniels."

There were better ways Simon could think of to fill his Saturday morning than sitting in a dingy office in the basement of Scotland Yard waiting for a detective sergeant who was already twenty minutes late. He wondered why he had been ushered into this scruffy, airless room. Even one of the walls had been left unfinished, with its bare brick exposed.

Apart from the chair he sat on, the only other furniture was a second chair and a wooden desk. On previous visits Daniels had met him in the large office he shared with another officer on the third floor overlooking the Thames. Simon stood and walked towards the door to look out into the corridor. Before he reached it the door flew open and Detective Sergeant Daniels strode into the room.

"What the hell are you doing in here?' he asked. "This is an interview room. What were they thinking of?"

"Perhaps they decided I'm a suspect," Simon replied.

"Wouldn't surprise me." Daniels slumped into a chair and swung his feet onto the desk. "There's not many a policeman as trusts a reporter. With good reason. We may as well stay here now. I've only got ten minutes anyway. I'm hoping to get off by twelve. It's my daughter's birthday this afternoon."

"It's very good of you to see me." Simon resumed his seat in the chair opposite Daniels. "I won't take up much of your precious time. I wanted to know if there's been any development in the murder investigation."

"Which murder?" Daniels took a match from his pocket and poked around in the bowl of his pipe.

"Have there really been that many since last Wednesday?"

"Oh God, you mean the stage door murder?" Daniels struck the match against the bare brick wall and lit his pipe. "I told you the other day. The investigation's not that easy when the victim's a woman like that."

"Is there nothing new I can report to our readers?" Simon coughed when Daniels exhaled a cloud of smoke in his direction. "I need to write something for the Sunday edition tomorrow."

"There's been no arrest if that's what you want." Daniels shrugged. "We've been asking around. Spoken to some of the girl's friends. Her *special* friend she lived with..." Daniels sniffed as though a bad smell had irritated his nostrils. "She wasn't at all helpful. Almost obstructive I'd say."

"Have you had the autopsy results?"

"She was strangled." Daniels shrugged. "With a sash cord. Not much more to say."

"Was no evidence of her attacker found on her body?" Simon asked. "Shreds of skin under the fingernails? Threads from a coat or something?"

"Regular little Sherlock Holmes, aren't you?" Daniels took the pipe from his mouth and pointed its stem at Simon. "Trying to accuse me of not doing my job properly again are you? No, Mr Sampson. There's nothing special in the autopsy report. And we searched that alleyway from top to bottom before you ask. Full of all sorts of rubbish. But nothing as would give us a clue to her murderer."

Daniels stuck his pipe back into his mouth. The tobacco

embers glowed red as he puffed on it. He pulled back the cuff of his jacket to check the time on his watch. It looked like Scotland Yard had already shoved the investigation onto the back burner. Without any fresh development Simon's story would soon be put on the spike by his editor. He was well aware of his promise to respect Grace Lucas's anonymity. But he needed to keep the story fresh.

"What if I was to tell you the killer has struck again?" Simon asked finally.

"When?"

"Last night," Simon replied. "In Soho. Shortly after midnight. Except this time he wasn't successful. The woman managed to escape."

"We haven't had any report of this." Daniels swung his feet off the desk and leaned across it. "How do you know about this?"

"I was there." Simon wafted away the smoke from Daniels's pipe. "I tried to persuade the young lady to report it to the police but she was afraid to do so."

"Hah." Daniels lent back in his chair and swung his feet back onto the desk, narrowly missing Simon's face. "Not much we can do if she won't report it."

"But it was the same modus operandi."

"Come again?"

"It was the same method used to try to strangle this young woman," Simon explained. "A length of sash cord."

"How come she wasn't killed then?"

"She's an expert in ju-jitsu. She overpowered her attacker who ran off."

"I'm not surprised he ran off." Daniels laughed. "She's not one of them suffragette women is she? Bloody terrifying. I'd run a mile as well if I bumped into one of them."

"The point is," Simon continued patiently. "It looks like the murder on Wednesday wasn't just a one-off. And this person could strike again."

"Now just a minute." Daniels wagged a finger at Simon. "I warned you about this the other day. Don't start making up stories about serial killers and go terrifying the public. If this woman was attacked like you say she was why hasn't she reported it?"

"I told you," Simon replied. "She's afraid."

"What of?" Daniels shook his head. "Oh, hang on a minute. You said it was Soho. What is she? A whore? A pervert? No wonder she won't say anything."

"But I'm telling you about it now," Simon protested. "Someone tried to strangle a young woman in Soho last night just before midnight. And the attacker used a sash cord. The same murder weapon used to murder Maureen Lyon. I saw it myself."

"What's this woman's name then?" Daniels asked. "And where exactly was it in Soho?"

"I can't tell you. I promised the young lady—"

Daniels swung his legs off the desk and shoved his face close to Simon's.

"Why are you protecting these people, Sampson? And why do you think we should be wasting valuable resources on them?"

JOURNAL ENTRY 20 JULY 1929

The cursed woman got away. And injured me in the process. I remember how they told us that these sons and daughters of Satan could have superhuman strength.

Now I've experienced it first-hand. I hope that it doesn't hinder me when I return to work tomorrow. I may be asked awkward questions.

If only I'd had my stick with me. Then I could have subdued the viperous woman easily. But it's too dangerous to carry it when I'm not on official business.

I really need to toughen up. That was my weakness on that night and I must not allow it to defeat me. The crusade has only just begun and there is much yet still to do. Next time I must arm myself with more than my God and my bare hands. I can't risk another one of them getting away to sin again.

But I will always have more time. Maybe after I have finished work and I am able to find that same accursed woman again. If I do, I will be ready for whatever defence she presents to me.

So that this time she will be silenced.

9

There was only ever one person who telephoned Bill on a Sunday morning. Well, perhaps her friend Daphne might call if she had an urgent question about seating arrangements for a forthcoming soirée. But Bill had spoken to Daphne three days ago at the drinks party after the opening of *Bitter Sweet*. No, she was confident who was causing the phone to ring so shrilly at nine-thirty this Sunday morning.

"There's really absolutely no need for you to hurry, my dear," said the voice at the other end when she finally reached the hallway and lifted the receiver. "I'd hate for you to feel I was being inconvenienced by your tardiness."

"Noël, it's first thing on a Sunday morning." Bill looked around and then cursed under her breath when she realised she had left her cigarettes in the sitting room. "Civilised people don't talk on the telephone at this time of day, let alone on a Sunday."

"Civilised people don't entangle themselves with the disreputable underworld of the gutter press," Noël replied sharply. "The swines only turn round and stab you in the back. Have you seen this morning's papers?"

"Noël darling, I got out of bed to answer your call." Bill

pulled the flapping edge of her silk wrap tighter around her. "I haven't had my first cup of coffee yet, let alone opened a newspaper. Let me say it again. It's Sunday morning."

"So it is," Noël replied. "And after you've been to church and confessed all your sins you can run along and buy the papers. All of them. Especially that bloody rag *The Chronicle*. Read it and call me later. I'm at the flat all morning. Cowering in a corner, staring at the wall in quiet desperation."

The line went dead.

"I can't do this any longer," Bill said to the silent telephone receiver. "Nursemaid to a spoiled little boy. He may be supremely talented but he's also a supreme pain in the neck."

She went into the kitchen, prepared the coffee percolator, and set it on the stove. While she waited for it to brew she telephoned the porter.

"Danvers, darling? It's Florence Miles here. Have the Sunday papers arrived yet?"

"I put them outside your door at seven this morning," Danvers replied. "I didn't ring the bell as I thought you might want a lie-in after the excitement of Mr Coward's show opening this week."

"What an absolute treasure you are, Danvers," Bill replied. "What would we do without you?"

"Mr Coward must be loving how much attention he's getting," Danvers continued. "He's all over the front page of *The Chronicle*. Mainly because of that murder. Enjoy your Sunday ma'am."

Bill settled herself in a chair on her balcony overlooking St John's Wood. It was going to be another scorching hot day and there was scarcely a breath of wind. She lit a cigarette, took a sip of coffee, and pulled *The Chronicle* from the pile of newspapers next to her.

"Good God, Simon," she exclaimed. "What have you dropped me in this time?"

The report was halfway down the front page with the headline 'Noël Coward Theatre Killer Strikes Again'. It went on to describe the events outside the club in Soho. Simon had been careful not to name Grace Lucas or the club. But the article mentioned Soho several times, included one more reference to Noël, and a mention of *Bitter Sweet*. The final two paragraphs accused the Metropolitan Police of failing to take the attacks seriously.

Bill took a final drag on her cigarette and stubbed it out, finished her coffee and went back inside to refill the cup. She paused by the telephone in the hallway for several minutes before picking up the receiver. After the operator connected her a sleepy sounding man's voice answered the call.

"Have you decided to give up on your job completely or is this some kind of professional suicide?" she asked.

"Good grief, Bill," Simon groaned. "Do you have to shout quite so loudly? I've not long woken up. Can I call you back in a while?"

"I have a very angry boss breathing fire down the phone at me and demanding answers," Bill replied. "Don't be long."

She was about to put the receiver back in its cradle when she heard another man's voice calling Simon's name.

"Do you have someone with you?" she demanded.

"It's really—I mean—I don't see how it's any of your business —" Simon began.

"You've got a man there, haven't you?" Bill chuckled. "Well, you're a sly one, Mr Sampson. And after all your denials at The Paradise Club the other night. I won't disturb you further."

She hung up the phone, lit another cigarette, and carried her coffee cup back out to the balcony.

So much for Simon's claim he was too busy to have a significant other in his life. She would enjoy watching him squirm later when she tried to prise the identity of the mystery man from him. Of course it could simply be an old university friend or a relative.

But somehow she doubted that

She picked up another newspaper from the pile next to her. There was no mention of Maureen's murder in it. She turned to the arts section and had barely begun reading the reviews when the telephone rang again. This was turning into an irritatingly busy Sunday morning.

"Well?" said a crisp voice in her ear. "Have you spoken to your little viper in the grass, yet?"

"Noël, I've only just poured my second cup of coffee. What exactly do you want me to do? Scold him? Remove him from my Christmas card list?"

"Good God you've not got to that stage of exchanging billets doux already, have you?" Noël's voice thundered. "I want you to tell him, politely of course but in no uncertain terms, that his absolute rag of a newspaper is to desist immediately from associating my name with the murders of these unfortunate women."

"Murder," Bill corrected. "There's only been one so far. The second woman managed to fend off her attacker."

"Very resourceful of her, I'm sure." Noël's voice was icy. "Dammit, Bill. I'm trying to run a respectable theatre company here. I don't care two hoots what the critics say about my productions as long as it's unqualified praise. But reporters really have no right to include my name in their grubby little articles about a murderer loose on the streets of London."

"I thought you were opposed to censorship, Noël," Bill commented coolly.

"When it's carried out by that puritanical prig the Lord Chamberlain, of course I am," Noël replied. "But I will not be the subject of slander or libel. Deal with it, Bill."

The line went dead.

Bill was about to head back to the balcony when the phone rang again.

"Oh, for goodness sake," she exclaimed. "Why did I ever have this infernal contraption installed?"

This time she lit a cigarette before she picked up the receiver. "Do you realise it's Sunday morning and it's not even ten o'clock? Decent people don't speak on a Sunday until after midday."

"I'm terribly sorry," said Simon in her ear. "I'll call back later."

"Do not hang up," Bill commanded. "Simon, are you there? Hello? Hello?"

"I'm still here, Bill," Simon said. "Are you all right?"

"Not in the least," she replied. "Noël's furious with you. Which means he's furious with me."

"Why's he so angry? All publicity is good publicity as the saying goes."

"That was P T Barnum's ridiculous assertion." Bill breathed smoke into the mouthpiece in exasperation. "Noël is not a circus owner. He's a highly respected playwright and theatre producer. He wants you to stop linking his name to your slanderous articles."

"It's libel not slander when it's written down," Simon corrected. "And it's out of my hands I'm afraid. That was the editor's decision."

"Well, tell him to stop." Bill stubbed out her cigarette in the ashtray so vigorously she knocked it onto the floor and scattered ash across the parquet. "Damn. I think I'll go back to bed and start this day again."

"Before you do let me give you some good news," Simon continued. "Somerskill rang a short while ago to say the Metropolitan Police are absolutely furious."

"I'm not surprised." Bill lit another cigarette. "Who the hell's Somerskill?"

"My editor," Simon replied. "I told you about him over dinner. Do keep up. Anyway, the commissioner rang Somerskill to say the Met is putting extra efforts into the search for the murderer. They're holding a press conference tomorrow morning to announce it. Imagine. One article from me gets the Met to leap into action. Unheard of."

"It's about time they did something useful." Bill knelt down and attempted to clear up the mess from the ashtray. "Are you going? And if so, can I come?"

Simon replaced the receiver and went back to the kitchen to finish making the coffee. Bright sunlight streamed through the open window but the traffic sounds of London on a Sunday were muted and distant.

"Who was that?" a voice called from the bedroom.

"That was Miss Miles again." Simon glanced at the clock on the wall. "Come on, Calvin. Haven't you got up yet? You're going to be late if you're not careful."

The kettle boiled. Simon turned off the gas and warmed the cafetière. He added two scoops of French roast coffee and topped it up with boiling water.

"That smells good." The voice came from behind him. "Do you have any pastries as well?"

"Calvin, you're not even dressed." Simon took down two

cups from the cupboard. "I thought you said you were on duty at twelve?"

Calvin tightened the towel wrapped around his waist, folded his arms, and leaned against the kitchen doorframe. "Miss Miles? The one who disturbed us earlier? Why is she so angry with you?"

"I've made peace with her now." Simon poured the coffee. "For the moment."

"Why are women in London always so difficult?" Calvin asked. "Where I come from they are much more relaxed."

"That's because where you come from women aren't given such a hard time. They have a place. Opportunity. They're treated differently."

"We treat them differently in the city. Yes that is certainly true." Calvin took a cup of coffee from Simon. "In the countryside it is still very traditional. But I do not think the way you treat Miss Miles would make any difference. It is just the way she is. In German we would say Sie erträgt Narren nicht so leicht."

"Oh, she certainly doesn't suffer fools gladly." Simon laughed. "But I find the way she deals with them rather endearing."

"Even when it is you?" Calvin asked.

"Are you calling me a fool?"

"But of course not." Calvin put his cup on the worktop next to the door. "Maybe she treats you like one sometimes, no? You have not known her long yet she seems very familiar already."

"I met her the week after you and I celebrated our three-month anniversary."

"And when am I going to meet her?"

"There's plenty of time for that." Simon gestured to the hallway. "Let's go and drink our coffee next door. Then you need to get going. And I do too."

Calvin leaned forward and kissed Simon. "Are you not coming back to bed for a while?"

"Herr Schatz." Simon laid a hand on Calvin's chest. "We both have work today. I certainly can't be late. My editor's expecting me. And I thought the senior officer you report to was a stickler for punctuality?"

"Stickler?" Calvin laughed. "What a strange language this is. How fortunate for me to meet a journalist. Now I can learn even more bizarre words."

"As if you need to," Simon replied. "Your English is perfect to my ear. Better than that of some Englishmen I know."

"Ah, but that is where you are wrong. I have much to perfect."

"Much to perfect." Simon ran his hand across Calvin's chest. "That's what the hours in the gym are for. I'm surprised you have time for anything else."

"It is essential for my work." Calvin grasped Simon's hand. "You know that if I am to do this good work I must be physically fit. I cannot afford to make mistakes when protecting our society against the bad ways of the world." His hand gripped Simon's even tighter.

"It's almost like you have a calling." Simon extricated his hand from Calvin's with difficulty. "Your passion is almost alarming sometimes. Come on. You need to get in the shower and be on your way."

Calvin smiled. "I will be late finishing tonight. May I come back afterwards?"

Simon picked up his coffee. "I don't see why not."

Calvin gave Simon one more lingering kiss on the lips before he headed for the shower.

There was something about Calvin's disarming frankness that both thrilled and unnerved Simon. It was very un-English. As they had got to know each other Simon had become increasingly curious about Berlin, the city where Calvin was from. A city that welcomed men who were other sounded far more appealing than London's oppressive society.

It made Simon restless. He was nearly thirty and yet he had never left England. Maybe now was the time. Perhaps, when Calvin returned to Germany he would go with him.

10

Bill's greeting outside Scotland Yard the following morning was brief and to the point.

"God, you look rough, Simon. Didn't you get any sleep last night?"

"It's too hot to be able to sleep much at the moment." Simon pulled his hat lower over his eyes. "What about you? Why the dark glasses and the headscarf? You look like Greta Garbo."

"It's in case there are photographers here," Bill replied. "If my picture ends up in the paper Noël will kill me."

"I thought you weren't so keen on working for him anyway?"

"If I leave I want it to be my decision not his." Bill held up a notepad and pencil. "Is this authentic enough?"

"Oh dear." Simon opened the door for Bill. "Not so much Greta Garbo as Dorothy Parker. Just keep a low profile when you're inside, will you? If the commissioner's there he's going to be looking out for me as it is."

Bill noted she was the only woman amongst nearly two dozen men in the smoke-filled, windowless room where they waited for the press conference to begin. The featureless space must have doubled as a classroom. Everyone sat at individual wooden school desks equipped with inkwells and hard wooden seats. It reminded her of the miserable years she had spent at a convent boarding school in Rhyl. If the session became too dull she would persuade the others to engage in an ink pellet fight to while away the time.

"Good morning, gentlemen."

A uniformed police officer sporting an enormous waxed moustache strode up to a large desk at the front of the room and sat. He was followed by someone Bill recognised instantly.

"My name is Chief Inspector Traynor and this is Detective Sergeant Daniels," the moustachioed officer continued. "We've all been called out on this bright sunny day thanks to a scurrilous report in one of your newspapers." He paused and slowly scanned the room. Bill lowered her head and raised her hand to screen her face from the officer's scrutiny.

"And I see the author of this work of fiction is amongst us this morning," Chief Inspector Traynor snorted. "Mr Sampson. I'm surprised you dare to show your face at Scotland Yard after your outrageous article in *The Chronicle* yesterday. Not the sort of thing the commissioner wants to be reading over his breakfast kedgeree."

Simon said nothing. Bill turned her head and saw him stare down at his notepad. His cheeks glowed crimson.

"Nothing to say for yourself?" The chief inspector's voice boomed in the cramped classroom. "Perhaps it's just as well. The commissioner has asked me to tell you, gentlemen of the press, that whatever the scurrilous *Chronicle* might publish, the Metropolitan Police force is doing everything in its power to catch the perpetrator of the heinous murder at the stage door of

His Majesty's Theatre five days ago. Extra men have been assigned to the case and summer leave has been cancelled for a substantial part of the force."

The chief inspector turned his head to address Simon directly. "You can imagine how popular that decision is amongst the brave, hardworking officers of this great institution. But we will not be accused of slacking or failing to do our job. Whatever the class or unusual proclivities of the poor unfortunate victim, the Metropolitan Police will work ceaselessly to ensure the killer is brought to justice."

He sat back in his chair, folded his arms, and glanced around the room with a look of defiance on his face. "Any questions?"

A man with a pipe clenched in his teeth raised his hand. "Jackson. *Daily Mail*."

"Ah." Chief Inspector Traynor smiled and nodded approvingly. "A quality newspaper. What's your question, Jackson?"

"What about the other woman who was attacked? Will you be investigating that incident as well?"

"We will not." Traynor shook his head. "Because there's nothing to investigate. It's another fabrication in the tissue of lies *The Chronicle* has published. Quite apart from falsely alleging laziness on the part of my esteemed colleagues, the paper has invented this story to further discredit the force."

"It's not a fabrication."

"What was that?" The chief inspector gripped the edge of the desk and leaned forward. "Who spoke?"

"I did." Bill stood. She removed her sunglasses and headscarf. Several reporters gasped and reached for their notebooks.

"And who are you, young lady?" asked the chief inspector.

"My name is Sarah Millick," Bill replied.

Simon chuckled and Bill suppressed the urge to smile. He

had clearly spotted her use of the lead character's name in *Bitter Sweet*.

"Well, Miss Millick," Traynor continued. "Would you be so good as to explain why you disagree with my assertion?"

"Because the article in *The Chronicle* is all true—"

"I hardly think—"

"It *is* true." Whether it was the tone of Bill's voice or the expression on her face but the chief inspector made no further attempt to interrupt. He sat back in his chair, folded his arms, and nodded for her to continue.

"The attack in Soho occurred exactly as described in *The Chronicle*. Shortly after eleven-thirty on Friday night a young woman was brutally attacked by a person, possibly a man, using a length of cord similar to that used in the murder of Maureen Lyon at His Majesty's Theatre. It was only because the young woman was skilled in ju-jitsu that she was able to fend off her attacker and escape."

When Bill stopped speaking there was no sound in the room save for the nervous tapping of Detective Sergeant Daniels' foot against the table leg. Chief Inspector Traynor slowly unfolded his arms and leaned forward.

"And how can you be so sure that this attack happened?"

"Because I was there." She held up the length of cord she and Simon had found in the Paradise Regained Club. "This is what the attacker used to try to strangle the victim."

The interview room was no bigger than twelve feet square. Lime-green brick walls extended to a high ceiling where a solitary light bulb hung from a frayed flex. Near the top of one wall was a small window. Bill was halfway through her second cigarette before she realised the window was closed and her smoke was adding to the airlessness of the room. She stood, strode across to the door, and grabbed the handle. It was locked.

"Let me out of here at once." She rattled the handle and banged on the door. "How dare you lock me in. Open up this minute."

After Bill's dramatic announcement at the press conference Detective Sergeant Daniels had invited her to stay behind and answer some questions. With all the reporters staring at her she realised she had little choice in the matter. A constable had escorted her to the interview room, assured her Daniels was on his way, and had shut the door. That was nearly twenty minutes ago.

She rattled the handle fruitlessly one more time and turned to resume her seat at the small wooden table in the middle of the room.

A key scraped in the lock and the door swung open. Detective Sergeant Daniels stood on the threshold with the constable behind him.

"Why was I locked in?" Bill demanded. "Am I under arrest?"

"Not at all. "Daniels gestured to the open door. "A simple mistake by the constable. You're free to go if you wish, but obviously I'd prefer you to stay. Would you like some tea?"

"Good God, no." Bill sat at the table and stubbed out her cigarette on the floor. "But tell him to get us an ashtray. It's the least he can do." She lit another cigarette and waved towards the closed window. "And get that thing open. I can't see my hand in front of my face with the fug in here."

"It's stuck." Daniels dismissed the constable with an order of a cup of tea for himself and sat opposite Bill at the table. "Miss Millick. When I met you at the theatre last week you told me your name was Miss Florence Miles. I also have reason to believe that you answer to the name of Bill–"

"Only to my close friends, sergeant. Not the Metropolitan Police."

"*Detective* sergeant," Daniels corrected. "Why did you give a false name at the press conference this afternoon? In fact, why were you at the press conference in the first place? You're not a journalist are you?"

"I was accompanying Mr Sampson." Bill blew a cloud of smoke across the table. "And I changed my name because I didn't want the less honourable members of the press to write about me in the shoddy rags they call newspapers."

"And you consider Mr Sampson to be honourable?"

"Of course. I do."

Bill reflected on her answer. She had responded instinctively but was it an honest answer? Yes, of course it was. Would she have said that about any journalist before she'd met Simon? Never. She would have parroted Noël's disdain for the profession.

"If it hadn't been for Mr Sampson your chief inspector would never have called that press conference. It seems like he's started to take my friend's murder seriously. And you're sitting here finally ready to investigate an attempted murder in Soho."

"Alleged attempted murder," Daniels countered. "And we were already taking the murder of Miss Lyon seriously, whatever Mr Sampson might claim." He took a pipe from his pocket and poked at the contents of its bowl with a match. "Let's start with the name of the alleged victim and where the alleged attack took place."

"Will you stop using that word 'alleged', please?" Bill tapped the ash from her cigarette onto the floor. "It makes me sound like a liar. And where's that constable with the ashtray? Between your pipe and my cigarettes we'll be knee-deep in ash in a minute."

"The name, Miss Miles." Daniels took a tobacco pouch from his pocket and restocked his pipe. "And the location."

"I can't tell you her name, detective sergeant." Bill nudged the ash and cigarette stubs around her feet into a tidy pile with the toe of her shoe. "We did try to persuade her to go to the police. But she didn't believe you'd take someone like her seriously."

"'Someone like her'," Daniels repeated. He struck a match and puffed on his pipe until the tobacco in the bowl glowed red. "Someone like her in Soho. That makes her either a prostitute or a pervert. I'm presuming the latter as you and Sampson have been attempting to link the two crimes. And it was late at night. So might I be right in assuming it took place at one of those clubs for women of a certain persuasion?"

Bill said nothing.

"I see." Daniels clenched the pipe between his teeth, opened the notepad to a fresh page, and picked up his pencil. "Let's assume I'm right and it's one of the female perverts clubs. That narrows it down to three. Which one is it, Miss Miles?"

"Do you have to be so offensive, detective sergeant?" Bill asked. "I resent you using that word pervert."

"Common parlance, Miss Miles," Daniels replied. "People like that can hardly be considered normal."

"Ah, 'normal'." Bill leaned back in her chair and crossed her legs. "Such a dull word for a dull existence. Don't forget that Freud concluded all humans are innately perverse. He found the origins of human perversions–"

"I don't give a damn about Freud and his ungodly theories," snapped Daniels. "If you want us to investigate this alleged assault you're going to have to cooperate. And that starts with giving me some information."

"I've already said, detective sergeant." Bill stubbed out her cigarette on the floor and lit another. "I have a duty to respect the confidentiality of the victim. She didn't want to go to the police—"

"Don't give me that." Daniels reached into his pocket and threw the length of window cord she and Simon had found onto the table. Its sudden reappearance caused Bill to take a sharp intake of breath. "You claim that someone tried to strangle a woman last Friday night with this length of cord."

"I'm not just claiming it—"

"And the attacker could strike again if you don't start helping us with information. If you won't tell me the woman's name, or the name of the club, then we'll visit all three clubs today, interview everyone we find there, and then shut them down."

"You can't do that."

"Oh, but we can, Miss Miles." Daniels wrote a list of names on the pad and turned it round for Bill to read. "Would you care to tell me which one it is? That way you can at least prevent the other two suffering the inconvenience of a police visit."

11

"How could you, Bill?"

Sylvia slammed a glass of gin and tonic down on the countertop between them.

Bill picked up the glass, took a sip, and peered into the gloom of the dimly lit interior of the Paradise Regained Club. It was empty save for her and Sylvia. Normally at this time of the evening the place would be crowded with women. Instead, the empty tables were testament to a brutal visit from the police earlier that day.

It was lunchtime when three police officers had arrived to close the club just as Daniels had promised. They had been ruthlessly efficient in their cross-examination of a dozen women who'd had the misfortune to be in the club at the time. After they had been turned out onto the street a closure order was nailed to the doorpost outside and Sylvia and Bill had been left alone.

"I told you before." Bill put her glass back on the counter. To avoid Sylvia's angry expression she stared at the condensation misting its side and swirled her finger around in it to write her name. "If I hadn't told Daniels the name of this place yesterday he'd have closed the Cherry Tree and the Honey Pot as well. It wouldn't have been fair."

"Is this fair?" Sylvia pointed to the empty tables. "What am I going to do now? More to the point, what are any of us going to do now? The police have really got us in their sights now, thanks to you and that idiot reporter friend of yours."

"Simon's not an idiot," Bill responded. "He's an ally. He's on our side. He knows how we feel because he's also 'other' as they so charmingly put it. And he's got a strong sense of moral justice. You know as well as I do that the police should be putting more effort into investigating Maureen's murder. And into the attack on Grace. Simon thinks the crimes are connected, he's sure they are. I think he's right. It can't be a coincidence that a cord was used in both attacks and that both victims are 'other'."

"But all he's done is draw attention to us. We were safer before. Keeping our heads down. Trying not to flaunt ourselves."

"'Flaunt ourselves'?" Bill almost knocked her glass over. "Is that what you're accusing me of doing? Wearing trousers and cutting my hair short?"

"No, but—"

"And if you're going to use that offensive word might I ask you if you're not doing the same? Wearing that workman's overall and—"

"It's not a workman's overall." Sylvia straightened and put her hands on her hips to model the outfit. "This is worn by women comrades in the Soviet Union. A friend of mine brought it back from a hand-of-friendship visit to Leningrad."

Bill laughed. "You'd better not 'flaunt' that piece of information if the police interview you again. Otherwise you'll be charged with being a Bolshevik." She reached for a cigarette and lit it. "I'm tired of having to keep a low profile. Why can't I be who I am? I hear it's completely different in Berlin. People like us aren't harassed by the police. There are hundreds of clubs there and no one bats an eyelid."

"Yes, but people like us are practically legal in Germany." Sylvia reached for a bottle of whisky and poured herself a double. "Here we're always only one step away from being arrested—"

"It's true, but on what charge?" Bill interrupted. "It's not like there's a special law for us like there is for the men. They can't arrest us for gross indecency because that law doesn't apply to women. When they drafted it last century they didn't think we were capable of such things. God bless the Victorians and their limited imaginations—that's all I can say."

"Well, they found an excuse to close us down today." Sylvia put her glass on the countertop. She walked around to Bill, slipped an arm around her waist, and kissed her on the cheek. "Oh, my dear Bill. I'm sorry to be so ratty with you. I know you were only trying to do what you thought was right."

Bill turned to her and returned the kiss on her lips. "I don't suppose you'd reconsider my invitation of last year?"

"I'm sorry Bill, dear." Sylvia slipped her arm away from Bill's waist. She walked over to one of the now empty tables and tidied the chairs scattered around it. "My heart is meant for another."

Sylvia bent down, picked up a small piece of card from the floor, and examined it. "Goodness, that's careless."

"What is it?" Bill asked.

Sylvia walked back to the bar and put the card on the countertop in front of Bill. "One of my customers. In her haste to leave she dropped her visiting card. She's the wife of Judge Soames. Thank goodness the police didn't find this or there'd have been a major scandal."

Bill picked up the card. "I'm sure they'd have hushed it up. The last thing they want is for the public to know that the judiciary, or their families, are less than perfect." She tapped the card on the rim of her glass. "But this gives me an idea."

"Oh my dear, no." Sylvia took the card from Bill and shoved it in her pocket. "You are *not* calling on Lady Cynthia Soames and threatening her with blackmail. She's been a very loyal client of this establishment and a very good friend to me." Sylvia took a swig of whisky. "A very loyal friend indeed."

Bill smiled. "Is she the one for whom your heart is intended?"

"No, it's not her." Sylvia turned away and tidied some glasses back onto the shelf behind the bar.

"It's all right." Bill lit a cigarette." I won't ask any more questions. Your secret is safe with me. No, I've got a far better idea. Simon introduced me to his aunt at the Salisbury the other day."

"What on earth were you doing in the Salisbury?"

"It's not important." Bill waved her hand dismissively. "The point is she's something very high-powered in the Home Office. If only Simon could persuade her to have a quiet word with someone in the Met about this closure order we might have a chance—"

She was interrupted by a loud banging at the main door. Sylvia strode across to it. "We're closed," she shouted. "Courtesy of the Metropolitan Police. I'm not allowed to let you in."

"It's all right, it's me," said a muffled voice.

"Speak of the devil," Sylvia said. "It's Mr Sampson." She unbolted the door and opened it a few inches. "I'm not allowed to let anyone in. You and your friend have managed to get me banned."

A hand appeared and pushed the door open a few inches. Simon's head appeared.

"Perfect timing, " Bill exclaimed. "We were just talking about you. Well, about your aunt. Do you think you could get her to reopen this place?"

"Bill," Simon smiled. "She's my aunt I don't know if I could ask a favour like that–"

"Well, really." Sylvia moved to push Simon's head back through the opening and close the door. "It's your fault I'm in this mess."

"Will you just let me in for one minute?" Simon pushed hard against Sylvia. Her foot slipped on the stone floor, and she landed flat on her back.

Bill strode across and knelt at Sylvia's side. "Are you all right, my dear? Anything broken?" She glowered at Simon. "Haven't you done enough damage already?"

"Me?" Simon leaned against the doorjamb and folded his arms. "I'm not the one who stood up in the middle of a police press conference and told them they were lying."

"I never said—"

"Will you just shut up, Bill?" Simon shook his head. "Why do you always have to argue? If you give me a minute I can explain my plan to get this place open again."

He bent down to Sylvia. "I'm very sorry to knock you over. I do hope you're not injured."

Sylvia sat up abruptly and Simon had to duck out of the way to avoid their heads clashing. "No damage," she said briskly. "Now what's this plan of yours? I'm in need of some good news today."

There was a loud tapping at the open door and the flash of silver from a distinctive walking stick.

"Hello?" Aunt Cynny stood on the threshold. "May I come in? It might be after sunset but it's still awfully exposing out here. I'd really rather not be recognised."

Simon straightened and extended an arm to his aunt. "Come in at once and I'll close the door." He turned around. "Sylvia? Allow me to introduce Aunt Buckingham. I mean, Miss Cynthia Buckingham."

"Cynny!" Sylvia jumped to her feet and embraced Simon's aunt passionately. "Thank goodness you're here."

<h1 style="text-align:center">12</h1>

There was such a thick cloud of smoke hanging above their table Simon was almost tempted to take up smoking rather than endure it passively. He had forgotten that Aunt Cynny smoked cheroots. She sat with Bill and Sylvia, lighting one after another as the three women talked about mutual friends, the state of the arts in Britain, and whether communism or fascism was a more potent threat to the future of the world.

They discussed anything except the reason Simon had brought Aunt Cynny to the Paradise Regained Club in the first place.

At first it had been difficult to persuade her to come out late on a Tuesday evening. When he had telephoned his aunt she had immediately said no. She was far too busy with an urgent policy paper she had to complete by the morning for the Home Secretary. When Simon had pressed her further she had added it would be unprofessional and undiplomatic for her to interfere in a police matter. Finally, when he had revealed the club to be the Paradise Regained she hesitated and Simon knew he had won her over.

"Can I get anyone a drink?" Sylvia walked over to the bar. "Are you sure you won't have another, Cynny?"

"Thank you, but I've got to keep a clear head, my dear. I've got this damned policy paper to finish by first thing tomorrow morning. I did try to explain it to young Sampson here."

"If you continue to call me 'young Sampson'," Simon protested. "I'll tell everyone what your real nickname was at home."

"Touché." His aunt slapped the back of her hand as if to reprimand herself. "Wouldn't do for people to know that, would it young man?"

Simon sighed. "Look. It's almost nine and I feel we really should make a start on the real reason we're all here and leave the gossiping for another time."

"'Gossiping'?" Bill exclaimed.

"It's all right my dear," Aunt Cynny responded. "Ever since he was a child Simon's always been a rather serious boy. Take no notice. Now young man. Tell me what's been going on."

Simon summarised the events of the past five days. His aunt leaned forward, rested her elbows on her knees, and cupped her head in her hands like a child listening intently to a bedtime story. When Simon had finished she stood, put her hands on her hips, and paced up and down the narrow space between the table and the bar.

"Tricky, tricky," she muttered.

"Do you think there's anything you can do?" Simon asked.

"Silence, my boy." Aunt Cynny stopped and raised a finger to her lips. "Aunty is thinking."

Bill chuckled. She reached across and patted Simon on the head as if he was a five-year-old.

"You know that's exceedingly irritating." Simon brushed Bill's hand away and glowered at her.

"Don't be so dull." Bill pouted. "Your aunt is delightful. I'm already falling in love with—"

"Tsk, tsk," Aunt Cynny interrupted. "Please remember the words of the great Pythagoras, *meaningful silence is better than meaningless words*. I need silence while I'm thinking."

Bill squeezed her lips between thumb and forefinger and nodded at Simon.

"Now, let me see." Simon's aunt continued to pace up and down. "It's going to be exceedingly difficult to get JR interested in this little domestic matter."

"Who's JR?" Simon asked.

Aunt Cynny stopped pacing and stared at him as if he had just asked her for the meaning of life.

"Why, my boss, dear boy. The Home Secretary. John Robert Clynes. Known as JR to those who are close to him. He's a dear man but a stickler for, how can I put it, the more conventional British way of life."

"You mean he's not one of us," Simon suggested.

"All I can say is he has a charming wife and two very well-behaved children–"

"Which doesn't necessarily mean he can't be 'other'," Bill interrupted.

Aunt Cynny sighed. "No dear. But in JR's case I'm pretty certain it does. Granted he's a very sensitive man. A remarkable man in many ways. He comes from a very poor background. Forced to work in a cotton mill when he was ten years old. Goodness knows how but he's risen from a lowly start to be Home Secretary. Very widely read. Loves his Milton, Shakespeare, Ruskin–"

"That's it." Simon jumped to his feet. "You know the name of this club, don't you?"

"Paradise Regained," Aunt Cynny answered. She slapped her thigh. "Good God, my boy. You always were a quick thinker. JR loves the writings of Milton. And Paradise Regained has become one of his favourites pieces. All I have to do is tell him the name of this place. I'm sure he'll be amenable to making a telephone call to the police commissioner and quietly suggesting his force reverse the closure order."

"Are you seriously suggesting," Bill began. "That you're going to persuade the Home Secretary that this club is devoted to the writings of John Milton?"

Aunt Cynny wheeled round and put her hands on her hips again. "Do you have a better idea?"

"I suppose not." Bill took out a cigarette and lit it. "But what happens when the commissioner tells him the real nature of the Paradise Regained Club?"

"JR's a very persuasive man." Aunt Cynny resumed her pacing. "And he does hold the purse strings for the Metropolitan Police. And they are in the middle of negotiating for extra funds. I'll go back and finish that urgent policy paper tonight. Tomorrow I'll hand it to JR first thing. He'll be in such a good mood because I've finished it that I'm sure I can persuade him to pick up the phone and have a quiet word with the commissioner. He trusts me. You never know, you could be open again by tomorrow evening, Sylvia." She took her seat back at the table. "That's sorted. Now. What about these murders? Any idea who's behind them, young Sampson?"

"Aunty Cynny, " Simon began. "You're doing it again."

His aunt slapped her palm to her forehead. "My God, I've forgotten already. I'm so sorry Simon. Dunce's cap for aunty."

She lit a cheroot and clamped it between her teeth. "You think the two murders are linked, don't you? What's your theory?"

"It's only one murder," Simon corrected his aunt. "But the other poor woman was also attacked by someone using a piece of window sash cord. It's the same weapon used in the murder of Miss Lyon. That's why I think they're linked."

"I stand corrected." Aunt Cynny puffed on her cheroot. "You don't think it was someone who'd read about the first murder in the paper and thought they'd have a go using a bit of window cord in the same way?"

"That bit about the window cord wasn't in any of the papers." Simon shook his head. "Because the police hadn't told us. And this afternoon Chief Inspector Traynor told us categorically not to publish anything about it for fear some maniac might copy our murderer's modus operandi."

"Very sensible of them." Aunt Cynny pointed her cheroot at Simon. "I'm sure they don't want another Jack the Ripper mess on their hands. I'm sure they're thinking about all the false leads the sensationalist reporting in the press created. Hundreds of them."

Bill jumped in to defend Simon before he had a chance to speak. "Simon has been extremely responsible in his reporting, Cynthia. If anyone's to be criticised I'd say it's the police themselves. That ghastly Daniels man actually told me he didn't want to investigate because Maureen and Grace are—different. Like us. He actually called us perverts. Vile man."

"He used the same word when he told me the press conference was cancelled," Simon added. "But I don't think it's just him. You hear it all the time."

"Excellent, excellent." Aunt Cynny was oblivious to the discussion. She clapped her hands delightedly. "There's a double connection between the two victims. The use of the window cord and the fact that both Miss Lyon and Miss Lucas are Sapphic sisters. Do you think that's the only motive? Have you had an opportunity to find out if Miss Lyon had any enemies?"

"Not that we're aware of," Simon replied. "Bill says she was very popular with the cast on productions. Always very hard-working."

"She came in here occasionally." Sylvia carried a tray of drinks over from the bar and handed them out. "Wasn't it here that you two first got together, Bill?"

"'Together'?" Aunt Cynny fumbled with the drink Sylvia had just given her. "Oh, my dear. Were you and Miss Lyon together as in 'together'?"

Sylvia laughed. "Sorry, Bill. Have I put my foot in it?"

"Not all." Bill lit a cigarette and blew out a cloud of smoke. "I was very privileged to be close to Maureen for a while, Cynthia. She had a very good heart and was a very sensitive soul."

"I'm so sorry for you, my dear." Aunt Cynny shook her head. "Simon, why on earth didn't you tell me when we met the other night? Poor Bill must have only just got the news. How devastating for her. And you and I were gassing on about trivia like your job and the BBC—"

"It wasn't trivia," Simon protested. "I didn't tell you because I didn't know they'd been together. And I wasn't sure if Bill was ready to talk about her to a complete stranger at that moment."

"Please don't talk about it anymore." Bill sighed. She looked almost embarrassed. "It really doesn't matter. It must be the compulsive secrecy of those of us who must live and love in the shadows I suppose. It's all in the past now."

"My dear." Aunt Cynny stood as if about to make a speech. "Our love is never something to be ashamed of. Whatever others in this world might say. We sisters must stand together. Perhaps there may come a day when our need for secrecy will come to an end."

"I salute your optimism." Bill turned to Simon. "I suppose if we're all in the mood for spilling secrets then there's something else I ought to tell you."

Bill explained about the existence of the letter appearing to implicate Maureen in blackmail.

"I see," Simon said. "I presume you didn't tell me about this before because you think I'm a journalist who's going to splash it all over the front page."

"Actually, no," Bill replied. "I did try to persuade Jenny—that's Maureen's housemate, Cynthia—to tell the police about it but she refused. Probably because she didn't like the way they ransacked Maureen's house when they looked for evidence. I promised her I wouldn't tell anyone."

"Well thank you for telling us now." Aunt Cynny sat and patted Bill's leg as if to reassure her. "We will all keep your confidence, including young Simon over there."

Simon opened his mouth to protest but then decided to ask a question instead. "You say this letter was addressed to Maureen?"

"No, I didn't say that," Bill replied. "Jenny found it among her things. But it didn't start with 'Dear Miss Lyon'. There wasn't even an envelope. We can't be certain it was meant for her."

"Well-observed. Capital," Aunt Cynny interjected. "If only they'd allow women with brains like yours into the Metropolitan Police then the crime wave would be over tomorrow."

"Bill, I understand that you don't want to believe Miss Lyon was a blackmailer," Simon began. "But if she's not, then why was the letter among her things?"

"I don't know," Bill replied. "But on the other hand, if blackmail was the motive for Maureen's murder, what's the killer's motive for trying to murder Grace Lucas? It's a bit of a coincidence if they were both up to blackmail."

"You're right," Simon said. "There's surely a common motive for both the attacks. And that's most likely the fact that they're both—"

"Sapphic sisters," Bill finished Simon's sentence.

"Wonderful!" Aunt Cynny clapped her hands again. "Listening to the pair of you talk through the logic of this conundrum is pure poetry."

Simon was about to protest his aunt's lavish praise in an attempt at self-deprecating modesty when the lights went out.

"Damn it." Sylvia exclaimed through the inky darkness. "The fuse must have blown again."

"Does it happen often?" Bill asked.

"This is only the third time," Sylvia replied. "Hold on everyone. I've got some candles behind the bar."

Simon peered into the gloom. The only lights were the glowing tips of Sylvia's cigarette and his aunt's cheroot. There was a crash that sounded like a chair falling over.

"Damn."

"Are you all right, Sylvia?" Bill asked.

"You'd think by now I'd know this place well enough to find my way around it in the dark," Sylvia replied. "Won't be a minute."

Bill lit a match, and held it up. Her face loomed out of the darkness. Simon held out his hands and laid them on the edge of the table.

"I feel in the mood for a séance," he said.

The match burned down to Bill's fingers. She dropped it on the floor and stubbed it out with her toe. Simon playfully walked his fingertips up her back.

"Will you stop that, Simon." Bill lit another match. Simon held up his hands in front of his face like Lon Chaney in *The Phantom of the Opera.*

"You're really such a boy still." Bill lit a cigarette. "And your aunt said you were so serious."

"I'm beginning to think it's a lot better than being a dreary adult in this world." Simon dropped his hands. "I thought you'd be more fun than that."

A match flared by the bar and Sylvia lit three candles in a brass candelabra. She carried it across to the table and set it down.

"I'll go and have a look at the fuses," she said. "It shouldn't take me long to fix it."

Aunt Cynny pulled out a large pocket watch from her coat, flicked open the cover, and peered at it in the candlelight. "Goodness, it's getting late. I'm afraid I must take my leave of you, gentle people. I have work to finish before morning."

"Yes, I think I ought to leave too." Bill drained her glass and stood. "I'll see if I can pop over to Jenny's again sometime this week. I'd like to ask her a bit more about Maureen. See if she can shed any light on why that letter was among her things."

"And if I manage to get the electrics sorted here," Sylvia began. "I'll go and meet Grace at the hospital and try to persuade her to report her assault to the police."

"And I'll convince JR that the interests of the poet John Milton are best served by reopening your club." Aunt Cynny picked up her enormous hat and pulled it down firmly on her head. "What will you be doing, Simon?"

"I'll be having a lie-in," he replied. "My editor's given me the morning off as I've been working hard today."

"Slacker." Bill collected her cigarette case from the table. "Honestly, men. You don't know what hard work is."

"How rude," Simon responded. "I was going to offer to escort you back to St John's Wood, seeing as there's a murderer on the loose. But now that you've said that..."

"Thank you but I'm perfectly capable of looking after myself," Bill replied. "And anyway, I'd appreciate some time on my own to think."

JOURNAL ENTRY 23 JULY 1929

What is it with these sisters of Satan who roam the streets? If one of their witches' covens is closed down they simply move on to the next one. They can't keep away. There is another one at the end of Old Compton Street.

I saw her go in. The one with the hand-chopping and the kicking legs who defeated me last time.

She will not avoid me again. Now I know how she can defend herself I can better prepare. How fortunate my work gives me the tools I need to carry out my task of cleansing this city.

This central area of London is home to those places for licentious and lewd exhibition.

Theatres.

They give employment to fallen women when the respectable establishments such as factories and shops reject them. I see many of these depraved females on my daily rounds.

There's a particular one I have tracked down. I have observed her on several occasions now. She appears to be a ringleader or spokeswoman for the others. A real troublemaker. She openly criticises and obstructs those who would clean up this sin-ridden city. Like the first one, she too works in the theatre. As a lackey for one of the sodomite men.

It won't be difficult for me to track her down. I've already become good at this. And I have another advantage.

I have found a way to get hold of her address. It's time for me to pay her a visit.

<h1 style="text-align:center">13</h1>

When Bill and Aunt Cynny emerged at street level they discovered the power cut was not confined to the club but seemed to have affected most of the West End. There was no moon. The only light to illuminate the pitch-black streets came from motorcar headlights.

"They should never have replaced the gas lamps with these new-fangled electric ones," Bill commented. "Do you want to share a taxi, Cynthia? I'm heading to St John's Wood."

"Thank you my dear," Aunt Cynny replied. "But my gaff's south of the river in darkest Kennington. Not as salubrious as St John's Wood but much handier for the House. And the cricket ground."

Aunt Cynny waved her cane commandingly above her head and two taxis drew to a halt alongside them almost immediately.

"I'll bag this one and you take that." She opened the cab door. "Toodle-pip, my dear. A delight to finally get to know one of Simon's friends. So pleased he's finally mixing with grown-ups."

Aunt Cynny climbed into the cab and it disappeared into the gloom of Shaftesbury Avenue.

When Bill's taxi reached Upper Regent's Street the street

lights were back on again as well as the lights in restaurants and pubs they passed.

"Very unreliable this electricity stuff," the cabbie commented. "If you ask me we're better off without it. Me and the missus still have the good old gas mantles at home. Much more reliable. And far safer than electricity in my humble opinion."

"Absolutely," agreed Bill. She pointed to a building site in Langham Place. "Have you seen this monstrosity going up opposite The Langham?"

"Yeah, love," the cabbie replied. "They say it's going to completely overshadow the old hotel. You know what it is, don't you?"

"I do." Bill lit a cigarette and opened the window. "My former employer's responsible. The BBC's going to move there from the Strand. It's going to be some big ugly new headquarters for them."

"You used to work for the BBC, love?"

"I did." Bill hated being called 'love', even though she knew no offence was intended. It seemed somehow overly familiar from a complete stranger. "I've no idea why they'd want to move from the Strand. It was so convenient for dining at Simpson's."

Twenty minutes later the taxi arrived at her mansion block. There was a different man behind the reception desk in place of the usual porter. He appeared to be in his early thirties with almost matinee idol good looks.

"Good evening, madam," he said. "May I help you?"

His manner of speaking was very precise, as if he was taking care to enunciate each word. Bill tried to place his accent.

"I'm Miss Miles," she replied. "I live here. Where's Danvers?"

"Ah, Miss Miles." The young man stood, clicked his heels

together, and nodded sharply in greeting. "My name is Darling. I was told by Mr Danvers to expect you. He has taken a few days off." He glanced down at a sheet of names on his desk. "I understand that you work for the famous Mr Coward, is that not right?"

The more Darling spoke the more Bill became fascinated with his way of speaking. It was perfect English, but almost too perfect in the way he pronounced each word.

She ignored his question. "Danvers didn't mention he was going away."

"He has not gone anywhere as far as I am aware," Darling replied. "He said he had some matters to deal with at home. I understand that his garden in particular is being dried out by the unusually hot weather we are experiencing in London."

"Funny. He didn't say anything about it this morning."

"Mr Danvers left a message for you. I will go and get it." Darling disappeared through a door to the left of the reception desk. Bill took out her cigarette case and lit a cigarette. There was a small settee for guests in the reception area with an ashtray next to it. Bill sat and reflected on the events of the day. The new young man on reception was an unexpected pleasure. He was a contrast to the elderly but likeable Danvers. Perhaps he had told her about the change this morning but she had been in too much of a hurry to absorb the news.

The meeting with Simon's aunt had also been an unexpected pleasure. She hoped they might have lunch together soon. Apart from being an entertaining and delightful person, Cynthia might also prove a useful contact at the Home Office, especially as Noël often needed to bring actors into the country at short notice. The immigration process could be tiresomely difficult.

Bill's priority was to visit Jenny again. She decided to use the pretext of finding out when the funeral would be to call her in the morning.

Darling re-emerged from the doorway and walked over.

"It does not say much I am afraid." He held out a piece of paper. "Mr Danvers gave it to me shortly before he went off duty this afternoon."

Bill read the note.

Miss Miles. A young gentleman called for you at midday. He would not tell me his name. He said he would call again later. Danvers

"Doesn't say much." Bill handed back the piece of paper.

"As I said."

"A mystery caller." Bill stubbed out her cigarette and strode over to the staircase. "How intriguing."

The hallway light in her apartment failed to come on when Bill flicked the switch.

"What is wrong with everything tonight?" She left the front door ajar while she crossed to the lamp on the hall table. It too failed to light. Exasperated she turned to head back to the reception and ask Darling for help with the fuse board.

She heard the *swish* of the cord through the air moments before it wrapped around her neck. She choked as it tightened on her windpipe. The cord was narrow and she failed to grab hold of it. The pain as it cut into her neck was excruciating and within seconds her air supply was cut off.

Her attacker breathed rapidly against the back of her head. She kicked hard and made contact with what she hoped was his shin. The grunt of pain that followed clearly came from a man. But the cord remained firmly around her neck. Bright speckles of light flashed in her vision. Her heart beat pounded in her ears.

She kicked back hard again. The man grunted but the cord

remained in place. Her legs weakened. She staggered forward as they buckled beneath her.

Someone called her name. The voice sounded far away. It was as if she were back at school and one of the nuns had caught her smoking round the back of the chapel. The voice was disappearing and the light was fading to blackness when the cord around her neck fell slack.

She collapsed to the floor. Someone's feet trampled past her head and voice called her name again. This time it was much closer and she recognised it immediately —Darling.

"Miss Miles. Are you all right?"

The rush of air into her lungs overwhelmed her and she coughed violently. The pain in her windpipe was excruciating each time she drew in more air. Darling rolled her onto her side and placed a small cushion under her head.

"Do not move, madam," he said with impressive authority. "Keep lying there until you are feeling a bit more like yourself once more. Might you have any idea who that man was?"

Bill tried to speak but it only brought on another fit of coughing.

"Do not worry, madam. There is no need for you to say anything for the moment. You have had a nasty shock. I do not know who he was or how he got in your place. He certainly did not pass me at the reception. I will call the police in a while. I need to make sure you are all right first."

It was several minutes before Bill felt well enough to sit up. She felt her neck gingerly. "Did you see what he looked like?" she asked hoarsely.

"I am afraid not, madam. It happened very quickly and he shot past me down the corridor to the stairs. He had a grey cap pulled low over his eyes and some sort of dark jacket with the collar pulled up. I am very sorry, madam. I should have gone after him but I was most concerned about you."

"It's quite all right, Darling." Bill choked again with the effort of talking. "I'm very lucky you were here. What made you come up?"

Darling held out his hand. He was holding her cigarette case. "You left this on the reception desk. I only found it after you had gone."

"One of the many benefits of smoking." Bill extended her arm. "Pull me up, will you? I need to rest on something a bit more comfortable than this parquet."

Darling helped her into the sitting room where she collapsed onto the chaise longue.

"Would you do me a tremendous favour and call the police from the telephone in the hall?" she asked. "And would you mind awfully if I ask you another favour? Will it inconvenience you to stay with me for a bit? Stupidly I don't feel up to being on my own just yet."

"Quite understandable madam," Darling replied. "But I will need to be back at reception in a while to let the police in. Is there anyone I can call to come over for you?"

"I can think of one man." Bill took a cigarette from her case and lit it.

Simon arrived at Bill's mansion block, panting for breath, almost fifty minutes later. He had failed to flag down a taxi and ran all the way from his flat. Two wrong turnings and a near fatal collision with a bus later he sprinted up the stairs two at a time to find Bill's front door open. He strode through the hallway into the sitting room.

"I can't leave you alone for five minutes." Simon leaned against the doorframe and tried to catch his breath. "First you're whisked away by the police for shooting your mouth off in front of the chief inspector—"

"Just a minute," Bill began, but Simon continued.

"Next thing I know you've carelessly come close to being the London strangler's next victim. Which reminds me, why's the front door wide open–"

"Simon–"

"Anyone could just walk in here–"

"Good evening Mr Sampson." Detective Sergeant Daniels emerged from the kitchen with a bone china teacup and saucer in his hand. "I left the door open because I knew you were expected." He put the teacup on a table next to the chaise longue. "And before you ask, no I won't be making you a cup of tea as well."

"Thank you so much, detective sergeant." Bill looked at the teacup warily. "Although I'd still prefer a gin martini."

"Not for shock, Miss Miles," Daniels replied. "Hot sweet tea is what they recommend." He sat in an armchair opposite Bill. "Before I leave you is there anything else you can remember?"

"I'm afraid not," Bill replied. "I think that new chap Darling will probably be able to tell you more than I can. It was dark and the man attacked from behind. I didn't see a thing."

"It was definitely a man?" Simon asked.

Daniels sighed. "Mr Sampson. I appreciate your concern as a friend of Miss Miles. But would you please permit me to conduct this inquiry? We'll all get along swimmingly if you do."

"Of course, detective sergeant." Simon crossed to the sideboard and picked up the whisky decanter. "Are you all right if I have a drink, Bill?"

"Help yourself. And you may as well pour me one too while you're at it." She smiled sweetly at Daniels. "Strictly medicinal you understand."

"Please feel free to ignore my advice." Daniels cleared his

throat. You say it felt like a cord round your neck? The same as the one you showed me."

"Exactly." Bill loosened a silk scarf to reveal a thin red weal where the cord had cut into her skin. "You can see for yourself."

"Thank you, Miss Miles." Daniels looked away. "But this time he didn't leave the cord behind?"

"No. But that reminds me." Bill took the glass of whisky Simon offered her. "Simon, darling. Pop over to the sideboard again and get the tie clip we found. It's next to that sweet little statue of Helen, goddess of beauty."

"She was also the goddess of sailors you know." Simon picked up the tie clip and handed it to the detective.

"How on earth do you know that?" Bill asked.

"One of the benefits of a good education," Simon replied. "Although how beauty and sailors are connected I really don't know."

"Oh, I can think of several." Bill laughed. "She was also the leader of the dancing Spartan women at—"

"Fascinating as this little history lesson might be," Daniels interrupted. "But could you tell me the significance of what Mr Sampson has just handed me?"

"We found it at the scene of the crime," Bill said dramatically.

"A tie clip." Daniels turned it over slowly between finger and thumb. "And why do you consider it relevant to my investigation?"

"It's a man's tie clip," Bill replied. "And we found it close to where the victim was attacked. Outside a women's-only club. After tonight I think we're pretty certain the attacker's a man. So who else could it belong to?"

"I presume this club receives visits from the usual trades people?" Daniels asked. "People like postmen, delivery drivers, and the like. It probably belongs to one of them." He put the clip into his pocket. "Don't mind if I hang on to it, do you? Routine checks."

"Feel free, detective sergeant."

Daniels stood. "I won't take up any more of your time tonight. You've had a nasty shock. But I must remind you we could make more progress if the previous victim were to come forward and identify herself."

He crossed to the sitting room door. "I'll go and talk to your porter now. Mr Darling, isn't it?"

Bill nodded. "He's not the usual one. Apparently Danvers had a sudden impulse to go off for a few days and do some gardening."

"Oh really?" Daniels put a hand on the door handle. "Don't you think that's a little odd? Are you sure he's not the man who attacked you?"

"Don't be absurd, detective," Bill retorted. "He was the man who rescued me."

"Thank goodness he was there," Simon added. "Would your usual chap have been up to challenging an attacker?"

"Danvers?" Bill laughed. "He's a hundred and two if he's a day. Lovely man but strong-arm stuff is definitely not his thing."

"Very well." Daniels opened the door. "We'll send a couple of fellows round in the morning to do a thorough search of the place for clues. Will you be in?"

"It's doubtful," Bill replied. "I've got a production meeting at the theatre at eleven. But perhaps that temporary porter Darling can accompany them. I trust him. After all, he saved my life tonight."

"Thank you very much, Miss Miles. That's very helpful. I'll let myself out." He nodded to Simon. "And I'll shut the door behind me."

When the front door slammed Simon jumped to his feet.

"That man is unbearable. How dare he badger you about Grace Lucas when you're in this state."

"A tot of whisky is helping a lot." Bill held up her empty glass. "Be a dear and pour me another, would you? Actually, I think he's got a point. Grace needs to pop into Scotland Yard and have a chat with him. You never know, she might recall something that could lead to this hideous man being brought to justice."

Simon topped up her glass. "How are you feeling? Are you going to be all right on your own here tonight? After all, you've got that good-looking porter on duty now."

Bill took a sip of her drink. "I was going to ask you about that."

14

"That chaise longue doesn't look any bigger than four feet long," Simon observed. "I can't sleep on that. My legs will be hanging over the end." He tapped the floor with his foot. "And this parquet looks like it would be very unforgiving on my back. Look, why don't you come over to mine? I can sneak you in by the back stairs."

"I wouldn't mind." Bill lay back on the chaise longue like a St John's Wood version of Cleopatra. "Do you have a spare bed in your apartment?"

"No, but my sofa's a lot longer. You'd be far more comfortable on it than I would on that."

"Certainly not, my darling." Bill picked small pieces of lint from one of the cushions. "Thoughtful as your offer is, don't you realise I'm really not interested in giving up my nice comfortable bed for a sofa? I really can't understand you. Why did you ask me about being alone tonight if you weren't prepared to sleep on my chaise longue?"

"Because when I asked I thought you might have a spare bed." Simon got up, crossed to the chaise longue, and held out his arms to gauge its length. "I suppose I could sleep on it. But

I'll get a terrible crick in my neck. Haven't you got any more cushions lying about somewhere? I could pile them up on the floor to make a sort of mattress."

"That's not a good idea at all." Bill swung her legs off the chaise longue and strode to the doorway. "I'm not having you sleeping on my silk cushions. You'd probably get hair oil or something on them."

"I don't wear hair oil," Simon protested. "And I can assure you I'm very clean. I take a shower every morning."

"How very modern of you." Bill walked into the hallway. "Follow me," she called over her shoulder.

"Are you sure you need me to sleep here tonight?" Simon asked. "After all, you've got that strapping young man downstairs guarding the entrance."

He followed Bill into the hallway.

"He may have rescued me but that was only because he came up to give me my cigarette case." Bill's voice came from the bedroom. "He didn't stop the man breaking in here in the first place."

"You're not seriously suggesting...?" Simon stood in the bedroom doorway. Bill was holding out both hands to her large double bed as if she were a salesman demonstrating its features. "That would be wholly improper."

"I'm only suggesting we share the bed. It's not a marriage proposal." Bill wrinkled her nose. "Neither of us has the slightest interest in each other sexually. No offence, Simon."

"None taken."

"As long as you don't snore, don't thrash about, and don't wet the bed—"

"Now *you're* being offensive, Bill." Simon folded his arms and leant against the doorframe. "And what about you? What are the chances you'll wake me up at two in the morning screaming blue murder because you've had a nightmare about your mystery strangler?"

"Ah, but that's why I need you here." Bill walked over to Simon, rested a hand on his arm and kissed his cheek. "You can be my knight in shining armour."

Simon experienced a frisson of excitement at Bill's proposal. On the one hand it was not something polite society could ever condone, even in the liberated twentieth century. But there were many aspects of Simon's life polite society would never condone. Bill was right. It was an entirely platonic arrangement.

He thought back to when he was fourteen years old and he had stayed with a school friend at the boy's family home during the summer holidays. He had shared a bed with him and no one had thought it improper. The family was not to know Simon had had a massive crush on his friend. A crush his friend had reciprocated. Sharing the bed had been a dream come true for both of them.

"And what will Noël say when he finds out you've been sleeping with his mortal enemy?"

Bill held her finger to Simon's lips. "You'll say nothing about this to anyone. Ever. If I find out you've been blabbing I'll turn you into a modern day Farinelli."

"The castrato?" Simon laughed. "My lips are sealed to protect my manhood. Do you have a spare toothbrush?"

"Several." Bill squeezed past him into the hallway. "Pink or blue?"

Simon climbed into Bill's bed. It was large with an elaborate brass headboard and a grey satin coverlet. He stretched out his legs and luxuriated in the expensive feel of the rich cotton sheets. Bill was still in the bathroom finishing her night-time ablutions.

The room was exquisitely decorated with Arts and Crafts features. Flowers and birds outlined in gold adorned the pale green William Morris-designed wallpaper. It was complemented by curtains with a similar motif. Wooden furniture, painted a dusky pink contrasted with the walls and curtains. To complete the rich décor, a three-panelled silk-covered vanity screen with a Japanese theme stood in one corner.

It was an altogether very feminine room and Simon scolded himself for assuming Bill would have more masculine tastes. He made a note to ask her where she had found the vanity screen. A similar one would look very good in his bedroom.

She appeared in the doorway wearing white silk pyjamas. Simon instinctively pulled up the bedclothes to cover his bare chest.

"How remarkably coy you are, Mr Sampson." Bill pointed to the opposite side of the bed. "Move over. You're on the wrong side. I can't possibly sleep next to the open window. I might catch a chill."

"Bill, it's one of the hottest summers in years," Simon protested. But he slid obediently across the bed.

Bill switched off the hall light and walked over to the bed. She pulled back the bedclothes to reveal Simon had kept his underwear on in the absence of any pyjamas that would fit him. He clasped his hands across his chest.

"Why Miss Miles I do declare," he began in a voice inspired by the writings of Jane Austen. "You are most forward in your manner. I sincerely hope it is not your intention to ravish me this night."

"I can't think of anything less inviting." Bill sniffed and climbed into the bed. She left the covers back where they lay. "I've never understood why the majority of women consider it their duty to chase after and marry a man. Women are far more alluring. And they're far easier to understand."

Bill's comment made perfect sense to Simon. He found women mysterious, contradictory, and even a little intimidating. Men were far less confusing. For several years he had been curious and even anxious about having sexual relations with a woman. They had never attracted him in that way and he was concerned how he might fulfil his matrimonial duties if he were to ever be obliged to marry. He knew of several men who, despite being more naturally attracted to other men, had married women and even had children with them to comply with the requirements of conventional society. He had decided several years ago it was not to be his destiny despite pressure to do so from his family at birthday and Christmas gatherings.

"Have you never been tempted?" Simon asked.

"What? Sex? With a man?" Bill sniggered. "Simon Sampson. Are you making improper advances now that I've invited you into my sanctuary?"

"Good God no." Simon slid away from Bill until he was in danger of falling on the floor. "But if we were normal it's my understanding it would be expected of me. The man, that's me in this situation, *would* be expected to make advances, improper or otherwise, to the woman. That's you. Those are the roles normal people are supposed to assume. Absurd isn't it?"

"'Normal'?" Bill sniffed. "That awful word again. The idiot policeman Daniels used it yesterday. I think we should be deliciously un-normal at every opportunity."

"I think you'll find the correct word is abnormal."

"Certainly not. Abnormal has all sorts of undesirable associations. Un-normal is a far better word. You know, I always had a soft spot for Humpty Dumpty. He said that words meant exactly what he wanted them to mean. Nothing more and nothing less."

"My dear Bill." Simon shuffled across the bed towards her and kissed her on the cheek. "Despite being an infuriatingly difficult person, in the short time we've known each other I've developed rather a soft spot for you."

Bill turned her head and gave him a very brief kiss on the lips. She quickly rolled away and pulled the covers over her.

"Good night, Mr Sampson. Let this be our little secret."

Simon listened to her regular breathing in the stillness of the room. It was comforting to share a bed. Another frisson of excitement sparked through his body. Was this what a normal man felt for a woman? Perhaps he was wrong. Perhaps he was attracted to women after all. Maybe he was attracted to both sexes. It was many years since the thought had even crossed his mind.

"Simon." Bill's voice was a whisper in the darkness. "Are you still awake?"

"Yes, Bill," he replied. "You only turned the light out a few minutes ago."

"Of course. Silly of me." She sounded unusually flustered.

"What is it?"

"Would you mind awfully if I cuddled a little closer to you?"

"Not at all. Do you want me to slide over to you? Or will you slide over to me?"

No reply.

"Bill?"

"I think I'm being ridiculous."

"You've had a nasty shock." Simon rolled towards the middle of the bed. He reached out. His hand made contact with Bill's shoulder and he squeezed it gently. "I have to tell you, Bill. You're one of the strongest people I've ever met. For a woman anyway."

"Hmm." Bill slid towards him and nestled her body against

him. He put his arm around her waist. "That's a backhanded comment. But I'll take it with good grace tonight."

"Why backhanded?" Simon asked.

Bill shifted her body against Simon's. It felt strangely erotic.

"My friend Amelia says women can't win. They're praised like hell if they achieve anything simply because they're women. And then they're crushed if they fail."

Simon chuckled. "Who's Amelia?"

"Amelia Earhart, darling," Bill replied. "That wonderfully adventurous American who keeps flying across the Atlantic. Lady Heath introduced me to her when she landed in Southampton last year. We had a bit of a thing until she went back to New York."

"A bit of a thing?" Simon asked. "So she's...?"

"Of course," Bill replied. "Like all the women who achieve anything in this life. Think of her as a role model."

She exhaled contentedly.

"Like me."

———

The streets around His Majesty's Theatre were packed with stationary vehicles when Bill emerged from her meeting with Noël and the stage crew shortly after eleven the next morning. The traffic jam of taxis and buses looked like it was never going to move again. She summoned up her courage and headed towards the Central London underground train at Tottenham Court Road.

Bill had steadfastly tried to avoid the underground trains. She found them an uncomfortable and smelly way of travelling. In the heat of the summer she knew the overcrowded carriages were going to be unbearable. But she had promised to meet Jenny Casewell at her cottage for eleven-thirty and she was already going to be late. Once the train arrived it would be no more than a ten-minute journey to Notting Hill and a five-minute walk from the station to Jenny's house.

To Bill's surprise there were very few people on the platform at Tottenham Court Road. She lit a cigarette and ruminated on the events of the night before while she waited for the train.

Noël had been horrified when she told him of the attack.

"You mustn't stay in that flat a moment longer," he had commanded. "Book yourself into a hotel and charge it to the company. At least until they catch this criminal."

"That might not be for a while," Bill had replied. "The police are hopeless. They haven't been taking the attacks seriously. It's going to cost you a fortune."

"I'm not suggesting the Ritz, my dear," Noël had said icily. "I'll pay up to a guinea a night. No more. That should be more than enough for you to find something reasonably clean. *Bitter Sweet* isn't doing *that* well. At least not yet."

The more she thought about it the less tempting Noël's offer became. The attacker was unlikely to return after being thwarted by the replacement porter and the prospect of sleeping in a strange bedroom without the comforts of her flat, possibly for weeks or even months, had no appeal. She decided to stay where she was and hope the replacement porter might stay for longer. If she was stricken by anxiety she could always call Simon.

That was a thought she would never have countenanced before last night. She had not slept well. Partly because her mind kept replaying the moment the cord tightened around her neck and partly because Simon had snored. Not continuously but he had woken her a few times with a noise she would have never have expected to hear except maybe from the elephant cage at London Zoo. She had poked him in the ribs each time and he had rolled away from her. Each time his snoring had subsided to a gently rhythmic breathing.

Bill chuckled. She realised she was deceiving herself. The more honest reason was the unexpected arousal she had experienced as they had lain cuddled together. But it had definitely not been the night to explore the sensation any further. If ever.

There was a thunderous roar from the tunnel and the train rattled into the station. Bill stubbed out her cigarette and lit another. If she had to share a confined space with complete strangers she at least needed something to mask the smell.

Jenny opened the front door and stepped out to greet Bill.

"There's someone here," she whispered. "I'm so glad you've arrived. I'm not very sure of him. He gives me the creeps to be honest."

"Who is he?" Bill asked quietly.

"He says he's a solicitor for Maureen's father. He's come to collect her things." Jenny looked to be on the verge of tears. "I'd be much happier if you'd talk to him."

"Of course." Bill put her arms around Jenny and gave a reassuring hug. "Lead on."

A short man wearing an unseasonal winter coat over his suit stood in the living room. He clicked his heels together and held out his hand when Bill entered the room. It was a very limp handshake.

"My name is Fisher," he began. "Jebediah Fisher. From Fisher, Bathurst and Ferris. I represent the interests of Mr Smith following the unfortunate demise of his daughter."

The man had a strange, clipped manner of speaking. It was as though he were trying to be very precise with his words.

"Smith?" Bill queried. "But Maureen's last name was Lyon."

"Indeed." Fisher coughed nervously. "It seems when she fled to London she forsook her family name and took her mother's maiden name."

"'Fled'?" Bill repeated. "What was she escaping?"

"A figure of speech, madam." Fisher coughed again. "Although I understand she had been unhappy in Bath and sought excitement and thrills in this unfortunate city. And your name is?"

"Miles," Bill replied. "Florence Miles. Miss Lyon worked with me on theatrical productions for Noël Coward. What's the purpose of your visit here?"

"My client is Douglas Arbuthnot Smith, Miss Smith's father. He seeks the return of her possessions."

"Do you have any proof of this?" Bill asked. "A letter of authority from Mr Smith? Evidence that Maureen's name was Smith? We've always known her as Miss Lyon."

"I can present you my business card, madam." Fisher reached into his pocket. "And I have a letter of introduction from Mr Smith in my briefcase. As to Miss Smith's surname, I do not have her birth certificate. I am afraid that you will have to take my word for it."

Bill barely glanced at the card. Fisher's tie clip glinted in the morning sunlight highlighting the small black cross in the centre of the cross bar.

JOURNAL ENTRY 24 JULY 1929

Last night was full of failure and triumph.

I was defeated in my attempt to remove that bitch ringleader. Worse, I cannot know if she recognised me or not. There were so many mirrors in her hallway. Even with the power knocked out and the lights off.

I may find out in time.

But I got the one with the hand chopping and the leg kicking who got away last time. It was really so easy.

It took very little time for that witches' coven of a club to reopen again. And the viperous bitches wasted no time in going back there.

Including the one who fights like a man.

I happened to be passing and saw her go in. All I had to do was wait until she finally re-emerged from her lair. Doubtless she committed a night of debauchery with her wicked sisters while she was inside.

I followed her up to Tottenham Court Road where she made the mistake of taking a short cut round the back of that new theatre they're building. The Dominion. Another home for licentious and lewd exhibition. It's fortunate I've taken to carrying a length of cord with me wherever I go. A brief struggle and this time she was no more.

Theatres. They are the devil's temples.

I will return to that bitch ringleader. It is not my intention to be defeated again.

15

Bill held Jenny's front door open.

"I'm waiting, Mr Fisher."

"I protest in the strongest possible—"

"Would you prefer we telephone the police?", Bill asked. "Jenny. Pick up the phone, there's a dear. Although we could simply shout for them. The local constable is usually no more than a few minutes away."

"I can get a court order—"

"Then go and get one," Bill interrupted. "Off you go. You're making the place untidy."

"You have no right to order me around," Fisher persisted. "I am an officer of the Supreme Court of—"

"Out!" Bill grabbed Fisher's arm, propelled him towards the door, and pushed him outside.

"I say, thanks awfully Bill." Jenny was curled up on the settee with a cushion clutched tightly to her chest. "I'm so glad you arrived when you did. Do you think he was a phoney?"

"I can't say for certain." Bill closed the door and examined the business card Fisher had given her. The office address for the firm of solicitors was in Bath. There was a telephone number

141

as well. "He had all the markings of a solicitor. Pompous, officious, and ultimately dreary. But how on earth did he expect to waltz off with Maureen's things without at least some kind of proof he had authority to take them? What concerns me more is the tie clip he was wearing."

"Tie clip?" Jenny asked. "What's so important about that?"

"It was the same as the one Simon and I discovered outside the Paradise Regained Club. You know. Where Grace Lucas was attacked."

Jenny's eyes opened wide. "You think he's the murderer?"

"Again, I can't really say. It's all very strange." Bill held up the business card. "Can I use your telephone? I want to check this out to start with."

"It's on the table in the hall."

Bill spent over twenty minutes persuading the receptionist at Fisher, Bathurst, and Ferris to describe the firm's partner Jebediah Fisher. Her description of him matched the man who had been in Jenny's house. She refused to disclose if he was acting for a client called Smith as Fisher had claimed, or that he had an appointment to see Jenny that day.

Bill returned to the living room and Jenny handed her a cup of coffee. "Do you still think he's the murderer?"

Bill shook her head. "It doesn't make sense. Why would Maureen's murderer come here and demand we hand over her things? It would be pretty brazen of him." She put the coffee cup down next to the phone. "No, I don't think he's the murderer. But the tie clip is puzzling."

"Perhaps it's a coincidence," Jenny replied. "There could be lots with that design."

She hugged the cushion again. "There seem to be many things we don't know about Maureen. Too many things. First we find out she was a blackmailer. Now it seems she lied to us about her name."

"Not quite a lie." Bill sat next to Jenny. "Fisher did say Lyon was her mother's name. I wonder why she changed it? Are you sure there isn't anything more about her family we can find out?"

"All her things are in cardboard boxes in the bedroom," Jenny replied. "I've been through them but do you want to have a go?"

Bill lit a cigarette. "I'm not sure you should keep them here anymore. If Fisher does what he promises and comes back with some kind of court order you'd have to hand them over."

"Can you keep them?" Jenny asked.

Bill shook her head. "Not after what happened last night. My place isn't safe anymore."

Jenny looked puzzled and Bill realised she had failed to tell her about the attack. After she had recounted the story Jenny slumped back on the sofa.

"None of us are safe anymore," she said. "What are we going to do? What am I going to do? If *you're* not safe in a building with a porter, I'm an easy target here on my own." She glanced towards the living room door as if expecting the murderer to burst in at any moment.

"You mustn't think like that," Bill said brusquely. "I think the police are finally taking this seriously. Certainly after what happened last night. It's only a matter of time before they catch him."

"And in the meantime?" Jenny asked. "I'm going to be tossing and turning in my bed wondering if he's going to break in one night. Or I'll come back late from a night out to find him lying in wait for me. I don't think I can deal with the worry."

"Would you consider going back to stay with your parents in the West Country for a while?"

"I don't think so." Jenny shook her head. "My aunt leaving me this cottage was the best thing that happened to me. Coming up to London did so much for my career. There are many more places I can work here. It's given me lots of possibilities. Back in the West Country there are fewer theatres where I can work. Less opportunity. And I'd be stuck with my parents."

"What about your brother? Didn't he move to London at the start of this year? You could stay with him for a bit."

Jenny laughed. "He's not very happy with me since Aunt Victoria left me this place in preference to him. And anyway, Bill. I'm surprised at you. Why do we women have to turn to a man for protection when something like this happens? I would have thought you of all people would see the defeatism in turning to them in an emergency."

Bill was chastened by Jenny's rebuke. She was right. They had fought so long for women to have equal rights with men. Last spring's General Election was a big step forward. Women under the age of thirty could finally vote. But it was only three years since Parliament had given them the right to own and sell property in the same way that men could.

The huge barrier remained the Marriage Bar preventing married women from working in the Civil Service. It infuriated Bill. She had argued about it at length with her former boss at the BBC. But like most men he could see no place for married women in the workplace.

"They would be too distracted and emotional about matters of home life," he had declared.

There had to be another way she and Jenny could protect themselves from the threat of the murderer returning without resorting to the protection of men like heroines in a Victorian penny-dreadful.

"I need a drink." Bill crossed to the kitchen. "Have you still got that gin? I think we both need one."

Simon had spent a busy morning working on a new front-page lead for *The Chronicle*. He had received news of the death of Grace Lucas during a routine call to Scotland Yard. Because her body had also been found outside a stage door the killer was now dubbed "The Stage Door Murderer".

The afternoon edition was due to go to press at midday. Simon's editor had promised him the majority of the front page for his story as long as he filled it with as much *"colour"* as possible. He had to find a new angle none of the other papers reporting the story would have. The dilemma he faced was including the attack on Bill in the story.

He knew Bill would be furious with him if she read about herself on the front page. It would probably infuriate Noël Coward as well and possibly sour her working relationship with him. But it was unavoidable and he convinced himself that if he failed to do so then all the other newspapers would. He had a head start on rival newspapers through his connection with Sylvia at the Paradise Regained Club. He was confident none of the other reporters working on the story would know about the club or the previous attempt on Grace's life.

The door of the Paradise Regained Club creaked open and Sylvia looked out suspiciously.

"Now what do you want?"

"Can I come in?" Simon asked. "I've got some bad news to tell you."

Sylvia sat at the bar, knocked back a shot of neat vodka, and poured herself another.

"When did it happen?" she asked.

"Last night."

"Grace was in here last night,"

"Perhaps the killer lay in wait for her and followed her when she left," Simon replied. "They found her body in the alleyway round by the stage door of that new Dominion Theatre in Tottenham Court Road."

"I didn't think it was even open yet."

"It's not." Simon fiddled with the coffee cup Sylvia had handed him. "Would that have been on her way home?"

"It's one way, yes," Sylvia replied. "She lives—lived—in a couple of rooms in Holborn, not far from Gamages department store. That would have been a shortcut for her." She knocked back another vodka shot. "I suppose her ju-jitsu failed to help her this time. Poor Grace. Such a kind soul. They're going to miss her at the hospital."

"Where did she work?" Simon asked.

"The Middlesex in Mortimer Street. She was in charge of a lot of nurses as far as I understand."

"So she had nothing to do with the theatre?"

"What a strange question." Sylvia laughed. "Are you trying to link her with Maureen's death at His Majesty's?"

"Yes," Simon replied. "And the attack on Bill last night."

"Bill?" Sylvia's hand froze as she reached for the vodka bottle. "He attacked Bill?"

"I'm so sorry Sylvia. I thought you'd been told."

"I knew nothing about it." Sylvia sat heavily on a bar stool. "Is she all right?"

"She's fine." Simon smiled. "You know Bill. Furious and even more determined to catch him. I just thought, as Maureen worked in the theatre and Bill does too—"

"Sylvia shook her head. "You've drawn a blank there. I think the Dominion was just a coincidence."

"What else can you tell me about Grace?" Simon asked. "Does she have any family?"

"None that are talking to her." Sylvia poured herself another drink. "I would think she was like most people who come in here. Either their family has shunned them or they've left them behind in some provincial corner of England to come to London." She knocked back the vodka and narrowed her eyes at Simon. "You're not going to write about The Paradise Regained Club in your story, are you? Not after Cynny pulled those strings to get us reopened again."

"If I don't then it's only a matter of time before one of the other papers does," Simon replied. "At least I'll write a fairer piece about the club than some of the other more sensationalist papers would do."

"Oh God, this is disastrous." Sylvia held her head in her hands. "None of the girls are going to come within a mile of this place if there are reporters hanging around the entrance. And if they've got cameras..."

"I'm sorry." It was at moments like these that Simon regretted his choice of profession. He knew several of the reporters on other newspapers who would gleefully write about the depraved nature of an all-women's club in the heart of Soho. However balanced his report might be, other newspapers would make outrageous claims about what happened behind the closed doors of the Paradise Regained Club. "It will only be for a while. They'll soon lose interest and move on to another salacious story."

"But we're not a salacious story," Sylvia snapped. "We're just a group of outcasts trying to keep our heads down in a society that hates us."

"I know, I know." Simon flicked over to a fresh page of his notepad. "What else can you tell me about Maureen Lyon? Did she come in here as well?"

"I don't know why I'm still talking to you." Sylvia stood and put the bottle of vodka back on the shelf behind her. "What makes you any more trustworthy than the rest of your thrill-seeking friends in Fleet Street?"

"I write the truth," Simon replied. "And I want this killer caught just as much as you do. To protect people like you and the other women who come in here. Look. If I hadn't made a nuisance of myself at Scotland Yard and written that story in the *Sunday Chronicle* about their incompetence they wouldn't be investigating this now." He leaned across the bar and reached for Sylvia's arm. "I'm on your side. Can't you see that?"

Sylvia sighed and sat back on her stool. "All right. What is it you want to know?"

"Tell me about Maureen Lyon." Simon readied his pencil to take notes.

"There's not much to tell," Sylvia began. "You've probably heard it all from Bill or Jenny already. She moved here from Bath a few years ago. Fell out with her family. Well, her father. Her mother had died years before when Maureen was only two. I think she said she was brought up by her grandparents. Not sure why she fell out with her father. It was a very religious family. You know. One of those new religions that's been springing up. I think they were very puritanical. Couldn't accept our modern life. Wanted things to go back in time."

"Was she working in the theatre when she lived in Bath?"

"Oh, no. Not until she got to London That was Jenny's doing. She was moving to London at the same time. From Bristol. They happened to meet when Maureen got on the train at Bath. An aunt had left Jenny that house where she lives and Maureen had nowhere to go and not much of a plan as far as I understand. So Jenny took her under her wing. Gave her a roof over her head and got her a job working at the opera house. Maureen blossomed from then on."

"And were they actually living together as a couple?"

"Don't ask me questions like that." Sylvia glowered at Simon. "How would you like it if some newspaper published details of the men you'd had affairs with?"

"I'm sorry." Simon held up his hand. "Is there anything else you can tell me?"

Sylvia picked up a cloth and mopped the bar top vigorously. "I think you need to speak to Jenny. I've got things to do here."

"Simon," exclaimed Bill when she opened the door of Jenny's house to find him standing outside. "What perfect timing. We've got lots of news to tell you. Jenny's had a visitor and we think he's connected with the murderer in some way."

"I've got some bad news I'm afraid," Simon began.

Bill ignored him and carried on. "Plus we've thought of a wonderful way that people like myself and Jenny and the other women of the Paradise Regained Club can protect themselves without having to rely on men."

"Bill." Simon tried again. "Would you just let me—"

"It's all thanks to Grace and her ju-jitsu," Bill continued. "She was able to stand her ground against this killer. And I could have done better if I'd been trained in her combat skills. It was only thanks to that man Darling standing in for Danvers that I didn't become another victim. But we're tired of relying on men to defend us. So we're going to—"

"Bill, will you listen to me?" Simon raised his voice. "Grace is dead."

16

Bill stood in Jenny's tiny kitchen and poured generous measures of gin into three glasses. It seemed like this was one of those days when life had decided to throw as much bad luck in her direction as it could. It was one of those days when it would be safer to return to bed, hide under the bedclothes, and wait until after the clock had chimed midnight.

Only there was no way she could do that. She had a responsibility to Jenny for a start. And then there was the argument she had to pick with Simon.

It was not enough for life to fling the shock of Grace's murder at her. But she also had to listen to Simon sheepishly admit his front-page story had given details of last night's failed attack and had named her. He had tried to defend his treachery by saying it was probable the other newspapers had carried the story as well.

She had made it clear his actions were indefensible and that the time was fast approaching when she would have to telephone Noël who was most likely already baying for her blood.

But she wasn't ready to do so just yet. She needed another

drink first. She picked up the three glasses from the kitchen counter and carried them into the living room.

"Are you still here?" She handed Simon his drink. "Haven't you got to write another article dragging both my name and Noël's into the gutter along with that rag you write for?"

"Come on, Bill. I've already told you. The other papers were going to be writing about you as well—"

"So you had to follow them meekly like a sheep." Bill handed a glass to Jenny. "How do you think for a moment that justifies your betrayal—"

"It's hardly a betrayal, Bill. I simply thought that by writing a more balanced version of the facts related to you—"

"'Simply' is the important word in that sentence," Bill interrupted. "This isn't the first time you've got me into a fix with Noël you know."

"If you weren't involved in the story then I wouldn't have had to mention you."

"Oh, so you think it's my fault I was attacked in my own flat last night—"

"Stop it," Jenny interrupted. "Stop it, both of you. Do you think that arguing like this is going to bring Grace back? Bring Maureen back? Have a little decency, can't you? Your petty quarrelling is doing nothing to…"

Her voice tailed off, she lifted her hands to her eyes, and sobbed. Her shoulders shook and she took short, staccato breaths between sobs. Bill sat on the settee beside her and put an arm around her shoulders.

"Now look what you've done," she said to Simon.

"Me?" Simon pulled a freshly laundered handkerchief from his pocket and handed it to Bill. "She was upset by our quarrelling. That takes two you know."

"She's upset by a lot more than that," Bill said quietly. "We all are. I was so convinced I'd got a good plan. I hated sitting around doing nothing. That's why I decided we should all learn ju-jitsu. But now that Grace has—"

"You *did* have a good plan." Jenny lifted her head. "After all, without the police on our side there wasn't a lot else we could do. But what with you being attacked last night. And now this news about Grace. It feels like the killer's getting closer. I don't feel safe in London any longer."

"What are you going to do?" Bill asked. "Have you thought about going back to Bristol?"

"Well, I was planning to go to Maureen's funeral in Bath. So I might as well go on to my parents afterwards. I'll just have to swallow my pride I suppose. They might be pleased to see me."

"I didn't know you had a date for the funeral." Bill tipped a cigarette from her case and lit it. "When did you find out?"

"I'm sorry, Bill. I forgot to tell you," Jenny replied. "That awful solicitor Mr Fisher told me before you arrived. It's the day after tomorrow."

Simon stood and walked out to the hallway. "Would you mind if I used your telephone, Jenny?"

"What are you doing?" Bill asked. "Ringing in another story to your bloody news desk?"

"Certainly not." Simon lifted the receiver. "I'm going to book a hotel in Bath for the next few days. It's time we found out a bit more about this shady fellow Fisher with the matching tie clip. And I can accompany Jenny to Maureen's funeral."

He dialled a number and held the receiver to his ear. "Would you care to join us, Bill? Or are you going to be too busy riding your high horse?"

The telephone call to Noël had not been as bad as Bill had imagined. He was in an excellent mood and singing the praises of *The Chronicle*.

Bill had failed to notice a full-page feature by *The Chronicle's* arts correspondent about the 'genius of Noël Coward'. She had been too blinded with fury at Simon's front-page story. The arts correspondent had included a glowing review of *Bitter Sweet* and references to Noël's plans to take the show to New York.

Fortunately, Noël had monopolised their telephone conversation and Bill had no need to draw his attention to what was on the front-page. He had given her four days off to attend Maureen's funeral straight away. "You can enjoy a little holiday in Bath. They have hot springs there. Maybe take the waters," he had added. "But I want you fighting fit in the following week. We've got lots to do. Cochran wants to take *Bitter Sweet* to Broadway while the show's still on here in London. Imagine. The same show on both sides of the Atlantic simultaneously. It will be even more of a triumph."

Charles Cochran was Noël's producer on *Bitter Sweet*. Bill hated the man. She considered him a frustrated actor who envied what Noël and his cast did and had only turned to producing when his acting career had failed to take off. He looked down his nose at her and avoided involving her in conversations. Instead he would approach Noël directly and cut her out of decisions. She was sure it was because she was a woman.

Simon's assistant in the newsroom had managed to get them the last three rooms in the Royal Hotel in Bath and booked them on the express train from Paddington the following lunchtime.

"How exciting," Bill lit a cigarette. "We're going on an adventure. I hope your assistant booked us a place in the dining car. I always find it thrilling to be eating when you're hurtling through the countryside at breakneck speed. Now, to more immediate matters. Where are we all going to sleep tonight?"

"I'm sure I'll be all right here," Jenny said. "It's only one night."

"I wouldn't hear of it," Bill replied. "You won't get a wink of sleep worrying. And I'm not spending a night alone in my flat."

"But you'll have that replacement porter on duty at yours," Simon reminded her. "The one who rescued you, remember?"

"Yes, but it was only through a stroke of luck that I'd left my cigarette case downstairs and he brought it up for me. He didn't stop the man getting into my apartment."

Bill blew out a smoke ring and smiled at Simon. "You can put us all up, can't you? You said before you could sneak me up the back stairs without the porter noticing. It's perfect. Your apartment's only ten minutes from Paddington so we can have a lie-in tomorrow morning."

"But it's only one bedroom," Simon protested.

"You said you had a settee," Bill responded.

"Yes, but—"

"That's settled then," Bill interrupted. "Jenny and I will share a bed and you can sleep on the settee."

"Don't I get any say in this?" Simon looked at her with puppy dog eyes. She presumed he thought it might win her round.

"Well, I suppose if you can't bear to sleep on your settee you can spend the night in my apartment. That way Jenny and I can invite some girls round and have a wild party Sapphic-style at your place."

Jenny giggled. "That sounds like fun."

"Absolutely not." Simon stood and walked to the hallway. "We've got lots of work to do. We need to take a look at those cardboard boxes of Maureen's things. Then we need to put them into a taxi to take over to mine to keep them safe in case Fisher comes back with some kind of court order. We've got a busy evening ahead."

Bill sighed. "Spoilsport."

———

Jenny had put together a simple buffet meal of cold meats and salad with a jug of fresh lemonade she had made earlier in the day. Simon carried the boxes from Maureen's old bedroom into the living room and the three of them sat on the floor picking at the food and discussing what they were looking for in Maureen's possessions.

"I've been through everything already," Jenny said. "I wanted to make sure the police didn't see the correspondence with Bill. It might have made things difficult for her."

"Would you prefer I wasn't involved in this?" Simon asked. "There's some very personal stuff here. And it's personal to both of you. I understand if you'd rather I left."

"Nonsense." Bill poured herself a glass of lemonade and added a splash of gin to it. "You're supposed to be the one with the journalist's eye. We can't be precious about this now. And we might just find some kind of clue as to why Maureen was murdered."

"But she's not the only victim," Simon replied. "There's Grace Lucas as well. Has she got any connection to her?"

"Apart from being found by a stage door?" Bill sniffed. "What's that headline I read about him in your newspaper? *The Stage Door Murderer*? Not very original is it?"

Simon ignored the jibe. "Grace Lucas didn't have anything to do with the theatre, did she? She was a nurse."

"I don't think Maureen even knew her," Jenny added. "Although I suppose she might have known her from the Paradise Regained Club. But that's about all."

"Perhaps the club is the linking factor," Simon mused. "Perhaps the killer is somebody from the club. But Bill's convinced it's a man."

"Whoever attacked me had a man's voice." Bill replenished her plate with some cold tongue and potato salad. "I can't believe the killer is one of the girls from the club."

"Even if they had a deep voice?" Simon asked.

"It was definitely a man." Bill put a forkful of potato salad into her mouth. "I just know. Anyway I'm beginning to think there isn't a link between the attacks. Remember that letter you found? About the blackmail? That's certainly more of a motive than some random person taking a dislike to women who go to the Paradise Regained Club."

She hooked her foot around one of the boxes and shoved it in Simon's direction. "Come on, senior crime reporter. It's time you earned your supper. We need something a bit more solid to go on."

Simon began to work his way through the layers of Maureen's life contained in the box. It was an intriguing mix of trivia—theatre programmes, scribbled to-do lists, a few black and white photographs. One of the photos showed what looked like a family gathering. Simon examined it closely before passing it to Bill.

"Is that Maureen in the front?" he asked.

Bill squinted at the picture. "Good God, she can't be more than about twelve. I wonder who all these people are. There must be a dozen or more in this picture. I didn't think she had such a large family."

She took the photograph over to a table lamp. "How strange."

"What is it?" Jenny stood and peered over Bill's shoulder.

"This boy standing next to her." Bill pointed at the photograph. "It's impossible I know. But I'm sure I've seen him before. This must have been taken over ten years ago. And yet I recognise him from somewhere."

"Who are all these other people?" Jenny asked. "Maureen doesn't look very happy. If it *is* a family gathering then it definitely shows they weren't a happy family."

Bill handed the picture back to Simon. "We'll take this with us to Bath. Maybe we can identify some of the people at the funeral."

Simon put the photograph to one side and carried on sorting through the contents of the box. He pulled out a large book of fairy tales and flicked through the pages. He'd had the same book when he was a child and a wave of memories of night times in the nursery with nanny came back to him. There was the story of *Hansel and Gretel* and *The Three Little Pigs*. He flicked through the book and it fell open at *The Boy Who Cried Wolf.*

Pressed between the pages were two thin pieces of paper. Simon carefully separated them.

"What have you got there?" Bill leaned across and ash dropped from the end of her cigarette.

"Careful, Bill," Simon warned. "You'll set fire to them if you're not careful. They're registry office certificates."

He squinted at the spidery writing on one of them. "This is a marriage certificate from Walthamstow Registry Office. The names are Alice Mary Lyon—"

"Maureen's mother," Jenny interjected. "I like the name Alice."

"—And Douglas Arbuthnot Smith—"

"That horrible solicitor man said that was his client," Jenny interrupted again. "Maureen's father."

"Fascinating." Bill exhaled smoke over the certificate. "So Maureen kept her parents' marriage certificate hidden away. What's the other one? Her birth certificate?"

"No, there's a man's name on it," Simon replied. "Charles Arbuthnot Smith."

"Poor thing." Bill shook her head. "Fancy giving a baby a name like Arbuthnot."

"He was born 17th December 1899," Simon continued. "That makes him thirty this year."

"He's four years older than Maureen," Bill added. "She never mentioned a brother to me. Did she ever say anything about him to you, Jenny?"

"She hardly mentioned her family," Jenny replied. "The only time she did say much was when we met the very first time. It was on the train coming to London. I was coming here to take on this house my aunt had left me. When the train got to Bath Maureen got into my carriage. We had some Lyons tea together and Maureen decided then and there that Lyon was going to be her new last name. It had been her late mother's maiden name. Her mother had died when Maureen was only two years old. She said her father always blamed Maureen for her death. He sounded like a frightful man. Maureen changed her name from Smith to Lyon that afternoon on the train. She said she was never going back."

"Well, sadly she is now." Simon held out the certificates to Jenny. "Have you got an envelope to put these into for safekeeping?"

"I'm sure I have somewhere." Jenny took the certificates. "I wonder why she kept them in that book of fairy stories?"

"So Maureen had a brother," Bill mused. "I wonder if he'll be at the funeral?"

JOURNAL ENTRY 25 JULY 1929

I have been spending more time with the Elder from the Mission in the past few days. Of course I have not revealed the true nature of the work I have been doing to cleanse the streets of London. In his position it would not be a good idea for him to know.

But he has been talking a great deal about the power of persuasion in our mission. He has told me that he senses an impulsiveness in me that may lead me to disobey one or more of the Commandments.

I have told him a little of what I want to achieve and he seems to support me. But he calls it a Herculean task. He believes passionately in the power of persuasion and education.

It has given me pause for thought.

The ringleader is one of those females who think they're entitled to more than they already have. As if they don't have far too much in this depraved society already.

She should sit down and read what the good book says about people like her. Lot's Wife was a lesson for all like her.

And that is what I believe I should do. It is a different

approach. I will use her to convince the others of the error of their ways.

I will capture her, force her to listen to the words of truth, and extinguish the breath of impurity. I will take her to somewhere secure, away from the crowds.

Where no one will find her.

Then I will begin the process of re-education.

That's what my father should have done with my mother. Instead he allowed her to get away with far too much until he finally kicked her out.

Men are too forgiving of the so-called weaker sex. After all, they are all spawned by that one temptress in the Garden of Eden.

They must be brought back into line.

And I will begin with the one who dares cut her hair short and wear men's clothes.

17

The following morning the platforms at Paddington station were bustling with families going on holiday. Porters pushed trolleys piled high with suitcases and the rest of the paraphernalia essential for a trip to the seaside. Children dressed in their best Sunday clothes carried buckets and spades or clutched teddy bears. They trailed along behind their parents or nannies and looked wide-eyed at the monstrous steam engines lined up and ready to take them at breakneck speed to Truro, Penzance, or Plymouth. One boy aged no more than seven had to be scooped up by a porter when he wandered over to one of the locomotives to examine it in more detail. He was given a stern lecture on the perils of venturing too close to the platform edge.

Sunlight streamed through the vast glass canopy of the roof and shafts of light cut through the fog of belching smoke. Bill strode down a line of brown and cream-liveried carriages of the Great Western Railway train on platform seven. She had dispensed with her usual black trouser suit in favour of a long grey skirt, tailored jacket, and a demure cloche hat.

Simon and Jenny hurried to keep up with her. Behind them

a porter pushed a trolley laden with luggage. Bill stopped by carriage number eight and waited for Simon and Jenny to catch up.

"I can understand why Jenny needed to pack so many bags." Simon pointed to the porter's trolley as it headed towards the luggage van. "But why do you need so much, Bill? We're only going to be in Bath for a few days."

"It may only be a few days but who knows what events we may have to attend while we're there?" Bill responded. "A masked ball, a cocktail party, hunting with the local master of the hounds."

"I never would have thought you had such a variety of outfits." Simon opened the carriage door for Jenny to climb into the compartment. "I thought you simply had a wardrobe of black trouser suits and you swapped from one to the other from time to time."

"What an impertinent remark, Mr Sampson." Bill climbed into the carriage behind Jenny and held out her hand to assist Simon. "I would have thought you of all people would know that disguise is essential when on an investigation. Provincial people dress differently to city-dwellers. Why do you think I'm wearing this ridiculous outfit? Skirts are so impractical. But it's not my intention to stand out over the next few days. It's essential that I blend in."

Simon smiled. He wondered how well Bill would blend in once she opened her mouth.

As the train left behind the grey grime of the London suburbs and steamed through the green fields of Berkshire the dining car attendant summoned them to lunch. The carriage looked and smelled brand-new with polished wood panelling lit by white globe electric lights in brass fittings.

They took their seats at a mahogany table laid with a starched white cloth and napkins. Jenny sat opposite Bill by the window with Simon alongside Jenny. Bill ordered a round of gin martinis from one of the several waiters hurrying up and down the aisle. She lit a cigarette and took out a large leather-bound notebook.

"Here are the notes I took last night when we were going through Maureen's things. I think we all need to think hard about what we know about the case so far."

"The 'case'?" Simon asked. "Have you been taking lessons from Detective Sergeant Daniels?"

"What an absurd idea." Bill opened the notebook and slid out a fountain pen from its spine. "The man's an incompetent. It would be like taking lessons from a fool. No, the reason why we're on this train is because the police have failed us so badly. We're the last hope for the women of London."

Jenny giggled. "You've got a very high opinion of us, Bill. I'm only here to go to Maureen's funeral. Then I'm running away to hide at my parents' house for a week or so."

"You mustn't think of it in that way," Bill scolded. "I'm convinced that together we know enough to work out who the murderer is. But the clues are stuck in our heads somewhere. That's why I want to write everything down."

"You'd better keep that enormous book away from prying eyes." Simon reached into his pocket and pulled out a much smaller notebook. "Mine never leaves me."

"Please don't treat me like a half-wit, Simon." Bill unscrewed the top of her pen and drew a line under the notes from the night before. "Now. What else do we know?"

Before anyone could speak, the waiter interrupted them to take their lunch order. Simon ordered braised beef with boiled potatoes and carrots for all of them and a bottle of Bordeaux wine recommended by the waiter.

"If we're going to have a combined racking of brains," Simon began after the waiter had left. "I think we should start with you,

Bill. You're the only one of us who's had a close encounter with the murderer. Think back to the night you were attacked. Is there anything you can think of that might help identify him?" He leaned back in his seat. "That's a good thought, actually. You said you heard his voice. Are you certain the murderer's a man?"

"Yes," Bill replied emphatically.

"You saw him?" Jenny asked.

"I got glimpses of him," Bill replied. "In the mirrors in the hallway. I can't say I noticed him that much. I was too busy trying not to die."

"Think hard," Simon urged. "Was he tall? Short? Dark-haired? Fair-haired."

"That's impossible to say," Bill replied. "He had this woollen mask over his head."

"There's got to be something about him you remember," Simon said. "Tell me again precisely what happened."

"It was all so quick." Bill closed her eyes. "I opened the door and discovered the lights weren't working. I turned to go back downstairs and I heard this swishing noise. Then the cord was around my throat."

She put her fingers to her neck.

"I couldn't breathe. I tried to grab the cord but it got tighter. I could feel his breath. I was pulling at his hands. His fingers were rough, like a gardener's."

She opened her eyes.

"He had a ring."

"Go on," Simon responded. "Describe it."

"It was large." Bill continued. "And there was some sort of shape moulded on it. It wasn't a smooth ring. It was on his right hand. I'm certain of it. Presumably a signet ring of some kind. It was such a bizarre thought going through my head in that terrible moment. I was thinking how unusual it was for a man to wear such an ostentatious ring. I must have completely forgotten about it when Daniels interviewed me."

She stared out at the English countryside as it sped past the window. By her calculations the train would soon be approaching the rural part of England where she had spent the first ten years of her life.

Her parents had owned a large farm in Gloucestershire and Bill had loved her childhood. It was an idyllic time for an only child who was inquisitive and loved the outdoors. She would spend summers with a small group of friends from the nearby village climbing trees, damming rivers, and building dens in the woods.

It had all changed when her mother died suddenly. Her father had announced he could no longer cope with the responsibilities of bringing up a child. Bill had been dispatched to London to live with her aunt and uncle in Belgravia. They were a childless couple and it had quickly become clear they disliked children. They had sent Bill to a convent boarding school in Wales. Her father had visited rarely. When she left the school she went to a secretarial college in London. On her twenty-first birthday her father had written her a letter to say he had bought her the flat in St John's Wood. She had never heard from him again.

As she peered out of the soot-grimed window at the sunlit day large, threatening clouds rolled across the sun and the light dimmed as if a curtain had been drawn. It looked as if the weeks of unrelenting sunshine they had enjoyed were about to end.

The rain held off until late that evening when a dramatic clap of thunder presaged a downpour on a tropical scale. The streets of

Bath became like muddy rivers and for a few hours the city's traffic ground to a halt.

By the following morning the rain had reduced to a persistent drizzle, the temperature had dropped several degrees, and it felt like the start of autumn.

The Royal Hotel was opposite the railway station. It was a fine Victorian hotel built by the creator of the Great Western Railway himself, Isambard Kingdom Brunel.

Maureen Lyon's funeral was to be at midday in a place called The Heavenly Hall in Avon Street. Debris from the previous night's storm had blocked or narrowed some streets and they were jammed with traffic. Simon had spoken to the hotel receptionist and had decided it would be quicker to walk to the Heavenly Hall rather than take a taxi.

"Walk?" Bill exclaimed. "In this ridiculous outfit? And Jenny's wearing the most beautiful Mary Jane pumps. They'll be ruined in the mud on those awful pavements. Not to mention the blasted cobblestones. Absolutely not. I demand we take a taxi."

After twenty minutes sitting in a taxi that had travelled less than a mile Simon suggested they reconsider walking. Bill peered through the partly misted windscreen of the cab. There seemed to be no imminent movement in the traffic. She wrapped her cloak around her shoulders and rapped on the glass behind the driver.

"Pull over here," she commanded. "We've got more chance getting there on foot. Although my skirts will be ruined."

She threw open the taxi door and stepped out into a large puddle.

Simon chuckled. Perhaps you should have worn your hunting outfit today," he suggested. "The boots would have been more practical."

"Pay the driver." Bill glowered at him. "And try to be of some help to Miss Casewell. It's treacherous out here."

Avon Street was no more than a five hundred yard walk from where the taxi had dropped them. As they drew nearer the houses became more and more dilapidated and the people around them looked noticeably poorer. Curious barefoot children came up to them, taunted them, and demanded money. An elderly drunk man collided with Bill and swore loudly at her.

"So this is where Maureen grew up," Jenny whispered. "I never knew. No wonder she ran away to London."

The Heavenly Hall was halfway along Avon Street. It was a solid red brick building that looked like a bus garage. A large peeling paper poster was stuck above the entrance. It read:

I pursued my enemies and destroyed them.

"That's a cheerful welcome," Bill commented. "I wonder how they classify us."

She pushed open one of the heavy wooden entrance doors. They stepped into a gloomy hallway lit by a single electric bulb strung above their heads. Bill strode towards another set of double doors directly in front of them. Her heels clattered on the tiled floor. A door to their left swung open and a man stood on the threshold peering into the gloom.

"Who's that?" he asked.

It was the solicitor Jebediah Fisher.

"Mr Fisher." Bill walked over to him with her hand outstretched in greeting.

"In the Mission Hall I am addressed as Elder Fisher." He refused to take her hand. "Why are you here?"

"For the funeral," Bill replied. "I'm Miss Miles. We met the other day. Don't you remember?"

"But why are *you* here?"

"Well, because we're friends. Miss Casewell's here as well. You remember her as well, I presume?"

"I do." Fisher folded his arms. "You two are the ones who stole my client's property."

"Oh no, we haven't stolen it." Bill tried a smile but Fisher remained impassive. "Might I add, we've travelled all the way here not only to come to the funeral but also to return Maureen's personal effects to her father. They're back at the hotel."

It was partly true. They had packed a few of Maureen's things in the expectation they might meet Fisher again. It was a prudent decision and now had the potential to let them trade a place at the funeral for their return.

"I see." Fisher unfolded his arms and pointed to the set of double doors. "The funeral begins in fifteen minutes. My client Mr Smith will not be attending."

"He's not here?" Simon asked.

"Who is this man?" Fisher posed the question to Bill.

"My name's Simon Sampson," Simon replied. "I'm also a friend of the family."

"I very much doubt that you are a friend of the family." Fisher sniffed. "But I presume that you mean you are a friend of Miss Smith. Very well. Go and take your seats. And please maintain a sense of decorum. Remember that you are in a place of worship."

Beyond the double doors was an austere hall. The walls were bare brick and the only illumination came from weak sunlight filtering through tall metal-framed windows. A plain wooden coffin rested on two triangular trestles in the centre of the hall with about thirty wooden chairs arranged around it. On top of the coffin lay a black wooden cross and a bunch of scruffy-looking chrysanthemums. There was no one else in the hall. Simon sat on one of the chairs close to the door. Jenny went over to the coffin and laid a hand on it. Bill joined her and put an arm around her shoulder.

"I hate funerals," she whispered. "So morbid. Why can't they make them jolly affairs? Maureen was such fun. She would have hated this."

"Where is everyone?" Jenny whispered. "And why isn't her father here? Or her brother? There must have been someone else who knew her apart from us."

The doors behind them creaked open and four men dressed in black walked in. They stood either side of the entrance as Fisher entered. He walked across to the coffin and nodded to Bill and Jenny.

"We are about to begin," he said. "Please take your seats."

Bill and Jenny returned to Simon and sat next to him. Fisher picked up the black wooden cross from the coffin and held it in front of him.

"We are gathered here today to return a damaged soul to the fold of the Mission of the Heavenly Host," he began. "Made sinful and evil in life, Maureen Rose Smith was uncongregated by this Mission when she rejected the Truth. Now that her body has yielded up its soul we will commit it to holy ground in the belief and faith that it will be restored to the goodness of God's creation with all evil expunged."

"Good grief," Bill whispered to Simon. "He's not only a solicitor but also a minister of this bizarre place. This is even worse than I thought."

Fisher glowered at her and she slid her finger and thumb across her lips to mime sealing them.

"Maureen Rose Smith was born into a good family of this Mission," Fisher continued. "But through the—"

"No, it's not true. It's all lies." A woman's voice interrupted Fisher from the doorway. She was dressed in black with a small pillbox hat and a veil covering her face. "Maureen was a good girl. She wasn't a sinner. It's her father who's the sinner. He's the one what killed her."

Two of the men standing on either side of the entrance stepped forward and grabbed the woman. One put a hand over her mouth and the other pinned her arms behind her. They spun her round and marched her out of the hall. The doors slammed shut behind them.

"Who on earth was that?" Bill whispered to Simon.

"I don't know," Simon replied. "But haven't you noticed something? Fisher's wearing a large black ring. Do you think it's the same sort of ring you felt on your attacker's hand?"

18

"As I was saying." Fisher cleared his throat and continued the address.

"Maureen Rose Smith was born into a good family in The Mission of the Heavenly Host. Early in her life she exhibited the signs of being possessed by Satan. The Mission had no choice but to uncongregate her. When she grew older the sins of the city to the east proved too great an attraction for this wayward young woman. She travelled there to seek a life of debauchery and depravity."

Now that Simon had mentioned the rings Bill became fixated on the one Fisher was wearing. She was also distracted by his strange accent. He sounded like someone who had arrived from a European country and was trying hard to speak very precise and correct English. She tried to place his accent's origin as he continued the address.

"But in her pursuit of evil, Maureen's fallen life was taken from her. God's punishment is vengeful and it is full of wrath. Her body has now been returned to the Mission to be cleansed of all lustfulness before it is burned in the fires of purity and returned to the earth from whence it came."

Fisher processed around the coffin. He stopped at each corner to lower the cross and gently touch it to the surface of the wooden box. Throughout the procedure he spoke quietly and Bill cupped a hand behind her ear to try to hear what he was saying. She caught the odd phrase such as, "sister of Satan" and "extinguish the breath of impurity" but the rest was impossible to hear.

The doors creaked behind them and Bill looked round to see who else had entered the hall. It was one of the four men. The other three walked towards the coffin and stood one at each corner. The fourth secured the main doors open before joining them.

"Come," Fisher intoned. "Place your hands upon here and allow the energy of purity to extinguish the breath of impurity."

The four men lifted Maureen's coffin, placed it on their shoulders, and processed slowly towards the exit. Fisher leaned the cross into an alcove behind him and turned to follow the pallbearers.

"Excuse me." Simon stepped forward. "Where are they taking Maureen now?"

Fisher stopped. He regarded Simon disdainfully. "It is now the city council's responsibility to dispose of her earthly remains," he said. "We have done all we can. They will cremate her."

"Why isn't her father here?" Simon asked. "Why isn't he at his own daughter's funeral?"

Fisher sniffed. "The young woman caused Mr Smith much trouble in her short life. He has done more than enough for her and he has no need to expose himself to her impurity one last time."

"And her brother?" Bill asked. "Why isn't he here?"

"The brother is away on important business," Fisher replied. "Which reminds me. You said you had Miss Smith's personal effects with you. Could you bring them to my offices please? I will be there later."

"We'd prefer to hand them to her father directly." Bill smiled sweetly at Fisher. "Could you give us his address, please?"

"There's no need for that," Fisher replied. "I am his lawyer and you can hand them to me."

"No." Bill smiled again. "By the way, *Elder* Fisher. Why the fancy jewellery?"

Fisher hastily covered the large black ring on his left hand with his sleeve. "It is merely a symbol of the authority bestowed upon me by the other Elders of the Mission. No more than that. Any one of us might wear it when we are presiding over ceremonies."

"And is that the only time you wear it?" Bill asked.

Simon laid a hand on her arm. "Come on old thing," he said. "Let's go. As there doesn't seem to be a decent wake organised we should go and get a drink to toast Maureen's memory."

The three of them headed for the exit doors with Fisher calling after them: "You are thieves. Vagabonds. God will seek you out and exact a terrible revenge."

Back in the street Bill took her cigarette case from her jacket pocket and searched unsuccessfully for her lighter. Nearby, the four pallbearers had finished loading Maureen's coffin into a hearse. They stood around smoking and talking with a fifth man. Bill strode over to them.

"Anyone got a light for a damsel in distress?"

The man talking to the pallbearers took out a box of matches and lit one.

"You're an angel, my darling," Bill said as she inhaled deeply on the cigarette. "I need this to clear my lungs of the hypocrisy I've just inhaled inside that bloody hall."

The man looked startled.

"You were inside? At the service?" he asked. There was a

crispness about the way he spoke. His accent sounded similar to Fisher's. It was definitely not the local accent of Bath. "Who are you and why were you there?"

Bill extended her hand. "I'm Florence Miles, and these are my friends Mr Sampson and Miss Casewell. We knew Maureen in London. And who are you?"

"My name is Smith," the man replied. "Douglas Arbuthnot Smith. I am Maureen's father."

***

Smith had refused to invite them back to his home. After much persuasion he had reluctantly agreed to join them later at their hotel on the promise he would get his daughter's possessions returned to him.

That afternoon Bill, Simon, and Jenny sat in the lounge waiting for Smith to arrive. A waiter appeared with their order of tea, a plateful of dainty sandwiches with the crusts cut off, and a selection of cakes. He unloaded his tray on the table in front of them and held up an envelope.

"I have a message for a Miss Casewell," he announced.

"That's me," Jenny said. She took the envelope from him, slit it open with a knife, and took out a single sheet of paper. She raised a hand to her mouth and gasped as she read its contents.

"What is it, Jenny?" Bill asked.

"My father." Jenny stood so quickly she knocked against the table and Simon had to grab the cake stand to stop it falling. "He's been rushed to hospital."

"What's wrong with him?" Bill asked.

"It doesn't say," Jenny replied. "I must go to him. I'm so sorry. I can't wait around here."

"Of course." Bill stood. "Can I help you with anything?"

"I'll be fine. I'll go and get my suitcases and catch the next train to Bristol. I think there's one every hour."

Jenny walked away from them towards reception.

"I hope she'll be all right," Simon said.

"Jenny's not the strongest of girls." Bill sat again. "And it's a hell of a blow to get news like that so soon after Maureen's death. Let's hope her father isn't seriously ill." She looked at the grandfather clock standing in the corner of the lounge. "It's ten past three already. Do you think Smith's going to turn up?"

"Who knows?" Simon reached for one of the sandwiches. "I must say he looked like a startled rabbit when we met him this morning. It'll be damned annoying if he sends that blasted man Fisher in his place again."

"Well, if he doesn't turn up we'll simply have to find out where he lives," Bill replied. "I've certainly got some questions to ask him. Like did he kill his daughter? for a start."

"The man's called Smith, Bill." Simon shoved the last of the sandwich in his mouth and helped himself to another. "How many Smiths do you think there are in Bath? It will take us forever to find him."

"Can't you use your special skills as an investigative reporter?" Bill asked. "Surely you've had trickier problems to solve in the past?"

"I'm sure I could," Simon replied. "I'd start with the local post offices. I can usually sweet-talk them. And it certainly helps that he's got unusual first names. I managed to find someone in London that way before now. But then I knew they lived in the Shepherd's Bush area so that narrowed it down quite a bit."

"Who do you think that woman was who came bursting in?" Bill asked. "They were very rough with her. She was the one saying it was Smith who killed his own daughter. Do you think she's right?"

"I think anything's possible with that lot," Simon replied.

"Ghastly crowd. But for what it's worth my gut instinct says he didn't. As I said he looked like a startled rabbit. I don't think he's got the bottle to leave Bath, let alone travel to London. There's certainly something very odd about this Mission of the Heavenly Host lot."

"There's something very odd about the way Fisher spoke at the service this morning." Bill lit a cigarette. "Did you notice his accent? And Smith talks the same way. I don't think either of them are originally from this country."

"I suppose they both speak in a very precise way," Simon agreed. "But if they're from overseas their English is flawless."

Bill looked at the clock again and stood.

"I don't think this blasted man's coming," she said. "I'll go out to the reception and make sure Jenny's okay. While I'm there I'll check to see if he isn't hanging around outside."

Simon reached for another sandwich.

"And don't eat all the bloody sandwiches," Bill added.

***

Jenny had already got her suitcases from the bedroom and was checking out when Bill reached reception.

"Will you be all right?"

"Oh, Bill. What else can go wrong?" Tears glistened on Jenny's cheeks. "I thought I was going to Bristol to escape the problems of London. It looks like I'm heading towards even more problems."

Bill put a comforting arm around her shoulder.

"I'll come with you to the station and wait until the train comes."

Jenny wiped away her tears.

"That's so kind of you. But there's really no need. You should stay here in case Maureen's father shows up."

"There's no sign of him so far," Bill replied. "I'll come across to the station with you and see if he's hanging around outside somewhere."

"Could you do something for me please?" Jenny opened her handbag, rummaged around, and produced a set of keys. "Could you look after the house until I get back? You don't have to go in every day. But with father in hospital I don't know how long I'll be in Bristol."

"Of course I will."

Bill took the keys and put them in her jacket pocket. A porter loaded Jenny's suitcases onto a trolley and they followed him out of the hotel. There was no sign of Smith. The traffic on the main road was busy once more and they stood on the pavement waiting for a chance to cross. On the far side of the road Bill recognised a man leaning against a lamppost smoking a cigarette.

"What on earth's he doing here?" she said out loud and waved her arm.

"Who is it?" Jenny asked.

"Darling," Bill called. "Over here."

"Another of your romantic entanglements?" Jenny smiled.

"Not at all." Bill stepped into the road and a bus driver honked his horn. "Darling's his name. He's the temporary porter at Wetherby Mansions. What on earth's he doing in Bath?"

"You mean the one who saved you that night?"

"Darling," Bill called out again. The man turned and walked rapidly in the opposite direction. By the time they had crossed the road the man had disappeared into the crowd.

"Damn," Bill said. "I'm sure it was him. How very strange."

Perhaps he's visiting friends," Jenny replied. She glanced back at the hotel. "Look. Isn't that Smith?"

The gaunt, angular figure of Maureen's father stood on the

steps of the hotel looking around nervously as if pondering whether to go in.

"God, so it is." Bill wrapped her arms around Jenny and gave her a kiss on both cheeks. "I'll love you and leave you, my dear. Don't want him running off just when we've managed to entice him here. Safe journey and call us as soon as you have any news."

Bill crossed back over the road and incurred the wrath of several taxis and another bus as they slammed on their brakes to avoid hitting her.

"Mr Smith," she said breathlessly. "So good of you to come. Would you like to come inside? We have tea waiting for you."

Smith shook his head. "I will just collect my daughter's possessions and go."

"Oh." Bill lit a cigarette and exhaled. "Well, at least do me the courtesy of coming into reception. There are several boxes and I don't plan carrying them out here on my own."

Without waiting for his agreement Bill continued into the lobby. She waited by the entrance to the hotel lounge until Smith caught up with her. Bill walked into the lounge and took her seat back at the table with Simon. Smith hovered in the doorway watching them.

"Surely he's not going to run off now?" she whispered. "After we've got him this far."

"I'll throw him a bone," Simon whispered back. He stood, picked up one of the smaller boxes of Maureen's possessions stacked by the table, and waved at Smith.

"Good move," Bill said. "I'll pour us some tea. Although a stiff gin and tonic would be preferable."

Smith walked over to them and stood by the table.

"I have come for my daughter's things," he said. "This lady tells me there are several boxes. How many exactly are there?"

"Would you like some tea?" Bill handed him a cup but Smith ignored it. She sighed and put it back on the table. "There are three boxes in total. Do you have transport?"

Smith shook his head. "I will carry them myself. I do not live far from here."

"Are you sure we can't tempt you to a sandwich?" Simon put the box down on his chair and held out his hand. Smith ignored the greeting. "Or a piece of cake. It's very good, you know."

"I have no desire to take food with you people," Smith replied. "Allow me to take my daughter's things and you can return to that sinful place to the east."

"London?" Bill asked. "It's not all sinful. Some of it's quite serious you know. We even have churches. Although I've never seen one quite like yours before."

"That is because your eyes are closed to that which is good and pure," Smith replied. "We have several Missions in London. And soon we will fill this country with purification."

He bent down to pick up the box.

Simon put his hand on top of it. "We'll need a receipt," he said.

"I beg your pardon?" Smith looked shocked.

Bill was surprised as well. What was Simon thinking? The man was already more than enough angry with them. Simon took a pen and a blank sheet of hotel notepaper from his pocket and placed them on top of the box.

"We don't want your Mr Fisher continuing to call us 'thieves and vagabonds' do we?" Simon said. "Just write a simple 'I have received from Mr Sampson all of my daughter's possessions.' And sign your name of course."

Smith stared at Simon for several seconds before snatching

up the pen and notepaper. He sat at the table and scribbled what Simon had suggested.

"There." He handed the paper and pen to Simon. "Now give me what I came here for and get out of my life."

"Of course," Simon replied. "Just one thing. Why did that woman this morning say you killed your daughter?"

19

Bill ordered a gin and tonic from a passing waiter and put another smoked salmon sandwich on her plate. She lit a cigarette and drummed her fingers on the arm of her chair. Simon had followed Smith out of the lounge when he left. Twenty minutes later he had still not returned. The man was infuriating.

She thought about Smith's accent and tried to replay Fisher's voice in her head when he was giving the address at the funeral that morning. Their voices both had the same clipped, precise intonation. Were they related? They had different surnames. And there was little similarity in their faces. Smith's was gaunt and angular with a long, almost hooked nose. Despite his wizened appearance there was a resemblance to Maureen Bill recognised.

Fisher had a more rounded face with a squashed button of a nose. Perhaps they were both from the same country. Or maybe their families were and they had chosen to settle in Bath. Perhaps it had no relevance and was a coincidence. With very little else to go on she was clutching at any scrap of information that might lead to the identity of Maureen's murderer. Their accents were very likely irrelevant.

And why had Simon insisted on a receipt for Maureen's possessions? It was very strange behaviour. Perhaps it was because Fisher was a lawyer and he wanted to be sure the man wouldn't pursue them through the courts even though they'd returned all the items to Maureen's father.

Almost all the items.

There were several they'd retained. The marriage and birth certificates, for a start. Plus of course the letter showing Maureen had been blackmailing someone. Maybe that was why Simon had insisted on a written receipt. To make sure Smith could not subsequently claim something was missing.

Her gin and tonic arrived. Bill gave Simon's room number for the bill and lit another cigarette. He had been gone nearly half an hour and she began to worry. Perhaps something had happened to him. An accident on the busy road outside. Or perhaps Fisher had been waiting for Smith. Together they had gone through the boxes of Maureen's possessions, found there were key items missing and whisked Simon away in a fast car to interrogate him in a deserted house somewhere.

She shook her head vigorously and took another sip of her drink. Her imagination was running away with her. On his last trip to New York Noël had brought back copies of a crime fiction magazine called *Black Mask*. It featured a new writer called Dashiell Hammett. Reading his stories had become her secret guilty pleasure. Perhaps she should stop.

"Hello old girl. Were you worried?"

Simon stood in front of her with a broad grin on his face. He was holding an envelope.

"Not at all," Bill replied. "I've just ordered a gin and tonic. Do you want one? The waiter's over there."

Don't you want to know where I've been?"

"No, but I'm sure you're itching to tell me." Bill took another sip from her glass. "I must find out what gin they use here. It's absolutely delicious."

Simon threw the envelope in her lap. She opened it and pulled out the letter they had found among Maureen's possessions accusing her of being a blackmailer.

"Yes, I've seen it already." She held it out for Simon to take. "What about it?"

Instead of taking it Simon handed her another piece of paper. It was the receipt Smith had written half an hour before.

"Compare the handwriting," he said. "It's the same. I'm certain of it."

He was right. The backwards-leaning spidery writing on both sheets of paper was identical and the signatures were the same.

"Maureen was blackmailing her own father? Why on earth was she doing that?"

"For money I imagine." Simon sat at the table. "Yes I will have that drink. This detection business is thirsty work." He took a sip from Bill's drink.

"Get your own." Bill took the glass from his hand. "Although I concede you deserve a drink. What made you think it could be him?"

Simon called the waiter over and ordered a gin and tonic.

"Lots of thoughts were buzzing round my head while we were in that awful service this morning. If Maureen was a good person like you say then why would she blackmail anyone? The only person I could think of was someone who'd been awful to her. Seeing those ghastly people this morning made me realise what she'd had to put up with. Especially when they bundled that poor woman out so unceremoniously. It was a bit of a wild guess I admit. But it was worth checking wasn't it?"

He took another envelope from his pocket and handed it to Bill. There was a triumphant look on his face.

"I also know what she was blackmailing him about."

Bill opened the envelope and pulled out two certificates. The marriage certificate for Maureen's parents and her brother's birth certificate. She studied the certificates. What was it Simon had seen? She was determined not to be beaten by him. The certificates appeared genuine. The names were consistent with what Fisher had told them. Maureen's brother, Charles Arbuthnot Smith, was born on 17th December 1899. She examined the marriage certificate for Maureen's parents. Douglas Arbuthnot Smith married Alice Mary Lyon at Walthamstow Registry Office on 7th June 1899.

"Oh my God," she said. "You clever man. You clever, clever man. The dates. So their first born, Douglas was conceived out of wedlock."

"At least three months out of wedlock."

The waiter arrived with Simon's drink. He picked up the glass and tapped it against Bill's.

"Chin chin, my dear." Simon took a long sip of his gin and tonic. "Interesting isn't it? I can't imagine the Mission of the Heavenly Host would be very happy if it ever became public that one of their flock had fathered a—"

"Exactly," Bill interrupted. "I think we've just made a breakthrough."

Simon raised an eyebrow quizzically.

"I mean *you've* made a breakthrough," Bill corrected herself. "I wonder when Maureen found out? And when did she start blackmailing her father about it? Did she leave home when she discovered the truth and took the certificates with her as surety? Or did she only start asking for money when she got desperate? I know she always flew a bit close to the wind when it came to spending money. I helped her out on at least one occasion. And I'm sure Jenny did too."

Bill stuffed the certificates back into the envelope and handed them back to Simon. "I think those certificates, together with the letter from Smith are pretty strong evidence of a motive for murder."

Simon shook his head. "I still don't think Smith's capable of travelling all the way up to London and murdering his own daughter."

"Fisher, then?" Bill suggested. "Acting on behalf of a member of his flock, or whatever he calls them. Or doing it for his client. It amounts to the same thing."

Again Simon shook his head. "It's a hell of a risk for a lawyer like Fisher to take. He seems such a cautious, pedantic man. And then what about Grace's murder? Or the attack on you, come to that? What possible motive could Smith or Fisher have to commit those crimes?"

"Maybe the murders aren't linked after all." Bill finished the remains of her drink and held up her glass. "Get me another will you? You drank most of it. Perhaps the solicitor Fisher murdered Maureen but someone completely different murdered Grace and attacked me."

"I've no idea." Simon shrugged. "I'm not sure this is quite the breakthrough I was hoping for. It's even more confusing if you ask me. There are even more unanswered questions."

"We need to track Smith down," Bill said. "Then we can ask him directly about this. How long do you think it might take you to use your investigative talents and find his address?"

The same triumphant look passed across Simon's face.

"You haven't?" Bill asked, although she sensed she was about to have to congratulate him again. His series of successes were getting irritatingly frequent. Simon pulled a scrap of paper from his trouser pocket and held it up like a judge displaying his score for a dance competition.

"How on earth did you manage that?" Bill asked. "You've only been gone half an hour."

Simon tapped the side of his nose. "That would be telling," he replied. "When you've finished your drink we can go for a walk."

Smith's house was in a street of terraced houses barely five minutes' walk from the Mission Hall. It was a small house with peeling paintwork on the front door and layers of grime on the windows. When Bill and Simon saw there were no curtains and they could be spotted from inside the house they walked past and stopped at the corner of the street about fifty yards further.

"I don't think we should both appear on his doorstep," Bill began. "We'll terrify the man, he'll slam the door in our faces, and that will be the end of our investigation."

"I'll go, then." Simon turned to walk back to the house but Bill grabbed his arm.

"Not so fast," she said. "He's less likely to slam the door on me. I'll go."

"Why do you think he's going to open his house to you and not to me?" Simon shrugged her hand away. "I'm not letting you go alone. You're a woman and—"

"And what?" Bill was irritated. "That is so patronising of you. I'm perfectly capable of looking after myself."

"You weren't the other night," Simon replied. "A man had to come to your rescue when you were attacked."

"Damn you, Simon Sampson." Bill resisted the urge to push him against the wall in her annoyance. "I really thought you were making an effort to be different. And not act like all the other men with their condescending claptrap."

"Why are you twisting my concern for your safety into an allegation of being patronising?" Simon's face was getting redder and he regarded her furiously. "Two women have been murdered in London. As far as we know. There could be more. You were attacked the other night and it was only thanks to a man's intervention that you got away with your life. If Smith is the murderer—"

"But you've already said you don't think he is," Bill protested.

"We don't know that for certain." Simon glanced over her shoulder. "Damn it. Don't look behind you. Just follow me up the street."

He turned and led them further away from Smith's house.

"What's the matter?" Bill asked.

"Whilst we were wasting time bickering Smith came out of his house and he's heading this way," Simon replied. "I wonder if he's going back to the Mission? It's in this direction."

Simon grabbed Bill's arm and led her across the street to an alleyway. They went a few yards down before turning to see Smith walk up the main street on the opposite side. They waited until he had continued thirty yards further on before they re-emerged from the alleyway and followed him.

"I'm very grateful for your concern about my safety," Bill whispered as they walked. "But I do think that sometimes you could be a little less patronising."

"I understand completely," Simon whispered back. "Next time you're in trouble don't bother to call me because I won't come running."

"There's no need to be like that. All I meant was..."

She was cut short when Simon pushed her into a doorway and leaned against her heavily.

"Mr Sampson," she whispered. "This is very forward of you. Just because we shared a bed the other night—"

"For once in your life Bill just shut up."

She complied with his request and they waited in silence. After several minutes Simon peered out from the doorway and released the weight of his body from hers.

"Why did you do that?" Bill whispered.

"Because I saw Fisher coming down the street and I didn't want him to see us," Simon replied. "But I think he must have been meeting Smith. They've both disappeared."

"Great." Bill took out a cigarette and lit it. "So now we've lost Smith, have we?"

"I don't think so." Simon peered up the street. "The Mission Hall is only another hundred yards along. It's my bet they've gone in there together."

"Well, Fisher's hardly likely to let us back in again after this morning, is he?" Bill exhaled smoke in Simon's face. "We'll have to wait until Smith comes back out again and follow him home. Or I suppose we could wait outside his house and get arrested for loitering by a passing policeman."

"No need." Once more Simon had the same triumphant expression on his face. "I know that the Mission has a back entrance that leads directly to the upstairs rooms. If they're in the main hall apparently there's a gallery where we can hide and overhear them."

"How on earth do you know that?" Bill asked.

Simon grinned. "I have my contacts in this city. Come on. Follow me."

20

A bright shaft of late afternoon sunlight fell on the front door of the Mission Hall and caused it to glow an unnatural fiery red. The building extended back from the main street for over fifty yards. At the rear was an alleyway linking the back yards and privies of the terraced houses. Simon led the way down the side of the Mission Hall to three large metal rubbish bins at the back. One of them had a goat tethered to it. The animal's fur was brown and white and remarkably clean. He sidled past it nervously and it bleated at him hopefully. Bill was a step behind him.

"If that thing chews my skirt I swear I'll take it as a sign from God to always wear trousers in future," she whispered.

"I don't think there's much risk of you ever wearing a skirt again after we leave Bath." Simon petted the goat on the head and it attempted to nibble at his sleeve. "What on earth is it doing here I wonder?"

"Perhaps they keep it for the milk." Bill slid along the opposite wall as far from the animal as she could get. "They say it's very healthy for you. I tasted some once when Noël took me

189

to a farm near the house he bought in the middle of nowhere down in Kent. It was disgusting."

"I can't imagine you drinking any kind of milk, let alone goats' milk." Simon tugged his jacket sleeve from the goat's mouth. A sinister thought had crossed his mind about the goat's presence. He decided to keep it from Bill for the moment. Instead he got down on his hands and knees beside the bins, which were on large swivel wheels. He stretched out his arm to reach underneath one of them.

"What on earth are you doing?" Bill asked.

"Got it." Simon withdrew his arm and held up a key.

"How did you know that was going to be there?"

"I've already told you." Simon scrambled to his feet and dusted down his jacket and trousers. "I'm very well-connected in this city."

"I don't recall you telling me you'd been here before."

"That's because I didn't," Simon replied. "My family's from Wiltshire. We might have come here on a day trip once or twice when I was a child but that's all."

"Then will you please explain to me how you've suddenly become an expert on the city of Bath?"

"I'll reveal all in due course." Simon smiled.

"You really are an exasperating man. It's as if you don't trust me."

"Not at all." Simon walked past the bins to a large wooden door set into the wall. "But a journalist has to protect his sources. And I'm also protecting you."

"From what?" Bill's voice went up in both pitch and volume as her frustration grew.

Simon raised a finger to his lips and pointed at the building. Bill was forgetting where they were. "Will you keep your voice down? I'm about to open this door and I don't want you announcing our presence to everyone before we've even had a chance to get inside."

"We'll talk about this later," Bill whispered. "Protecting your sources indeed. Secrecy is the death of friendship. I hope you realise that."

She inhaled a large lungful of smoke from her cigarette. The goat bleated again and she gave it a withering look. "If that thing bites me I won't be held accountable for my actions."

"Just ignore it and follow me." Simon turned the key in the lock and put his hand on the door handle. "And don't either of you make any more noise. I'm about to open this door."

On the main road outside the Mission Hall a bus driver struggled to change gear. The double decker's gearbox made a loud screeching sound like a sawmill. Simon took the opportunity to pull open the door. If its hinges had creaked the noise of the bus would have masked them. He stepped inside and beckoned Bill to follow. She stubbed out her cigarette, went through the doorway, and gently pulled the door closed behind her.

They stood in a cramped, unlit hallway. To their left was a door that probably opened into the main hall. From behind it Simon could faintly hear men's voices. To their right was a steep flight of stairs. Simon led the way up to another door at the top. He tried the handle and it opened easily. The men's voices became louder. He stepped through the doorway, ducked down, and motioned Bill to do the same.

The staircase had brought them to a gallery at the far end of the hall. It was about ten feet deep and extended along the length of the back wall. It might have been the architect's half-hearted attempt to recreate a minstrel's gallery in the Victorian hall. In front of them was a carved wooden rail supported by balustrades placed at regular intervals.

Simon crept forward and peered through the gaps between the balustrades. In the Mission Hall below a small crowd of men stood around talking. They were dressed in black suits with black ties. Simon leaned over to whisper in Bill's ear.

"They're speaking German. So they could be from Germany. But it's an odd accent so they could be from Austria or Switzerland or somewhere."

He counted thirty-two men in the hall. Fisher and Smith stood to one side of the main group. They leaned towards each other and spoke conspiratorially.

"No women here," Simon whispered. "But after what we saw this morning I suppose I'm not surprised."

"Can you speak German?" Bill whispered back.

"No but I understand a bit," Simon replied. "I've been getting lessons from a friend recently. I'm certainly not fluent. But I can catch the gist of—"

His answer was interrupted by the thunderous sound of a horn directly below them. The single blast was followed by two more. The murmur of conversation stopped, the men moved to their seats, and sat down. The person responsible for blowing the horn walked forward with the instrument in his hand. It looked as though it might have been used by Joshua to destroy the walls of Jericho.

Behind him another man followed, dressed in a long black cloak with a hood partially obscuring his face. He was stooped and walked with a stick. A large high-backed chair was placed in the centre of the circle. The elderly man lowered himself into it with slow, deliberate effort. Fisher held out the same cross he had carried at the funeral service that morning. The old man leaned forward and kissed it. He raised his arms shakily in brief supplication before lowering them again. He turned his head to stare at each of the men.

"Guten Abend, liebe Missionare," he began. His voice was tired and slow and he paused frequently to catch his breath. "Wir befinden uns in einem Moment der Krise. Eines unserer treuen Mitglieder had Maßnahmen ergriffen, die die Existenz der Mission gefährden."

"What's he saying?" Bill whispered.

Simon raised a finger to his lips and leaned close to her ear. "I'll tell you later," he replied.

The man continued in German. In his opening comments he had talked about the crisis caused by one of its members risking the existence of the Mission. He went on to talk about the truths of the teachings of the book of Leviticus and how the Mission was guided by its holy words. He recited a long list of those who were damned by failing to follow the teachings of Leviticus including women who were temptresses and men who lay with men.

He then warned that a series of recent events in London risked exposing the actions of the Mission to the authorities. The more the man said the more Simon was convinced someone from the Mission was responsible for the attacks in London. But Simon's German was far from fluent and the man spoke in a dialect he had never heard before.

The man raised his hand and beckoned Fisher to approach him.

"Fellows of the Mission of the Heavenly Host," Fisher said in English. "I speak for all of us when I give thanks to the Great Teacher for the wisdom he enlightens us with. His wisdom in bringing this great movement to these benighted islands and for his wisdom in showing us the way forward to protect our work. We will now begin the service of purification."

He raised his hands in supplication and nodded to one of the men seated in the circle.

"Bring out the sacrifice."

"Sorry Mr Goat," Simon muttered to himself. "We should have let you go when we had the chance."

He looked across to Bill for her reaction but she had disappeared. Perhaps the thought of watching a blood sacrifice was too much for her. It was not something he relished seeing himself. But as he wanted to find out as much as he could about this bizarre religious sect he steeled himself for the grisly spectacle.

The horn blower produced a long curved knife. He knelt before the Great Teacher and held it out horizontally in both hands. The elderly man leaned forward, placed the flat of his hand on the blade and muttered something inaudible.

The main door burst open and a man wearing a brown butcher's apron entered the hall. He strode up to Fisher and spoke in German. Fisher was startled and walked over to speak to the Great Teacher who hauled himself to his feet and pointed a bony finger at him.

"Schwachsinnig."

Simon had never heard the word before but by the way the Great Teacher said it he knew it wasn't a compliment.

Fisher shook visibly. He placed his hands together in prayer, lowered his head, and turned to the rest of the group.

"I regret to inform you, fellows of the Mission of the Heavenly Host, that a terrible thing has happened." His voice quavered and he kept his head bowed. "The sacrifice prepared for the service of purification has escaped. We are unable to continue without an offering to the prophet. We will try to reconvene tomorrow evening at the same time."

A murmur of conversation grew louder until the clamour of angry voices echoed off the brick walls of the Mission.

Simon chuckled and crept over to the door at the back of the gallery. He knew exactly what had happened to the goat.

"So now what are you going to do with it?"

The former sacrifice was tethered to a drainpipe running down the back wall of the Royal Hotel. It munched contentedly on the flower border of geraniums and marigolds. The evening sun was surprisingly warm and Bill sat in a steamer chair on the terrace with her back to the animal. She wore a pair of sunglasses, had a gin and tonic in one hand, and a cigarette in another. She looked like a passenger on the first-class deck of a steamship.

"It's all being sorted," she replied. "The hotel manager says there's a farm about a mile and a half from here. He's telephoning the farmer for me as we speak."

"Does he keep goats?"

"How should I know?" Bill shrugged. "But he's a farmer and it's an animal so I'm sure it will fit right in."

"And how are you going to get it there?"

"Me? Get it there?" Bill emptied her glass. "Oh, no. I've done my bit. I rescued it. If the farmer won't come and collect it I'll pack it into a taxi."

Simon smiled. He imagined the startled face of the taxi driver when he arrived at the hotel to collect his fare.

Bill tried to get the attention of a waiter at the far end of the terrace. "Do you want a drink? I'm certainly going to have another. We should celebrate. A very successful day's work I'd say. We've almost uncovered the identity of the killer. Another couple of days here and the case will be wrapped up."

"You think so?" Simon sat in the chair opposite. The waiter arrived and Bill ordered a gin and tonic for them both. "I'm sure it's true that this Mission lot are in it up to their necks. But I've got no idea how. Or which one of them is the killer. And I've got no idea how we're going to find out."

"We'll think of something." Bill replied. She lifted the arms of her chair to recline the seat until she was almost horizontal. "I could get used to this detection malarkey. It's much easier than working with the dreaded Noël and his capricious whims."

"We haven't solved anything." Simon tried to do the same with his own chair but the arms refused to budge. "And I don't think I can stay in Bath much longer. I rang my editor when I got back just now and he's getting agitated that I haven't filed anything for several days. The weekend's looming and he wants something for the Sunday edition. I'm not sure I've got enough to put a feature piece together."

"You'll think of something." Bill stretched her legs like a cat luxuriating in the evening sun. "Didn't you tell him that investigations take time?"

"I tried to," Simon replied. "But when I told him about what we've found out here he was very sceptical. He's worried about publishing anything that attacks the church. He says his readers would desert the paper in droves."

"The Mission of the Heavenly Host isn't a church." Bill waved her hand dismissively. "They're a bunch of crackpots who are somehow linked to the London murders."

"I agree. But my editor doesn't see it that way." Simon tried again without success to lean his chair back. "He wants me in the office the day after tomorrow. Anyway, I'm not sure it's safe for us to stick around here much longer. They're awfully angry with you for stealing their sacrifice."

"It's not a sacrifice it's a goat." Bill turned to watch the animal. "You know they're rather adorable once you get to know them."

"I'm discovering a whole new side to you." Simon smiled. "I thought you were the woman of steel, battling against our male-dominated society. And yet you've actually got a soft heart."

"My dear Simon." Bill peered at him over the top of her sunglasses. "I've *always* had a heart. And that's how us women are going to make this world a better place. After all, it's men who cause all the problems. They're the ones who start wars. They're the ones who invented all those so-called sports like boxing or duelling. They created the ridiculous adversarial system in our courts and in our parliament. Women are far more prepared to collaborate, to discuss, and to work towards consensus."

"So are you going to go back to the Mission and get them to agree to stop sacrificing animals?"

"Don't be ridiculous." Bill pushed her sunglasses up her nose and lay back in the chair. "Their minds are closed. They're men. There's a Greek word for it all. Patriarkhēs. It means the rule of the father."

"Patriarchy?" Simon nodded. "Yes I know. But it's actually a benevolent term. The men in charge protect you and look after you."

"Oh really?" Bill sniffed. "I don't think that bunch of stuffed shirts in the Mission Hall had an ounce of benevolence in their bodies. Remember that Patriarkhēs is about the father. That's a man not a woman. And it's also about ruling, not consensus. Patriarkhēs, or patriarchy if you like, is the root of all problems in this world. If you ask me—"

"Miss Miles?"

The waiter interrupted Bill before she could continue.

"Yes, what is it?" She peered up at the nervous young man. "Where are our drinks?"

"They're coming," he replied. "But you're wanted on the telephone. There's an urgent call for you."

"Oh, God it must be Noël." Bill stood. "Show me where the phone box is young man."

"Yes, Miss Miles," he replied. "And there's one more thing."

"What?"

The youth coughed awkwardly. "The manager's asked me if you could stop feeding the hotel's flower borders to your goat. Several of the guests have complained."

21

Bill sat on the hard wooden stool in the cabin next to the hotel reception and lifted the telephone receiver.

"Connecting you now," a voice said in her ear. There was a click and then loud crackling like damp wood on a fire. It obscured the voice at the other end almost completely.

"You'll have to speak up," Bill shouted into the receiver. "It's a terribly bad line."

"…Jenny…" a female voice said. "…Bristol… House… burgled…"

"Is that you Jenny?" Bill rattled the telephone cradle in the hope it would clear the line. "Whose house is burgled? Your parents?"

She rattled the cradle again and there was a loud buzz.

"Bill? Bill? Can you hear me?" The crackling had stopped and the line was clear. "It's Jenny here. My house has been burgled. It's terrible. My next door neighbour rang my mother to tell her about it. She told me as soon as I got here an hour ago."

"Oh my dear that's terrible." Bill leaned heavily against the wood panel of the telephone cabin. "Have they taken much?"

"I don't know," Jenny replied. "Miss Tewson saw my front door was open this morning and called the police. You remember her, don't you? She's eighty-two and awfully frail so she didn't dare go in. The police told her it's been ransacked. I was wondering when you might be going back to London? As you've got my key could you possibly check everything for me when you return? I don't think I can face returning to London just yet. My nerves are in shreds."

"Of course I will." Bill peered through the glass panel of the door at the grandfather clock standing in reception. "It's nearly eight now. I can leave first thing in the morning. I'm sure Noël is champing at the bit for me to be back anyway. I haven't called him today and I just know he'll be furious."

"Thank you so much," Jenny replied. 'You don't think it's related to everything that's been going on?"

"Without a doubt." Bill stood and opened the door of the cabin. "Now don't worry. I'll go and take a look tomorrow lunchtime when my train gets in. I'll telephone you then. I'll go and tell Simon why I'm leaving early. He'll be very understanding about it. Then I need to call Noël. I have to make constant phone calls to him or he gets furious. He's like a spoiled child. He's never accepted the imprisonment of being an adult."

Bill's second phone call was as disastrous as she had suspected.

"Do I know you?" Noël asked when they were connected. "You've been absent for days without so much as a telegram to let me know you were safe."

"I only left London yesterday," Bill retorted. "And I telephoned you yesterday evening when we got here. Anyway, I'm calling to say that I'll be back tomorrow so you can stop fretting."

"'Fretting'?" Noël's pronunciation of the word was explosive with the 'r' rolled extravagantly. "My dear Bill, I never fret. I merely make alternative arrangements. New York needs to be planned. Quickly. It's coming up to the weekend and nothing's been done. Nothing. And seeing as you weren't around I've decided to give it to Charles to deal with."

"Cochran?" Bill almost dropped the receiver in her fury. "What on earth did you do that for? He's incompetent. He's got no more ability to organise a complicated itinerary than I have of boiling an egg. I know you're sweet on him but this is—"

"I have no affection for Charles whatsoever," Noël retorted. "He minces when he walks. Far too effeminate. But he's a brilliant producer. You really should stop being so jealous, my dear. And something had to be done or *Bitter Sweet* would never make it to Broadway."

"Are you sacking me, Noël?"

"I do hope it doesn't come to that, my dear Bill. But you must admit you've been remarkably absent in the past couple of weeks. Both physically and mentally. And your loyalty has to be questioned when you persist in a relationship with that hack writer."

"Mr Sampson is not a hack writer." Bill cradled the receiver against her shoulder while she struggled to light a cigarette. "He's a very principled journalist who's standing up for the rights of women and challenging the indifference of the Metropolitan Police force."

"He's nothing of the sort," Noël replied. "He's a common little man who's dragging my name through the gutter and has associated me with those murders. It's a simple choice, Bill. Either you're loyal to me and the great theatre works I stage, or you allow yourself to be seduced by the dark forces of Fleet Street. I'll leave you to make your decision."

The line went dead.

Bill stared at the receiver. "I think I may have just made my decision."

She slammed it back in its cradle and left the telephone cabin.

—————

Bill left for London on the eight o'clock train the following morning. Simon had mixed feelings about her departure. He had enjoyed her company and her intelligent observations on the investigation. On the other hand she was remarkably temperamental and it would be a relief to be alone for a few days.

Well, not quite on his own.

Shortly after Bill had left for the station Simon checked behind the loose brick at the end of the garden wall of the hotel. He was pleased to discover his message had been collected and replaced with another. It informed him that his rendezvous was to be in Sydney Gardens, a short walk from the hotel. He returned to the dining room for another coffee and then set off.

His route took him along Stall Street and ran close to the grand portico of the Roman baths. He decided to make a ten-minute detour to view the outside of the eighteenth century Pump Room where visitors to Bath had long sampled the healing waters in elegant surroundings. The building's impressive entrance reminded him of Jane Austen's novel *Northanger Abbey.* He recalled how its heroine Catherine Morland would visit the Pump Room daily on the pretext of taking the waters. But in reality she was in search of a man. What strange rituals nineteenth century women had had to endure to find the security of a life partner. For a brief moment he considered that women in the twentieth century were far more fortunate. But then he realised Bill would have undoubtedly taken a contrary view if he had spoken the sentiment out loud.

Damn it, he was already missing the woman.

Simon arrived at Sydney Gardens half an hour later. As he strode towards the bridge over the canal at the far end a park keeper wished him good morning. There was no one else to be seen in the gardens. When he reached the bridge a figure emerged from behind a tree. It was Calvin.

"Herr Schatz." Simon stopped and checked to see there was no one else around. "Have you been waiting long?"

Calvin smiled. "Long enough to know that we are all alone here."

He stepped forward as if to kiss Simon, who pulled away. He looked around again nervously.

"It's broad daylight, Calvin. Are you mad?"

"I forget that I am not in Berlin." Calvin shook his head and took out a packet of cigarettes from his jacket pocket. "Instead I am in Victorian England. The country that destroyed Oscar Wilde, one of its greatest writers, through pig-headed puritanism."

"I'm sorry, Calvin," Simon replied. "But you know we have to be careful. Anyone might see and report us to the police. I can't take that risk. Neither can you."

"I understand." Calvin lit his cigarette and exhaled. "But it's very frustrating. If only you would come to Berlin. Things could be so different."

"Maybe one day," Simon replied. "Bill went back to London first thing this morning. Jenny Casewell's house has been burgled. She's gone back to find out what's been taken."

"She went on her own? Are you mad?"

"I couldn't stop her going." Simon was taken aback by Calvin's reaction. "And besides, I can't play nursemaid to her all the time. It was fortunate you were able to take the place of her porter the evening she was attacked. Without you being there things could have been very different."

"I was very pleased to help you." Calvin nodded his head and tapped his heels together. "But I only wish I could have stopped the murderer escaping."

"You did more than enough." Simon rested his hand nervously on Calvin's arm. He desperately wanted to show greater affection but the risk of being seen was too great. "You were there at the right moment and you stopped another murder. By the way, why did you use the name Darling?"

"Your German is still not very good, is it?" Calvin smiled. "Schatz? My last name? Translated into English?"

"But I thought Schatz meant treasure?"

"It can also mean darling."

Calvin rested his hand on top of Simon's. The feel of it gave Simon a sudden frisson of excitement. That such a simple gesture carried out in public should carry so high a risk highlighted the continued absurdity of civilised society, even in this modern age.

"Please explain something." Calvin gripped Simon's hand a little tighter. "Why do you want to keep me hidden from her? Are you ashamed of me?"

"Not at all," Simon replied. "But I think Bill's a very proud person. I'm sure she'd be furious if she knew I'd sent you to protect her."

He leaned closer to Calvin. How he wished he could put an arm around the man's waist. But he knew it would be madness.

"I want you to know that I'm very grateful for what you've done, Calvin. You saved her life that night. And thanks to you we might be getting closer to identifying the killer."

"It is my pleasure." Calvin nodded. "But I must now follow Miss Miles back to London. She is not safe. You know that."

He removed his hand from Simon's.

"I almost forgot. I have more information for you. There was a woman who was thrown out of the funeral service yesterday. I saw her when I was waiting outside. I thought she might be of interest so I followed her back to her home. I have the address where she lives."

"Excellent," Simon replied. "That was the strangest thing. She came bursting in shouting about Smith. She said he was the man who killed Maureen. No idea who she was."

"I may have the answer to that question." Calvin handed Simon a piece of paper. "You should talk to her. This is her address. I think she is Maureen Lyon's mother."

"That can't be right." Simon looked at the piece of paper Calvin had given him. "I remember Jenny telling us that her mother had died when Maureen was only two."

Calvin shrugged. "Now is your chance to find out."

* * *

The cab driver carried the last of Bill's suitcases into her apartment, leaned against the doorframe and mopped his brow with a handkerchief.

"'ow many weeks you been away, then?" he asked.

"Oh, just a couple of nights." Bill fumbled in her wallet for some coins. "Wait a minute while I find you a tip."

"A couple of nights?" the cabbie pointed at the pile of suitcases. "With this lot?"

"My trip was cut short," Bill explained. "It was supposed to have been nearly a week."

"Bleedin' 'ell. 'Ow does your 'usband put up wiv it?" The driver shook his head.

"Impertinent man." Bill dropped the coins back into her wallet and snapped it shut. "I'm not foolish enough to have one. Please leave."

She shooed the cabbie out of the front door and slammed it shut. "Damned cheek," she muttered to herself.

The telephone rang.

"Oh, dear. I do hope that's not Noël," she said out loud. "I really don't feel strong enough to speak to him right now."

Her hand hovered over the receiver for a few moments before she took it from its rest.

"Good day," said a woman's voice at the other end. "Is that Miss Miles?"

"It is," Bill replied warily. "Who are you?"

Please wait one minute," said the woman. "I have the director-general for you."

"Who?" Bill asked.

"Sir John Reith," the woman said. "The director-general of the BBC. He wishes to speak to you. You are Miss Florence Miles, aren't you?"

"Oh. Yes that's right." Bill lit a cigarette and leaned against the wall. "What does he want?"

"I think that's for him to say," the woman replied.

There was a click and then silence for several minutes during which time Bill hunted for an ashtray. She was about to place the receiver on the hall table and go in search of one in the sitting room when the line clicked again and she heard a familiar gruff voice.

"Is that you, Bill?"

"Sir John." To her embarrassment Bill realised she had snapped to attention and the sudden movement sent a shower of cigarette ash over her jacket. "How lovely to hear your voice."

"Really? I seem to remember you said you never wanted to see me again when you left my employment."

"Heat of the moment, Sir John. I'm sure I didn't mean it."

"Poppycock." The gruff voice ascended an octave in its register. "I seem to remember you always said exactly what you meant. One of the reasons I liked having you working for me. Can't abide yes-men. Or yes-women come to that."

""I'm sorry Sir John," Bill began. "What I meant to say—"

"Just be quiet for a moment," the director-general interrupted. "I've got something to say that will be of great interest to you."

JOURNAL ENTRY 27 JULY 1929

I've been keeping watch on her place over the last days and she's finally returned.

I think it's time to put my re-education plan into action. I have the holding cell prepared for her. It won't be particularly comfortable but the warm weather should make it tolerable. And I must remind myself that it's more than enough for an undeserving sister of Satan like her. I've stocked it with the bare necessities. She'll have what she needs. And if I'm to persuade her of the error of her ways she needs to at least be fed and watered.

The manner in which I was going to transport her to the cell has proved more of a problem than I expected. But I've been ingenious and now I've got the means to gain access to a vehicle. It won't be missed for quite some time. I can return it before anybody notices that it's gone. Benny at the pound is a good man. He swallowed my story about how I needed it for training without asking any awkward questions.

Everything is ready.

All I need to do is get her into the van. And this time I

think the uniform is going to be the perfect asset. It's a risk of course.

Because then she'll know. But it might mean she'll have a bit more respect for me.

We'll find out.

22

Simon's taxi pulled over to the side of the road opposite a turning to a narrow street of small terraced houses. He peered out of the window. It had started to rain again and the outside world looked grubby, cold, and uninviting. Across the street a rag and bone man struggled to load a bulging brown sack onto his cart. The horse stamped its hooves and shook its head. Rain dripped from its harness. A group of half a dozen workmen stood under the makeshift shelter of a derelict house smoking.

"Are you sure this is where you want to be?" the taxi driver asked. "I wouldn't want to hang around here after dark. The area's got a reputation you know."

"Aren't you going to drive me down to the address?" Simon asked.

"Not likely, mate," the driver replied. "This is as far as I go. You can walk the rest. Good luck getting back."

Number thirty-seven was a hundred yards along the narrow street on the left. The house was larger than he expected with a short flight of stone steps leading up to a front door covered in peeling paint. Another set of steps led down to a basement area. He banged on the door and waited. The wind and rain battered his umbrella and he struggled to stop it from blowing inside out. After several minutes a short woman with a cigarette hanging from the corner of her mouth opened the door and squinted up at him. She wore a frayed smock and a pair of workman's trousers. From behind her came the sound of children shouting.

"Does Alice Lyon live here?" Simon asked. "Or Alice Smith?"

"She might do." The cigarette bounced on the woman's lower lip as she spoke. "Who wants to know?"

"My name's Simon Sampson. It's about her daughter Maureen."

"You'd best wait here." The woman slammed the door shut.

A curtain lifted at a window to the left. Three children aged no more than four or five stared out at him. A young woman appeared behind them and the children disappeared from view. The woman stared back at Simon for a moment and then the curtain fell back into place. The rain had got heavier and Simon shivered as the cold wind whipped at his umbrella. The summer weather had definitely changed.

The door rattled and creaked open a few inches to reveal a woman's face. It was the same person Simon had seen thrown out of the funeral.

"Mrs Lyon?" Simon asked.

"Who are you?"

"My name's Simon Sampson. I was at Maureen's funeral. I saw you there. And I saw those brutes who forced you to leave."

"How do you know Maureen?"

"I've come to offer my sincere condolences," Simon replied. "Maureen shared a house with a friend of mine in London. It must have been a terrible shock when she died."

The woman said nothing.

"You are Alice Lyon, aren't you?"

The woman nodded. "What do you want?"

She continued to hold the door open only a few inches.

Behind her the children shouted to each other in what sounded like a game of tag.

"I wanted to ask you about Maureen. Look. Could I come in for a few minutes? It's pouring out here."

Alice moved to close the door but Simon shoved his foot in the crack between the door and the doorframe. He felt the weight of the door squeeze his shoe.

"Go away," Alice said. "There's nothing more I can do."

"She was murdered," Simon continued. "You know that, don't you, Alice? But Maureen wasn't the only victim. I'm trying to find out why she was killed. And I think you can help. If you don't talk to me then there's a risk that more women in London will be in danger. Please. You've got to help."

Simon felt the pressure on his shoe ease.

"You don't leave me any choice, do you?" Alice opened the door. "You've got five minutes. And no funny business. Or my friends here will throw you out."

The woman Simon had first encountered appeared in the hallway.

"Is everything all right, Alice?" she asked. "This man causing you trouble?"

"Don't worry, Elsie," Alice replied. "He's not staying long. Keep everyone out of the front room for a few minutes would you? And get the kids to play a bit more quietly."

Elsie scowled at Simon, turned, and disappeared into the gloom of the house. Alice led Simon into the front room, closed the door, and stood with her back to it. The room smelled strongly of damp.

"No one told me my Maureen was murdered," she began. "But I know they're responsible for her death somehow. They weren't going to tell me anything. I only got to know she'd died when one of the nosey parkers from the Mission came round and said they'd organised her funeral. I wouldn't have known anything otherwise."

"I'm so sorry." Simon leaned against the back of a battered armchair. "That's so cruel. But I only found out you were alive a few hours ago. I was told you'd died when Maureen was only two."

"Well, I'm not dead, am I?" Alice cleared her throat. The cough developed into a fit of choking and her whole body heaved.

Simon stepped forward. "Are you all right?"

Alice shook her head and waved him away. The coughing subsided and she leaned heavily against the door.

"It's this bloody place," she replied when she could speak again. "Six of us living in this hell hole. It's not fit for an animal let alone a human. It ought to be condemned. But there's nowhere else for us to go."

She pulled a grubby rag from her sleeve and wiped her mouth. "I'm still alive all right. Sometimes wish I wasn't. They told little Maureen I was dead when I was sent away. When they uncongregated me as they so charmingly called it."

"That's what Fisher said at the funeral," Simon replied. "He said it about Maureen. What does it mean?"

"It means you're no longer part of the Mission." Alice's rasping cough erupted again. "But it means far more than that. It means no one can ever talk to you again. Your friends, your family. Your children. No one. I was told to leave and keep away from my husband Douglas, from Maureen, and anyone else in the congregation. They told me I was dead to them. And I was dead to Maureen."

"That's horrible." Simon shook his head. "What kind of people are they?"

"They call themselves Christians." Alice snorted. "Well

they're not. I believe in God and in our Lord Jesus and I know I'm a good Christian. I'm better than any of them will ever be."

She heaved herself away from the door, shuffled past Simon, and sank into the armchair he had been leaning against. Another fit of coughing shook her body. Simon knelt at her side and watched helplessly as she breathed deeply and mopped beads of sweat from her brow.

"Are you sure there isn't anything I can do?" he asked.

Alice shook her head and cleared her throat.

"We can't afford a doctor," she whispered. "And if I go to the hospital they'd most likely threaten to take me away from Elsie and the family. I'd die if they did that."

"Does Elsie look after you, then?"

"You could say that." Alice chuckled. "Elsie's my friend. My *good* friend. You know what I mean?" She chuckled again. "You men don't know nothing. Tell me, Mr Simon Sampson. Are you married?"

Simon shook his head.

"Lady friend?"

"I'm afraid not," he said. "I'm not the marrying kind really."

Alice cocked her head on one side. "And what does that mean? Not fond of the ladies are you?" She leaned back in the chair and closed her eyes. "I see. Then maybe I'm wrong. Maybe you are one of those men who might understand."

"I think maybe I am," Simon replied. "Are you and Elsie...together?"

Alice did not reply. Instead, she began to sing. Her voice was faint and her lips barely moved. The tune was the hymn 'Abide With Me'. After quavering her way through the first two lines she stopped, opened her eyes, and smiled at Simon. A tear trickled down her cheek.

"Such a lovely hymn. I used to sing it to Maureen to get her to sleep. I've never sung it again until just now. And now I'll never ever be able to sing it to her again."

She blew her nose on the rag and wiped a tear from her cheek. "No good being sentimental, is there? What's done is done. Crying won't bring her back."

Simon tentatively rested his hand on Alice's arm. She looked down but made no effort to brush it away. "Why did they send you away?" he asked. "Why did they uncongregate you?"

"Because of her." Alice nodded towards the closed door. "They found out about me and Elsie. Another of them nosey parkers from the Mission."

"But you were married, Alice. Surely you knew you were taking a risk seeing another person? Especially someone who's... not a man."

"'Married'." Alice sniffed. "I was owned, more like. My husband's not a very nice man, Mr Sampson. He's a cruel man. Like the rest of them in that Mission. He thought he could do what he liked to me. To me and to the children. A brute he was. Elsie taught me it didn't have to be like that."

"Did he beat you?"

"And the rest."

Alice pointed to the mantelpiece.

"Get something for me, will you?" she said. "That picture over there."

Simon stood and crossed to the fireplace. He picked up a wooden picture frame. Behind its cracked glass was a photograph that was clearly Alice as a young woman. She cradled a child in her arms. A small boy stood at her side holding on to her skirt and behind them stood a younger version of her husband Douglas Smith. Simon picked up the photograph and took it to Alice.

"She was a lovely baby." Alice wiped the glass with her

sleeve. "Like an angel. Good as gold. I'd sing hymns to her and she just lay there chuckling and giggling. Good as gold she was."

"Is that her brother in the picture?" Simon asked.

"Difficult boy." Alice breathed on the glass and rubbed it again with her sleeve. "Always was. Always will be. Takes after his father. Only far worse."

"Why didn't you leave your husband?" Simon asked. "Take the children and go away somewhere."

"Where would I go?" Alice rested the picture frame in her lap. "My parents were long dead. I had no one else to turn to. Except Elsie. Her husband had upped and left as soon as their daughter was born. I used to come round here with Charley and Alice. The kids would all play happily together. It was a proper family. A home filled with love."

"Couldn't you stay?"

"Oh, no." Alice handed him the picture frame. "Put it back where you found it, will you?"

Alice smoothed down her skirt and pulled her shapeless cardigan tighter around her body.

"They said this wasn't a normal home. They said families always had to have a man at the head. And Doug kicked up something rotten when he found out. Next thing I know I'd been summoned to the Mission Hall. I was told to pack my bag and that I was never to see Doug or the children again."

"Weren't you tempted to sneak over to where they lived and see them?" Simon asked. "It's probably no more than a half hour's walk from here."

"They'd thought of that," Alice replied. "The local magistrate is a member of the Mission. He made some ruling that if I was seen within a mile of the children I'd end up in gaol. Not only that but Charley and Maureen would be sent to a Mission in London. I couldn't risk their lives being turned upside down like that. And I liked the idea of them being nearby even if I couldn't see them."

Simon could think of nothing to say in reply. It seemed inconceivable that a group calling itself Christian could behave in this way. And yet he had no doubts about what Alice had told him. He had witnessed the behaviour of the members of the Mission firsthand.

The sound of children singing a nursery rhyme echoed down the hallway outside the door, led by a woman's voice.

"Whose children are those?" Simon asked.

"Elsie's daughter's," Alice replied. Her husband pushed off as well. It seems to be a bit of a habit among men. Or maybe we just pick the wrong ones. The weak ones."

"You said your son was worse than his father," Simon said. "Charley's his name, isn't it? What did you mean worse?"

"He and Maureen stayed with Doug after they kicked me out," Alice replied. "But really it was Doug's parents who brought them up. Doug didn't have the first idea what to do with kids. Elsie says Charley got very dedicated to the Mission in his teens. Spent all his time there. He was obsessed with their teachings. You know, the sinfulness of man. And woman. The sickness of Sodom was in our midst and all that. Took it very seriously. Very literally. An eye for an eye and so on."

"Is he still there?" Simon asked.

"No, he left Bath some years ago," Alice replied. "He went to a Mission in London. Someone told me he'd joined the Metropolitan Police force."

23

Bill stood outside the mews cottage in Notting Hill and lit a cigarette. She needed a moment to prepare before entering the little home where her former lover had once lived.

During her recent visits there with Simon she had kept her emotions under control. But now she was alone. Even Jenny wouldn't be in the house. There would be no distraction from the memories it held.

This was where she had spent nights with Maureen when Jenny had been away on a production. Curled up on the rug in the cosy living room in front of the coal fire. Here they'd talked about a future together. Happy evenings making plans to create an all-woman theatre company. Of staging plays written exclusively by women and touring the country to bring their ideas to a wider population beyond London.

From the outside the house was calm and undisturbed. No sign of the recent break-in. The late morning sun gave its shabby paint a false radiance. The front door was locked, the curtains at the downstairs windows drawn. Bill finished her cigarette and took Jenny's door key from her pocket.

"Who are you?"

The downstairs window of the house next door was open and an elderly woman peered out.

"Hello Miss Tewson," Bill said brightly. "It's Miss Miles. Do you remember me? I used to stay here with Maureen sometimes to keep her company while Jenny was away."

"Miss Miles?" Miss Tewson squinted at her through a pair of heavy-lensed spectacles. "You're another one of those theatre people, aren't you? You know she's dead, don't you? Murdered they say."

"I'm afraid I do, Miss Tewson," Bill replied. "I was at Maureen's funeral in Bath only yesterday."

"And Miss Casewell's gone away and the house has been burgled." Miss Tewson shook her head. "It's a bad do, that's what I say. I shouldn't have to be living next to all this trouble. Not at my age. What are you doing here?"

"Jenny's asked me to check the house for her. She said you were the one who discovered the burglary. She's very grateful to you for letting her parents know."

"It was me who called the police." There was a note of pride in Miss Tewson's voice. "I saw the front door was open and I knew that Miss Casewell had shut it when she went away. I might be old but I'm not daft. I don't miss much living here on my own."

"I'm sure you don't," Bill replied. "Did you hear the burglars?"

"I couldn't have done, could I? It was my night for the Cock."

"I beg your pardon?"

"The entertainment," Miss Tewson explained. "At the Cock pub. I always go. It's a good old singalong. Lovely time I had. When I got back the front door was wide open. They must have got in while I was out."

"Do you think they had a key?" Bill examined the front door closely. "The door doesn't look damaged."

"How would I know?" Miss Tewson shrugged. "The policeman wasn't saying anything. Young fella he was. Not long out of nappies. Very abrupt and haughty. Didn't stay more than ten minutes inside the house. If that. Came out, shut the front door, and he was off."

"Did you get his name?" Bill asked. "Only, after I've checked inside I might go down to the police station and tell them I've been here."

"Like I said, he wasn't telling me nothing," Miss Tewson replied. "He didn't tell me and I didn't ask. Not a pleasant fella either. Not like the regular bobby. But then that one's much older."

"Very nice to see you again, Miss Tewson." Bill put Jenny's key into the lock. "I'd better get going."

"Do you want me to bring a cup of tea over for you, love?" Miss Tewson asked. "I'm making a brew."

"It's very kind of you," Bill replied. "But I'll be fine on my own."

"Suit yourself."

Miss Tewson slammed the window shut and a net curtain fluttered back into place.

Bill turned on the living room light before she shut the front door behind her. She decided against opening the curtains. It would stop Miss Tewson from being able to see in.

The burglars had destroyed the ordered calm of Jenny's living room. The settee had been upended, side tables tipped over, and piles of books strewn across the floor. The contents of every drawer had been tipped out and a beautiful Art Nouveau lamp had been knocked over and its glass globe smashed.

Bill perched on the arm of the settee and lit a cigarette. The devastation was shocking and she was relieved Jenny had not seen it first. It would have broken her heart. Bill steeled herself for a long afternoon imposing order on the chaos.

Strangely, the kitchen had been left undisturbed. She remembered there was a loose floorboard in the pantry. Jenny kept valuable items such as emergency cash and the pearl necklace from her mother beneath it. When she lifted it the few items that lay underneath appeared undisturbed. She would telephone Jenny later to get an inventory of exactly what should be there.

She checked the back door into the little courtyard garden and found it unlocked. The key was still hanging on a hook by the window. This must have been how the burglars had got in. It was a very unsophisticated lock. It would take little more than a hairgrip to get it open. Why the burglars had left by the front door leaving it wide open was strange. Perhaps they had been disturbed. She took the key from its hook and locked the door.

Bill took a small dish from one of the cupboards to use as an ashtray and climbed the cottage's narrow staircase to examine the two bedrooms. Maureen's room was directly in front of her at the top of the stairs. Its door was wide open and revealed a chaotic scene similar to the one in the living room. On the bed lay piles of clothes, papers, and books scattered across the eiderdown. Bill cleared a space, sat at the foot of the bed with the makeshift ashtray cradled in her lap, and stared at the mess.

It was more than likely the burglary had been carried out by someone connected with the Mission. Perhaps it was the murderer who had broken in. If so it was possible he might return. Bill hurried back down to the living room and slid the top and bottom bolts on the front door to secure it.

How stupid of her not to have thought of that earlier. Before she examined the devastation wreaked by the burglars it was time to call Jenny. She stood by the telephone in the narrow hallway and called her parents. Jenny answered the phone.

"Is it really terrible?" she asked.

"Oh no." Bill lit a cigarette. "Things have been thrown about a bit and it needs a good old tidy but there's nothing damaged as far as I can see."

"That's such a relief," Jenny sighed. "Thank you so much for going. And don't worry about tidying. I can sort it all out when I get back."

"I wouldn't hear of it," Bill replied. "It won't take me long and it will be as right as ninepence by the time you return. I'm only calling to find out if there's anything really valuable I should check for. I know about the loose floorboard in the larder and I think everything's still there. Was there anything else valuable on display?"

"You know how little I earn," Jenny laughed. "I don't have any priceless Ming vases or anything like that if that's what you're thinking. It's all sentimental tat to be honest."

"Then I think you've got off lightly." Bill looked at the broken lamp in the living room. She knew of a shop in Portobello that would probably have a replacement.

"Do you think they were disturbed before they could take anything?" Jenny asked. "I mean, if there's nothing missing then what were they doing there?"

"No, I think they were here quite a while," Bill replied.

"Then what were they after?" Jenny asked. "You don't think it's that awful solicitor man, Fisher? Did he come back for the birth and marriage certificates? Thank goodness Simon took them away."

"I don't think it was Fisher." Bill stubbed out her cigarette in the makeshift ashtray. "He's far too cautious to risk being caught in the act of burgling a house. But I think it's very likely it was someone from that awful Mission place. Don't worry your head about it anymore. I'll be here another hour or so. If you think of anything I need to check on then just give me a quick call. Otherwise enjoy your time in Bristol and let me know when you're back."

Bill ended the call, went back upstairs, and pushed open the door of Jenny's room. It was in a similar state of disorder to Maureen's. She pulled the door closed and returned to Maureen's bedroom. She would make a start on clearing up and perhaps call Jenny again in a while when she needed a break.

The door of the wardrobe was open and all the clothes were either thrown on the bed or scattered on the floor. Clearing them would make more space. She picked up several hangers of Maureen's pretty blouses from the bed to hang on the rail. Beneath them lay the fox fur coat Maureen had been given by Noël after she had worked on the costumes for his revue show *His Year of Grace* the year before.

Bill hung the blouses in the wardrobe and picked up the fur coat. The faint smell of Maureen's eau de toilette filled her head with memories. She hugged the coat, closed her eyes, and swayed back and forth in the same way they had slow danced in the living room late at night to music on the wireless or the gramophone.

Irving Berlin's 'Because I Love You' came into her head. They had danced to it the first time they had met at the Paradise Regained Club just before Christmas, 1926. Bill had been reluctant to betray her lack of coordination but Maureen had insisted. She had been so patient and had made no criticism of Bill's clumsiness as they stumbled between the tables of the nightclub in an approximation of a slow dance.

Snatches of the lyrics returned to her. A song about lost love and the lover who had tried but failed to erase it from their memory. At the time it was no more than a pretty tune to dance to. Now its irony enveloped Bill in sadness.

As she sang to herself she slipped her hand into one of the pockets of the coat to hug it tighter and her fingers made contact with an envelope. She opened her eyes and pulled it from the pocket. It was a lemon-yellow-coloured envelope. The same colour as the writing paper Maureen had used for what she called "*special letters*". It was still sealed and simply addressed *To Bill.*

The coat slipped from Bill's arms and she sat heavily on the bed. Her fingers trembled as she tore open the flap of the envelope and withdrew a single sheet of lemon-yellow notepaper. It was written in Maureen's perfectly shaped cursive script and dated the fourteenth of July. Just three days before her death.

My dearest Bill

It has taken me a long time to compose this letter and many failed attempts at writing it have been banished to the wastepaper basket. After all this heartache I may never hand it to you. But I needed to write down how I felt, how I still feel, after you said what you did at the beginning of this year.

I know that what you said was entirely sensible and that you had no intention of hurting me. You are the most wonderful person in the world. I love you and I felt sure that you loved me. In fact, I know that you loved me.

Because I love you I had no intention of disagreeing with you and I accepted your decision that we should part as being for the best.

Our love is forbidden. If it were ever discovered we would certainly face censure. You took a great risk while you were working at the BBC and I would not like you to face a similar risk again. Whilst I may be in a lowlier employ than you there is still a risk that I could endanger Jenny in her tenancy of this house. As you rightly said, the neighbours are already dangerously curious.

I have done as you asked and avoided having anything more than professional contact with you. That has been so difficult when we are in the same theatre together. We will be working together on Bitter Sweet in London very soon. That will be so hard for me and I respect your wishes of course.

But...

I am still in love with you. I cannot get you out of my heart. You are locked in there as surely as a linnet in a gilded cage (do you remember the first time we read Christina Rossetti's poem? It was when I knew.)

My dear Bill, if I do pluck up the courage to hand you this letter please be assured I have written it with love. I have no wish to hurt you. But the pain of being separated from you is unbearable.

With all my love, always, Maureen

"Oh, my dear Maureen," Bill sniffed. "How can I ever forgive myself?"

She wiped away tears but more took their place. She remembered the evening she had told Maureen of her decision. It had all seemed so logical at the time. Their relationship was too dangerous and a threat to their careers. She had overheard at least one casual comment from an indiscreet member of the company. There could easily be more. It was better that they avoid seeing each other any longer. She hoped that Maureen would understand.

Maureen had cried. Bill had held back her tears at the time, not wanting to betray her true emotion and make the moment worse for Maureen. Now she felt the grief for what was gone and could never come back. She allowed the tears to flow.

After several minutes she wiped her eyes. She folded the sheet of writing paper, put it back in the envelope, and shoved it into her trouser pocket.

"Come on old girl," she said out loud. "What's done is done."

She picked up the fur coat, hung it in the wardrobe, and buried her face in its sleeve to inhale Maureen's scent one last time.

There was a loud knock at the front door. It was probably

Miss Tewson returned with a cup of tea to poke her nose in once more.

A policeman stood on the doorstep. It was the same young man she had seen at the theatre with Detective Sergeant Daniels on the day of Maureen's death.

"Good afternoon, ma'am." He saluted smartly and smiled. "I'm Constable Smith. It's Miss Miles I presume? I'm here to collect you. Would you come with me please?"

24

Constable Smith held open the rear doors of the police van and gestured to Bill to get inside.

"You cannot seriously expect me to ride in the back of that thing?" she said.

"I'm sorry, ma'am," Smith replied. "No member of the public is permitted to ride up front. Police regulations."

Bill took out a cigarette and leaned against the door of the van. "Then I'll wait while you go away and return with a proper police car." She lit the cigarette. "Better still, I'll flag down a taxi on Holland Park Road and meet you at Scotland Yard. I'm not a common criminal you know."

"I'm sorry ma'am, but I have my orders," Smith replied. "And this is the vehicle I've been provided with. You're not allowed to ride in the front with me. It's regulations."

"And I have my standards, young man." Bill exhaled a plume of smoke. "You really can't be serious that I'm supposed to climb in the back of that thing."

"Begging your pardon, ma'am. But you leave me no choice."

Smith stepped forward and grabbed her around the waist. He lifted her off the ground and threw her into the back of the van. She landed on a pile of blankets and her head hit the floor. The crushed cigarette still smouldered on her lips. The doors slammed shut behind her and she was plunged into semi-darkness. The only light came from a few thin shafts of daylight shining through a vent above the driver's cab.

"Let me out of here at once," Bill yelled. She got to her knees and scrambled across the blankets. They smelled strongly of horses. The driver's door slammed shut and the engine rattled into life. She slid her fingers frantically over the contours of the rear doors to search for a handle. Finding nothing, she struggled to her feet and banged on the metal partition at the front of the van behind the driver's seat.

"I said let me out," she shouted. "I know who you are. You're the one who was in my apartment. You won't get away with this. Mr Sampson is only a few minutes behind me. He'll have seen what you did and—"

The gears screeched and the van lurched forward. Bill was thrown backwards. She tripped over the blankets and banged her head against the rear doors.

"Please keep quiet." Smith's muffled voice came through the partition. "Otherwise you'll put me off my driving. Make yourself comfortable. I'm really not going to hurt you. And please don't do anything stupid."

Bill stood and reached up to steady herself. But the gears screeched again, the van lurched to the right, and her feet slipped from under her. She fell sideways and the side of her head hit something sharp buried under the blankets. She sat up and spat out what she thought was a mouthful of straw but quickly realised was the remains of her cigarette.

She gingerly dabbed at the injury on her temple. It felt sticky and when she touched the tip of her finger with her tongue she experienced the metallic taste of blood.

"Damn," she said out loud. "That's all I need. An open wound in a filthy horse box."

She got to her knees and reached under the blanket to find the cause of her injury. It was the sharp edge of a spade. By the looks of it the spade had been used recently in a stable yard.

"Wonderful." Bill regarded the grubby blade with distaste. "So I'm going to die from an infection contracted from horse manure."

She cast the blankets aside, grabbed the handle of the spade, and used it to help her stand up. A glimmer of daylight shone through the gap where the rear doors met in the middle. She lifted the spade, inserted its blade between a flange of metal on the right hand door that overlapped with the left, and tugged on the spade handle. The left door moved slightly. Encouraged, she pulled harder. The blade flipped out of its position and Bill was catapulted across the van. The spade flew out of her hands and crashed against the van wall.

"Hey, what's going on back there?" Smith called out. "Sit quietly or you'll make me drive off the road."

"Why don't you come back here and make me?" Bill shouted.

She picked up the spade and weighed it in her hands. "At least I've got something to hit you with," she said to herself.

She returned to the rear doors and inserted the spade into the small gap between them again. Three times she tried and three times it flipped out of position. On the fourth attempt she was able to secure it in place. She yanked hard on the spade handle but the van swung wildly round a corner and she was thrown off her feet against the sidewall. A motor horn sounded loudly outside.

"Hey, what are you doing?" she shouted. "Are you trying to kill us both in this thing?"

"Please keep quiet, ma'am." Smith sounded agitated. "And stop messing around back there. We've almost arrived."

Bill picked up the spade and concentrated hard on fixing it as securely as possible in the crack between the two doors. She pulled back on the spade handle and the left door flexed. She tugged harder and it moved a little more. With her feet wedged against the bottom of the doors she pulled as hard as she could.

There was a loud crack. Bill fell backwards and lost her grip on the spade. Daylight flooded into the interior of the van through the now open door.

"Success!" She clambered to her feet and took a step towards her escape.

The van screeched to a halt. Bill was thrown onto her back and the door slammed shut again. The driver's door opened and footsteps approached the rear of the van. She got onto all fours and reached for the spade. The rear door swung open and Smith appeared in the doorway. Bill scrambled to her feet holding the spade in front of her.

"What the hell's going on?" Smith demanded. "Put that down or you're going to get hurt."

"Stay right there." Bill raised the spade. "If you think I'm going to let you near me after everything you've done you're very much mistaken."

Smith lunged forward, grabbed the edge of the blanket Bill was standing on, and pulled hard. As she fell back he grabbed one of her legs and dragged her towards him. His speed and strength were overwhelming, and with a few quick moves he had his arm around her neck and squeezed hard.

"Don't make any more stupid mistakes like that," he whispered harshly in her ear. "Or you'll be sorry."

Her legs banged against the floor of the van as he hauled her out, held her arms behind her back, and handcuffed her wrists. In the distance a horse neighed and the smell of manure filled Bill's nostrils. Smith led her towards a dilapidated wooden hut. He opened the door, pushed her inside, and followed her in.

"You weren't supposed to do that," he said. "This is supposed to be a civilised meeting. I'm sorry about the vehicle but it's the best I could get. Look, there are important things I have to tell you. And you're going to have to listen to me. You *must* listen to me. Otherwise something terrible might happen to you again. And you don't want that."

The inside of the hut was hot and stuffy. The heat of the sun had beaten down remorselessly on its tin roof and the only window was sealed shut. There was a pile of blankets on the floor, two wooden chairs, and a table improvised from an open-sided wooden box, with a jug of water and a mug on it. Smith had removed Bill's handcuffs and she sat on one of the chairs smoking while Smith paced up and down.

"Could you just stop that for a moment?" Bill reached forward and poured a glass of water. "And are you sure you haven't got anything stronger? I badly need a drink after everything that's—"

"Will you keep quiet?" Smith stopped pacing. He picked up the spade he had brought in from the van and stood in front of her. "I'm the one who's supposed to be doing the talking."

"Don't wave that thing at me, please." Bill put the water jug back on the box. "You're making me nervous. If you're supposed to be doing the talking then fire away. And you'd better make it quick. I'm sure Mr Sampson isn't far away."

"You can't keep saying that. I know full well we weren't followed. It's just you, me and Sir Duke out here."

"Who's Sir Duke?"

"My horse." Smith leaned the spade against the wall. "Or rather he's the Elder's horse, but he lets me look after him."

"Which Elder do you mean?" Bill asked. "Elder Fisher? That

unpleasant solicitor? And where exactly are we? We didn't drive far and yet we seem to be in the countryside. It's much quieter. I can't think where that could be in the middle of London."

"This is my little secret." Smith grinned. "But it's beautiful. A world away from the vermin who inhabit Notting Hill. And that's what I've brought you here to talk about."

Smith reached into one side of the box, took out a bible, and held it in front of him.

"Have you read this? Everything you ever need to know is in this book."

"Not recently." Bill cleared her throat. "Tell me, Mr Smith—"

"Constable Smith."

"I'm sorry, *Constable* Smith," Bill corrected herself. "You're from Bath originally aren't you? I think Mr Sampson and I met your father at your sister Maureen's funeral just a few days ago. Tell me, why weren't you at the funeral?"

Smith dropped the bible to his side. "It wasn't possible for me to be there."

"Is that because you couldn't get time off from work? I doubt it because I'm sure the Metropolitan Police are more understanding than that. Or was it because it was actually you who murdered Maureen?"

Smith opened the bible and flicked rapidly through its pages.

"Why did you murder your sister, Constable?" Bill persisted. "You're a religious man. You're a policeman. A public servant who should uphold the law. Why did you—"

"Leviticus chapter eighteen, verse twenty-two," Smith interrupted. "*You shall not lie with a man as with a woman, it is an abomination.*" He waved the open bible in front of Bill. "And that goes for women as well. The answers are all in this book. What she did was an abomination. She was an abomination. And she refused to seek forgiveness for her sin. She could not be allowed to go on living. Just as God struck down our mother for her abomination, my sister had to be struck down for hers."

He turned over two pages. "You don't believe me? Read Leviticus chapter twenty, verse thirteen: *If a man lies with a man as with a woman, both of them have committed an abomination; they shall surely be put to death; their blood is upon them.*"

He flicked through more pages. "And see here. In Deuteronomy chapter twenty-one. It's all there. *A rebellious child must be stoned to death.*"

He snapped the bible shut. "And our mother was just as sinful as my sister. She was like Lot's wife. God could not allow her to go on living. That is why she died."

"And what about the sixth commandment?" Bill asked. "I seem to remember that in the bible God tells you: *Thou shalt not kill.* It couldn't be more plainly written."

"Ah, but it was God's will." Smith sat in the chair opposite Bill and rested the bible in his lap. "God will forgive that. Of that it is certain."

"Is this really your justification for two murders and one attempted murder?" Bill's hand shook as she lit a cigarette and inhaled deeply. "Because when you get to court I think the judge is going to take a very different view. You can't take the law into your own hands and then simply claim that you're doing God's work."

"You're wrong." Smith grinned again. It was unnerving to see. His face betrayed the absolute conviction of someone who knew he was right. "We've been doing precisely that for centuries. Think of the Crusades and their victories against the Moors in Spain. Or the Conquistadors in their glorious conquest of the heathens in America."

"Never been much of a fan of the Spanish." Bill sniffed. "Ever since they persuaded Guy Fawkes to try to blow up the Houses of Parliament." She tapped the ash from her cigarette onto the floor. "Do you really feel no guilt for Maureen's murder? She was a beautiful woman. Beautiful in every way. Inside and out. And she had a capability to love that I discovered far too late."

She pointed the cigarette at Smith. "You murdered a woman I once loved. And she loved me. It was only this morning that I discovered she had always loved me. But because of what you've done I have no way of reciprocating that love any more. I will never forgive you for that."

Bill leapt from the chair and stubbed her cigarette on Smith's neck. In the few seconds he was distracted by the pain she reached past him and picked up the spade. She swung it at his head but he ducked and the spade struck the wall harmlessly.

Smith lunged forward to grab the spade but Bill swung it towards him again. This time it made contact with his head. He staggered backwards, hit the table, and fell sideways onto the floor. Bill stepped forward and raised the spade above her head.

"Never underestimate a woman," she said. "Now. Don't make a move or I'll use this again."

25

By the time Simon's train from Bath arrived at Paddington the rain had stopped, the clouds had cleared, and steam rose from the pavement as the heat of the sun returned London to summer. He walked to Lancaster Gate and took a Central underground train to *The Chronicle* offices in Fleet Street. An hour later he was in his editor's office with the draft of a story in his hand.

"There you go, Frank. I think you'll find this an interesting new angle on the murders."

Frank Somerskill took the two sheets of paper from Simon, sat back in his chair, and swung his feet onto the desk. Simon sat opposite and waited for his reaction. No other paper in Fleet Street would have the story. Simon was confident his name would be on the front-page of the next morning's edition with a possible follow-up for the evening edition.

"We can't print this." Somerskill tossed the pages onto the desk. "You're accusing the Met of harbouring a murderer. Where's your evidence?"

"I'll explain it again," Simon said patiently. "Maureen Lyon was the first victim. She was murdered at His Majesty's Theatre. When we were in Bath we found out her family was part of a bizarre fundamentalist religious cult. They threw her out. 'Uncongregate', they call it. They didn't just throw her out from the church but from the family as well. That's how she ended up in London. After Maureen was murdered the chum she shared a house with found evidence of blackmail. It looked like Maureen was blackmailing her own father over the illegitimacy of her brother."

"Doesn't sound like a very pleasant young lady," Somerskill replied. "Blackmail. Nasty business."

"But the father had been pretty unpleasant to her," Simon argued. "When Maureen was a child he told her that her mother was dead when in reality she wasn't. While I was in Bath I found the mother was very much alive. I interviewed her. And it's pretty clear the father was a brute to Miss Lyon. Doing all sorts of unspeakable things. Despite all that the church and the family cut her off and threw her out. I imagine she was pretty desperate for money when she arrived in London. It's a strong motive for murder."

"Maybe." Somerskill took a pipe from his pocket and shoved it unlit into the corner of his mouth. "If the father was a brute and she was blackmailing him then it could well be a motive for him to kill her. But you're not saying it's the father. You're saying it's the brother. Who happens to be an officer in the Metropolitan Police. I find that hard to believe. He's a public servant. Why do you say it's him?"

"Because he's got the opportunity," Simon replied. "To start with he's in London. At some point he probably found out where his sister was living. Maybe even tracked her down. But the blackmail wasn't the only motive for her murder. I told you I interviewed the mother in Bath. She told me her son Charley, the police officer, was obsessed with the weird religious cult and all its teachings. In his eyes his sister was a sinful person. A wicked person. And because this cult teaches the bible so literally he believed it was his job to punish her for her sin."

"I'm sure we're all sinful in the eyes of a cult like that." Somerskill struck a match and struggled to light his pipe. "But murder is a very extreme form of punishment."

"Yes but I'm pretty certain that in his eyes Maureen was *really* sinful. He would probably say that she should be damned." Simon coughed awkwardly. "You see she enjoyed the company of women."

"What's so sinful about..." Somerskill dropped the match as it burned his fingers. "Oh, I see what you mean. Sapphic leanings you mean?" He lit another match. "But from my dim and distant past I don't seem to remember there being any mention of that in the bible. And it's not even illegal in this country for women to be...Sapphic...as far as I know. The law's just obsessed with buggery. You know. Between chaps. The ladies are left alone."

"I discovered It wasn't just Maureen who was sinful." Simon noticed Somerskill's dropped match had set light to the pages of his draft. He threw them on the floor and stamped out the flames. "Her mother was also living with a woman. She told me that was why they'd uncongregated her as well."

"Did you say this lot claim to be Christian?" Somerskill puffed on his pipe. "Because they sound pretty un-Christian to me. So you reckon the brother was so obsessed with his sister's sinfulness that he decided to murder her. Why didn't he do the same for the mother?"

"Because, like his sister, he'd been told she was dead," Simon explained patiently.

"Oh, yes. Of course." Somerskill looked down at his desk. "Where's that article of yours?"

"You set fire to it, Frank."

"Did I? Well, probably just as well. I'm afraid you're asking our readers to believe a lot of conjecture. And Pipkins in legal will be extremely upset. Have you even checked if there's a Constable Charles Smith on the Met's payroll? Smith is an awfully common name you know."

"Actually, I haven't been able to confirm that," Simon admitted. "Detective Sergeant Daniels isn't returning my calls. But I have confirmed there was a Constable Charles Smith present at His Majesty's Theatre the day Maureen Lyon's body was discovered. And we found a tie clip with the inscription *To Charley* on it near the scene of the attempted murder in Soho."

"Why's that significant?"

"Because several of the people in the Mission of the Heavenly Host were wearing the same tie clip."

"This is all very circumstantial." Somerskill took a tobacco pouch from his pocket and refilled the bowl of his pipe. "If you want to publicly accuse a Metropolitan Police officer of murder you're going to need a hell of a lot more evidence than this. I'm not risking this newspaper's reputation on your gut instinct, Sampson." He waved towards the door. "Go on. Make some calls. Find me a story I can publish without risk of libel."

Simon returned to his desk. There were no messages waiting for him from Detective Sergeant Daniels. There was also no message from Bill. It was strange not to have heard from her by now. He thought back to what Calvin had said to him about leaving her to visit Jenny Casewell's house alone. He decided to put a call through to His Majesty's Theatre.

The man who answered told him brusquely that no one had seen Miss Miles for several days since she had gone on holiday. Simon managed to persuade the man to give him the phone number for Jenny Casewell. He tried the number twice and got no reply. He tried Bill's number. Again there was no answer.

Finally, he flicked through his contacts book and called a number he had secured through a colleague on the Arts desk.

"Is that Mr Coward?" he asked when a man answered the phone.

"Who wants to know?" demanded a voice instantly identifiable as that of Noël Coward.

"My name's Sampson, sir," Simon replied. "Simon Sampson. I'm sorry to bother you but—"

"Sampson? The rat from the newspapers?"

"Well, I—"

"How dare you call me on this private—"

"It's about Bill, sir."

"What is it about Bill?"

"The reason for my call, sir. She's missing."

"Missing? She's always missing. Never been there when I need her."

"With all due respect, sir. I think that's a bit—"

"People who begin their sentences with the words *With all due respect,* young man, usually go on to be anything but respectful." Noël sneezed. "There you are. Sneezing you see? I'm allergic to newspaper rats like you."

"I'm very worried about Bill," Simon said quickly.

Noël sneezed again. "Well don't be. She's a very capable woman. Irritating, offensive, downright rude, and, as you've just pointed out, generally absent. But very capable all the same I'm forced to admit. She'll turn up. Like the proverbial bad penny. Now I have a show to write. Don't interrupt me again on this number."

There was a *click* and the line went dead.

"How rude." Simon put the receiver back on its cradle and stared at the telephone. "It's about time Bill left your employ. You really don't deserve her."

He was about to reach for the receiver to call Detective Sergeant Daniels once more at Scotland Yard when the phone rang.

"Sampson here," Simon said with the receiver cradled to his ear.

"Simon, it is Calvin. You have got to get down here now."

"Calvin, where are you?" Simon replied. "What's happened?"

"Bill has been kidnapped."

"Dammit," Simon said. "I knew something was wrong."

"And now try to guess who the kidnapper is," Calvin continued.

"Constable Charley Smith of Scotland Yard," Simon replied promptly.

"Well, it is a policeman," Calvin said. "And he took her in a police van. How did you know?"

"I'll tell you later." Simon stood with the phone still pressed to his ear and unhooked his jacket from the back of the chair. "Where are you?"

"Chiswick," Calvin replied. "It is close to Chiswick House. There is a patch of land with stables and a hut on it. He has got her inside the hut."

"I'll call Scotland Yard," Simon replied. "They can get the local bobbies to go out there. They'll get there much quicker than me. A taxi's going to take at least an hour. Possibly longer if the traffic's bad."

"You must go now," Calvin said. "I will go back to the hut. If there is a possibility I will get her out. He is a madman."

"Be careful, Calvin," Simon cautioned. "Don't do anything until the police arrive."

"I will do whatever I must to keep her safe," Calvin replied and hung up.

That's what I'm afraid of Simon thought. He called Scotland

Yard and this time Detective Sergeant Daniels picked up the phone.

"Daniels, you've got to get your officers down to Chiswick," Simon began. "Miss Miles has been kidnapped by your Constable Smith. He's holding her in a hut next to Chiswick House."

"Which particular Constable Smith are you accusing of being a kidnapper?" Daniels asked. "There are several Smiths in the Metropolitan Police."

"His first name's Charles," Simon replied. "Charley. I presume he's the one who was with you at His Majesty's Theatre the day Maureen Lyon was murdered. Didn't have far to travel, did he? Seeing as he was the one who murdered her."

"Don't be ridiculous, Sampson. First you accuse one of my officers of kidnapping. Now you say he's a murderer."

"Double murderer," Simon corrected. "I'm certain he's responsible for the death of Grace Lucas as well. And the attempted murder of Miss Miles in her apartment. And now he's holding her hostage in Chiswick."

"These are absurd accusations," Daniels replied. "What evidence do you have for this nonsense?"

"I don't have time to explain now, Daniels." Simon slipped an arm through the sleeve of his jacket and swapped the receiver to his other ear to finish putting on his jacket. "Miss Miles is in danger. Can I meet you out there?"

"Certainly not," Daniels replied. "I've got an important meeting with the commissioner this afternoon. Nor will I be sending any of our valuable officers on such a wild goose chase."

"Damn you Daniels," Simon replied. "If anything happens to Bill I'll make sure you're sacked from the force without a pension."

Simon hung up the call and headed out of the newsroom.

"Mr Sampson?"

One of the newsroom secretaries waved a telephone receiver in the air. "Call for you."

"Can't it wait?" Simon paused in the doorway. "Who is it?"

"She says she's from the Home Office," the secretary replied. "Her name's Miss Buckingham. She says it's urgent."

26

For one brief moment after Bill hit Smith with the spade she felt triumphant. The man who had tried to kill her lay immobile on the floor in front of her. But then he drew his knees up to his chest in a foetal position and covered his face with his hands. His shoulders shook and he let out a wail like a child who had been punished.

"Don't hit me," he whimpered. "Don't hit me again. I'll do it right this time. I'm sorry, I'm sorry, I'm sorry. I promise to be good. Just don't hit me."

Despite everything Smith had done, despite everything he represented to her, Bill felt a pang of sympathy for him. The feeling irritated and confused her but she could not deny its presence.

"Sit up," she commanded. "Slowly. Don't make any sudden moves. Remember I've still got this spade in my hands."

Smith did as she asked. He dropped his hands from his face and shuffled back to lean against the wall with his legs outstretched in front of him. He looked down at his chest, sniffled, and wiped his nose with the back of his hand.

"Do you know what a pitiful sight you make?" Bill lowered

the spade. "I came *this* close to killing you. I imagine in your twisted view of the world that would have been justified. But not in mine. I don't believe in all that nonsense about an eye for an eye. If we start along that road then where do we stop?"

She stepped back and rested her shoulder on the wall opposite Smith. There was enough distance between them to give her time to defend herself if he suddenly lunged forward.

"You're a pathetic man, you know that don't you? You must take after that father of yours."

Smith glanced up and Bill raised the spade. He whimpered and turned his head away.

"You know we met your father in Bath?" Bill continued. "When we went to your sister's funeral. But of course you weren't there, were you?"

Smith grunted.

"Even your father wasn't at the service. Such a coward. He waited outside until the whole charade was over." Bill lowered the spade again. "Good God, I've just thought of something. You and I have something in common."

Smith glanced up at her.

"We both lost our mothers when were very young." Bill shook her head. "We must have been about the same age. Except somehow that tragedy in my childhood didn't turn me into a murderer. Even when I could have killed you a moment ago I resisted the temptation. What's the difference between us do you think, Smith? What makes you want to kill people and I don't? Was it that father of yours? What did he do to you?"

Smith shivered and he started to whimper once more.

"I think perhaps it was." Bill leaned on the handle of the spade. "Or was it that nonsense religion you were forced into? Run by all those men saying foolish things?"

"It's not nonsense," Smith mumbled. "And they're not foolish. It's the truth. The only truth in this world."

"How on earth can it be? Surely if those people were good Christians they wouldn't tell you to murder your own sister,"

"But that sinner was responsible for our mother's death," Smith replied. "When she was born everything changed. Mother changed. She was no longer the same person. It was Maureen who did that. They said it was because of Maureen that Mother died."

"Who's 'they'?" Bill asked.

"Elder Fisher," Smith replied. "And Father. They both said that her birth put such a strain on Mother her spirit could no longer survive." Smith raised his head and glowered at Bill. "It was Maureen who killed our mother. She had to be avenged."

"An eye for an eye?" Bill sniffed contemptuously. "Is that what you're saying? Is that the way you give some biblical justification to what you did? What nonsense. I think you were simply jealous of your sister. You were the older brother who gets his nose put out of joint with the arrival of a younger sibling. Except you couldn't stop after you'd murdered her, could you? Then there was Grace. And then you tried to kill me. What happened, Smith? Got a taste for killing did you?"

Smith scrambled to his feet and took a step towards her. She raised the spade and he held up his hands.

"All right, all right," he said. "I won't come any closer. But you've got to understand it's not like that. What was done was right in the eyes of God. These women are sinful. Wicked. They are an abomination in the world."

"If you say that then you actually mean that *I'm* an abomination in the world." Bill tightened her grip on the spade. "Do you think I choose to be this way? That any of us choose to be this way? If your God made me and you say he's a perfect God then why would he make me an abomination? That doesn't make any sense."

There was a loud crash from outside the hut. Bill turned to

see the entrance door buckle and splinter around the lock. From the corner of her eye she saw Smith step forward. He grabbed the spade handle and tried to twist it from her hands. She clung on to it as she heard a familiar voice from the other side of the door.

"Bill! Are you in there?"

"Darling?" Bill was shocked to hear his voice. "What are you doing here?"

There was another crash and the door flew open. Standing on the threshold was the man she knew as the temporary porter from her apartment block. He dropped his shoulders and charged headlong into Smith who groaned, released his grasp on the spade, and staggered back. Darling followed, wrapped an arm around his neck, and pulled him into a headlock. Smith lashed out with his leg and tried to kick Darling. Bill lifted the spade and swung it with all her strength against the back of Smith's legs. He howled in pain and collapsed onto his knees with Darling's arm still wrapped around his neck.

"Thank you," Darling said. "I cannot believe you had so much strength."

"You men are always underestimating us," Bill replied. "Keep hold of him. I'll get those reins hanging on the wall over there and secure his wrists. He won't cause us any more trouble after that."

When she unhooked the reins from a rusty nail she found them tangled and knotted. She picked away at the knots in frustration until the strips of leather were loose enough to untangle.

"Scheiße," Darling said impatiently. "Why are you taking so long?"

"Why do you think?" Bill asked. "I just thought I'd take my time to irritate you. Stop moaning and hold him still while I tie his hands."

It was at moments like this Bill wished she had been in the Girl Guides. She wrapped the reins several times around Smith's left wrist and tied what she hoped was a decent knot. Then she looped the reins around his right wrist and pulled tight. When Smith struggled against her she brought her knee up smartly between his legs and heard a satisfying yelp of pain. Touching Smith's hands brought a wave of nausea to her throat. His were the hands of a murderer. They were the hands that had so nearly killed her.

She tied a series of knots she hoped her school friend Freckles Fiona, a keen Girl Guide, would have been proud of and backed away. Darling dragged Smith around to the chair and forced him to sit. He threaded the ends of the reins through the slats at the back of the chair and tied them together.

"You have done a good job," Darling said to Bill. "Did you learn that in the British Girl Guides?"

"Certainly not." Bill took out a cigarette and lit it. "Now tell me what on earth you're doing here."

"Protecting you," Darling replied. "Simon sent me."

"Why on earth would he send you?" Bill asked. "No offence, Darling. But you're just a porter."

"I am not offended but that is offensive to porters." Darling shook his head. "No I am not *just* a porter as you say. And my name is not Darling. It is Schatz. Calvin Schatz. I am from Berlin and I am working temporarily in London."

"Good God." Bill leaned against the wall and tried to make sense of the information. It would explain why she thought she had seen Darling, or Schatz as she now learned he was called, in Bath. "How long have you been stalking me?"

"Now that is offensive," Calvin replied. "I have not been stalking you. I have been protecting you. And I would hope that you would be grateful. If I had not come to your rescue that night in your apartment—"

"Yes, yes," Bill replied hastily. "I am grateful. Of course I am. It's just a bit of a shock. Simon said nothing about it. I wish he'd told me."

"He said you would have refused any offer of help if he had told you."

"Ah." Bill inhaled on her cigarette and blew a smoke ring. "He seems to know me better than I thought he did. How awkward."

"It is true, then?"

"Possibly. Perhaps he's a more perceptive young man than I give him credit for."

"He is certainly perceptive." Calvin smiled again. "And also very kind, despite being a journalist and part of the rat pack of your gutter press. He understands people. He is sensitive. I would go so far as to say—"

"Now I understand." Bill laughed. "You must be the one whose voice I heard in the background when I called him the other day. It all makes sense now. You two are romantically entangled. My God, Simon's a dark horse."

"Such perversion."

"Oh, I forgot you were here." Bill rounded on Smith. "Do shut up you tiresome individual."

She smiled at Calvin. "Would you be so kind as to search this abomination of a man? I really can't bear to touch him."

"It would be my pleasure." Calvin bent down and went through Smith's pockets with remarkable efficiency. "He has handcuffs and a truncheon. Some keys and a whistle. No weapons that I can find. Of course your English bobbies do not carry guns, do they?" He fumbled in the inside pocket of Smith's jacket. "This is strange. He has two notebooks. Perhaps one became full and he needed a second."

"Give that back," Smith shouted. "It's not for your eyes. Get your hands off it."

Bill ignored him, took the two notebooks from Calvin, and flicked through the pages. One of the books contained a series of carefully dated journal entries. Her hands shook and she gasped as she read through them.

"What is it?" Calvin asked.

Bill waved the notebook in Smith's face. "It's your confession, isn't it? You'll hang for this. And now I've read what's in here I can't wait for that day. Your hatred for women leaps off every page. What you've written is positively gleeful about the despicable crimes you've committed."

She handed the notebook to Calvin. "This apology for a human being has kept a journal of his murderous intent. All his vile thoughts, all his planning, and worst of all his delight in the deaths he caused is written down in that notebook. It's the clear evidence of a twisted mind."

From outside came the rapidly approaching sound of bells. Bill looked out of the door and saw a police car racing towards the hut. It screeched to a halt and Detective Sergeant Daniels climbed out of the passenger seat.

"Just in time," Bill said. "Although how on earth he knew to come here I have no idea."

"I called Simon," Calvin explained. "He must have called the police. As you say, it is very timely."

Daniels walked up to the hut and stood in the entrance.

"What the hell's going on here?" he asked. "Miss Miles. Why is Constable Smith tied to a chair?"

"Good of you to show up, Detective Sergeant," Bill replied. "Constable Smith was holding me prisoner. This is Mr Calvin Schatz. He rescued me."

"Constable Smith held you prisoner?" Daniels shook his head. "I can't believe that for a moment. Constable Smith is an officer of the law. Why would he take you prisoner?"

"Because he's the murderer." Bill took the notebook back

from Calvin and handed it to Daniels. "And here's the evidence. Smith kept a journal. It's all in there. Two murders and his plans to murder me."

"Thank you." Daniels put the notebook into his pocket. "That's extremely helpful of you Miss Miles. Now untie Constable Smith while I caution Herr Schatz."

"What on earth are you doing?" Bill asked. "You've got the wrong man. It's Smith who should be arrested."

Daniels ignored her. "Calvin Schatz? I arrest you for the murder of Maureen Lyon. I also arrest you for the murder of Grace Lucas and the attempted murder of Florence Miles. You do not have to say anything unless you wish to do so, but what you say may be given in evidence."

27

Daniels reached into his back pocket, took out a pair of handcuffs and advanced on Calvin. Bill stepped between them.

"Over my dead body."

"Please, Miss Miles." Detective Sergeant Daniels sighed. "It's been a long and trying day. I had a very difficult meeting with the chief commissioner this afternoon. A meeting I had to cut short in order to come out here. The commissioner wasn't pleased."

"I don't care whether he was pleased or not," Bill replied. "You're arresting the wrong man. Constable Smith is the murderer. This afternoon he came to collect me from the house where Miss Lyon once lived. How he knew I was there I have no idea. But I have my suspicions he's been stalking me for weeks. He threw me bodily into the back of that van where there were no seats so I was tossed around on filthy horse blankets while he drove like a mad man through the streets of London. Then he locked me in here and recited the bible at me. He's mad. Completely mad. And dangerous."

"Have you finished with your wild and baseless allegations,

Miss Miles?" Daniels asked. "Because I'm certainly finished listening to them."

"But sergeant—"

"Stand aside, Miss Miles," Daniels ordered. "Or I'll put you in handcuffs as well as Herr Schatz. Now go and be useful. Untie Constable Smith immediately."

Bill glowered at him. She walked over to Smith, crouched down behind his chair, and fumbled with the knotted reins binding his wrists.

"As for Herr Schatz," Daniels continued. "We've been watching him ever since he entered this country a little more than a year ago. You know he's not English, don't you? He comes from Germany,"

"What's that got to do with anything?" Bill asked. "The King's grandfather was German as well. It didn't stop Queen Victoria marrying him."

"That flippant comment is tantamount to treason." Daniels rattled the handcuffs threateningly. "We know that Herr Schatz came to this country by very dubious means. There's no official record of his entry through the normal channels. We believe he was smuggled in by a boat landing somewhere off the east coast of England. Possibly arriving from the Hook of Holland under cover of darkness. Isn't that right, Herr Schatz?"

Calvin said nothing.

"We were given notice that Herr Schatz was a potentially dangerous man by the German authorities," Daniels continued. "They advised us to keep him under observation. Which we did. The German police believed he may have been involved in the mysterious deaths of two women in Berlin last year."

Bill was confused by what she was hearing. Everything she had experienced at the hands of Smith that afternoon led her to conclude he was the murderer. And yet these new revelations about Calvin planted doubt in her mind.

"Is any of this true, Calvin?" she asked.

"It is true I arrived by boat," Calvin said quietly. "And it is also true I crossed the North Sea from Hook of Holland to Suffolk. But you must believe me when I say I have nothing to do with the murders in London. And it is also true I came here on important business that I am not able to tell you about."

"I think the time for keeping secrets is over, Calvin." Bill finally loosened the ropes securing Smith's hands. Smith flexed his arms stiffly and stood. "If you want to avoid arrest you'd better start talking."

"I am afraid I cannot say any more, Miss Miles," Calvin replied. "But I can assure you I had nothing to do with those two murders in Berlin. Nor with the recent murders in London."

"So, it's true what Daniels says about the two women murdered in Berlin?" Bill lit a cigarette. "And you knew about them?"

Calvin nodded. "But I am afraid I cannot tell you anything about my work. What I can say is that the wrong person is being arrested here. I appeal to you, Miss Miles. You know what Smith did to you this afternoon. He is undoubtedly the man who attacked you in your apartment. If I had been able to catch him that evening we could have revealed the identity of a very dangerous man—"

"Enough." Detective Sergeant Daniels opened the handcuffs. "Put your hands behind your back, Schatz. I'm taking you to Scotland Yard. Constable Smith, drive the van back to the depot and have it cleaned out. Thoroughly cleaned out."

Calvin obediently put his hands behind his back. Daniels hooked the handcuffs over his wrists and secured them.

"You can't do this," Bill protested. "Calvin's right about what Smith did to me this afternoon. He's a mad man. All the evidence is in that notebook I just gave you. And if Calvin's right about that then I also believe him when he says the reason he's in England is legitimate. Although I wish that you'd tell me more, Calvin."

Calvin shrugged. "I am afraid it is not possible."

"Then if they're taking you to Scotland Yard I'm coming with you," Bill replied.

"You will not, Miss Miles." Daniels put a hand on Calvin's shoulder. "You'll stay here while Constable Smith and I take Herr Schatz into custody."

"And how am I supposed to get back to London?" Bill asked.

"You're only in Chiswick, Miss Miles," Daniels replied. There are several buses you can catch."

"I can't be seen on a bus looking like this." Bill brushed manure from her trousers. "I have standards to maintain. Look, Daniels. None of this makes any sense. How can I be certain something terrible isn't going to happen to Calvin once you and Smith drive away with him? I've already told you what Smith did today. He's a madman. I fail to understand why you're trusting his word over that of Herr Schatz."

"Because they're in it together."

Simon appeared in the open doorway.

"Damn you, Sampson." Smith lunged at Simon and rugby-tackled him to the ground. He rolled him onto his front, sat astride his back, and reached for his handcuffs.

"Oh no you don't."

Bill stepped forward and wrapped her arms around Smith's neck. She squeezed tight and tried to lift him away from Simon. Smith grabbed at her arms and shook her from side to side but Bill hung on grimly. She leaned over to use her weight to pull Smith away from Simon. Smith half lifted himself to pull in the opposite direction, overbalanced, and fell sideways on top of Bill.

Calvin kicked back hard between Daniels' legs. He groaned and doubled over. Calvin kicked back again and this time his foot made contact with Daniels' head. The detective sergeant staggered backwards, tripped over the chair, and fell against the wall.

"I wish you'd done that a few minutes earlier, Calvin." Bill pushed against the weight of Smith lying on top of her. "Because it's certainly the best way to disarm a man." She lifted her knee sharply into Smith's groin and grinned with satisfaction when she heard him yelp. He rolled away from her and pulled his knees into his chest.

Bill scrambled to her feet and picked up the chair. She put its legs on either side of Smith's body so its crossbars pinned him to the ground, and sat on the seat.

Simon walked over to Daniels and held out his hand.

"Keys, Daniels," he commanded. "You've seen what Miss Miles is capable of. You don't want her to remove them from you."

Daniels grunted. He reached into his pocket and handed Simon the keys for his handcuffs. Simon unlocked the cuffs on Calvin's wrists and tossed them over to Bill.

"Go on," he said. "Now you can get your revenge on your attacker."

"I don't need revenge," Bill replied. "Far better that we get justice. Not only for me, but for every woman subjected to men's violence against them."

She reached down to Smith's arms and secured his wrists with the handcuffs.

"Now, Herr Schatz," she continued. "Would you explain precisely what is going on between you two?"

Calvin looked sheepishly at Simon who stared down at his feet. Bill laughed and lit a cigarette.

"I'm such a fool," she said. "An unobservant, self-obsessed fool."

"Do not be harsh on yourself, Miss Miles." Calvin pulled Simon towards him and put an arm around his waist. "Like all men in our position we must go to great lengths to conceal our..." Calvin paused as if considering his next words carefully. "...our special friendship."

"But why conceal it from me, Simon?" Bill asked. "Don't you trust me?"

"I'm sorry, Bill." Simon continued to stare down at his feet. "You and I have really only just met. And given the nature of Calvin's work it was best that he kept as low a profile as possible."

"Yes, what exactly is your work?" Bill asked. "You're very mysterious about that. The other day you were a part-time porter in my apartment block. And a moment ago you admitted to smuggling yourself into the country on a boat. Are you working here illegally?"

"No, he's not."

"Good grief, Cynthia." Bill choked on her cigarette when she saw Simon's aunt standing in the doorway. "What on earth are you doing here?"

"And I'm pleased to see you too, Miss Miles." Aunt Cynny strode into the hut. "Herr Schatz telephoned me earlier to alert me to what was going on here. Sorry we've taken so long to arrive. I've had the devil of a job getting the authorisations needed to sort this mess out. The Home Office is a tad bureaucratic you know. Especially when it involves corruption in the Metropolitan Police."

Daniels pushed past Aunt Cynny and ran out of the door. A moment later he reappeared, held securely by two police officers.

"That was very foolish, detective sergeant." Simon's aunt jabbed her walking stick into Daniels' chest. "You've as good as admitted your guilt in this ghastly affair. The question is: how many more of your colleagues in the force have collaborated in this conspiracy of hate?"

28

The case finally came to trial in the autumn of 1929. On the day the guilty verdicts were returned by the jury at the Old Bailey the story was pushed from the front page of *The Chronicle* by news of the stock market crash on Wall Street. Simon's detailed report was relegated to the inside pages as a much greater event unfolded around the world.

Smith was sentenced to hang for the murders of Maureen Lyon and Grace Lucas. Daniels was sentenced to ten years imprisonment for perverting the course of justice. There were no further prosecutions. Simon had been tipped off that there was a bigger story to tell. That the cover-up of Smith's murderous activity went much higher in the ranks of the Metropolitan Police. But he was never able to gather enough evidence to prove it.

Simon's editor promoted him to chief reporter and gave him free rein to work on whatever story he chose. But his passion for journalism had been dampened and his idealism tarnished. He had been shocked at the speed at which the establishment had moved to conceal the corruption he sought to uncover inside the

Met. He concluded he had been naïve to ever believe he could make a difference. The forces ranged against him were too great.

On the first of November Simon arrived for lunch with Bill at the Ivy restaurant. It had been months since he had last seen her. Noël had changed his mind and begged Bill to go to New York when *Bitter Sweet* transferred to Broadway. With Simon's extra workload at *The Chronicle* it had made it impossible for them to get together. That morning she had called to say she had important news to tell him.

The Ivy was crowded. It was now one of the most fashionable meeting places in London. The waiter apologised that their table was still not ready. He showed Simon to the bar where Bill was perched on a stool smoking a cigarette.

"I've left Noël," she announced when he took his seat.

"I'm surprised it's taken you so long," Simon replied. "What are you going to do instead?"

"I'm going back to the BBC."

"But I thought you hated it there?" Simon ordered two martinis from the barman. "Sounds like you're leaping out of the frying pan straight back into the fire."

"It's going to be different this time." Bill stubbed out her cigarette and lit another. "This time I'm on the board. The first woman director of the Corporation. In fact I'll be one of the first women directors of any organisation in Britain."

"My, my," Simon replied. "So now you're part of the establishment. They've suckered you in. I presume that means you'll be closing ranks with the rest of them."

"Now, now," Bill chided him. "Just because I've got a senior job in the BBC doesn't mean I've surrendered myself to the establishment. And it certainly doesn't mean I share their views. I intend to change things from within."

"Such idealism." Simon raised his glass. "Here's to it. But please excuse me if I don't share your optimism. I've seen too much of how the establishment rushes to protect itself recently. I wish you luck. You're going to need a lot of it."

"Don't be like that." Bill rested an elbow on the bar and twirled the stem of her glass. "What's the matter with you? When I first met you this summer at His Majesty's you were a fearless reporter. Doggedly exposing corruption. Highly principled and standing up for what's right. I don't mind saying I was deeply suspicious of you to begin with. I thought you were just another dog from Fleet Street, as Noël would have said. But when you told me how much you wanted to help find Maureen's killer I realised you were different. You seemed to be the genuine article. A journalist with a heart. What's changed?"

Simon finished his martini and summoned the barman to order another.

"Well my birthday's coming up in two weeks' time. I'm going to be nearly thirty. That doesn't fill me with joy."

"Such an old man." Bill snorted. "Why should that be so significant? It's only a number."

"But I've got to the end of my twenties and I haven't achieved anything," Simon replied. "What I uncovered—I mean what we uncovered—in the Mission of the Heavenly Host was shocking. Not only did it preach hatred towards people like us and towards women in general, but it had actually infiltrated the British establishment. Its members were in the Metropolitan Police. Daniels was not only a detective sergeant but an Elder in the East London Mission of the church. He helped to drizzle the church's hatred into the day-to-day activities of the police. And I'm convinced there are more of them, not only inside the Met, but in other institutions across Britain. They've been put there to poison this country with their distorted morality. It's just that I can't prove it."

"Well we know they had their tentacles inside the Berlin police force." Bill stubbed out her cigarette in the ashtray.

"That's why Calvin was sent over here. To liaise with the Home Office. Which reminds me. Why did you have to be so secretive about him?"

"I told you before, my personal life is—"

"I don't mean about you being lovers," Bill interrupted. "I mean about him being a German police investigator. I was surprised that you kept that from me. I thought we were working together on the investigation."

"He asked me not to tell you. The fewer people who knew the better. And if his cover was blown then you couldn't have been blamed for revealing the secret."

"That's a convenient way of putting it." Bill jabbed at an olive with her cocktail stick. "And yet Calvin was quick to tell you everything. Pillow talk I presume."

"Don't be bitter."

Bill transferred the olive to her mouth and chewed it. "Are you still seeing him?"

"He's gone back to Berlin."

"That doesn't answer my question." Bill spat out the olive pip into her hand and tossed it into the ashtray.

Simon picked up his drink. "I might be."

"Now that's intriguing."

"Look, I'm tired of this country, Bill." Simon set his glass on the bar top. He gestured to the other diners in The Ivy. "Look at this lot. The elite of London. Money, position, they've got it all. Privileged people who don't care a jot if there's corruption in the Metropolitan Police. Just so long as they can be seen dining in the right places with the right people. In the past four months I've learned that what I've been doing doesn't seem to matter to most people. Having principles doesn't seem to matter."

Bill leaned towards Simon and blew a smoke ring above his head. "Oh look, Mr Sampson. You have a halo. Stop being so bloody virtuous. And as for criticising these people. Don't forget that you're about to eat lunch in The Ivy alongside them."

"I'm only here because you invited me."

"Pardon me for being so generous. Next time I'll treat you to a meal at the fish and chip van outside Billingsgate."

"I'm sorry, old thing." Simon put a hand on Bill's arm. "But I'm feeling terribly jaded. I uncover a major scandal that reaches up to the highest echelons of the Metropolitan Police. A scandal involving the murder of innocent women. Surely that's the moment when the powers that be should knuckle down and sort it out? Get rid of the rotten apples. Instead they see me as an inconvenience and they close ranks. And I'm sure it's not just in the Metropolitan Police. It's happening in institutions across this whole benighted country."

"Goodness, you are jaded." Bill handed him a menu. "Order whatever you want. Our table will be ready in a moment. I need you to cheer up."

Simon took the menu and scanned the choices. "I'll have the beef and sauerkraut," he said. "I might have to get used to eating the stuff."

"Come again?"

"I'm thinking of moving to Berlin."

Bill choked on her martini.

"But you can't."

"And why not?"

"Because I was about to offer you a job at the BBC."

Simon threw back his head and laughed.

"Now that's cheered me up," he said. "Although I don't think I'll be taking you up on it. So if you decide to withdraw your offer of a free lunch I quite understand. I thought you just wanted to catch up, not soften me up to get me into the establishment."

This time it was Bill's turn to laugh.

"Neither of us is paying for this meal. I'll be charging it to the BBC. So enjoy it and see if you change your mind by the end."

The waiter came over to announce that their table was ready. They followed him across the restaurant and took their seats. Bill lit a cigarette and sat back in her chair.

"You're actually going to go to Berlin, aren't you?" she said. "Of course you're not going to take my job offer. And it's a very good offer too. Setting up the first broadcast news operation in Britain. But I can see why it's not tempting you. A sexy man like Calvin waiting for you in that city of sin."

"It's not a 'city of sin'," Simon retorted. "It's a progressive city with liberal values, as far as I can make out. People like us don't have to hide in the shadows like we do here. Good God, they're even about to repeal Paragraph 175."

Bill looked up from her menu. "You'll have to enlighten me on that one."

"It's the law that makes homosexuality illegal in Germany," Simon answered. "Like the buggery laws here."

"You mean you'll be legal?" Bill asked. "I can see the attraction of moving there."

"Exactly," Simon replied. "So if I end up going, why don't you come with me?"

"Is that a proposal, Mr Sampson?" Bill shook her head. "I think that's a very bad idea. For one thing I'm just about to start an important new job with the BBC which I'm very much looking forward to."

"And the second?"

"I honestly can't think of one." Bill laughed. "It's just bad timing. Maybe if the BBC doesn't work out I'll think about it. After all, who knows how long this broadcasting thing might last? It could just be a flash in the pan. Aren't you going to miss dear old England?"

"Not in the least." Simon shook his head. "This country is

becoming far too right wing for my liking. We've got that nasty little fascist Moseley in the government at the moment. And the right wing is on the ascendancy. Germany's a far more liberal country."

"So what are you going to do? Live with Calvin in Berlin?"

Simon looked down at his menu. "We haven't talked about those sorts of practicalities yet," he said. "But, yes. If I decide to go. Why not?"

"How wonderful." Bill patted his arm. "I'm genuinely happy for you, Simon. To be able to live in an enlightened society like that. I can see why you can't wait to leave here."

She leaned forward and kissed him on the lips.

"Keep in touch Mr Sampson. I'm going to miss you."

"Of course I'll keep in touch." Simon smiled. "Maybe our paths will cross again one day."

THE END

AUTHOR'S NOTE

I'd like to thank several very important women in the creation of this novel:

Sue Laybourn for her editing help in the UK,
Barbara Senden for her editing help in the US,
Garret Leigh for her fabulous cover designs for this series.

Florence Milnes, MBE, who is the real-life inspiration for Bill. She established the first reference library for the BBC in the 1920s and was a stickler for detail.

Eleanor Rathbone, MP, who is the real-life inspiration for Cynny. She was a social reformer and campaigner for women's rights. Online historical references coyly refer to her 'longterm friendship' with another force in social reform Elizabeth Macadam.

One day the history we are taught might more accurately reflect the true role that women have played in shaping and improving our society. Until then we will have to peer critically through the skew of a centuries old male perspective.

ABOUT THIS BOOK

London 1929: The stage is set for murder

It's the summer of 1929 and there's a serial killer on the streets of London.

Bodies of young women are dumped at the stage doors of London's theatres.

Noël Coward's Assistant Florence Miles, known to her close friends as Bill, is dragged into the investigation when the body of her former secret lover is found outside His Majesty's Theatre.

Bill forms an unlikely alliance with the *Chronicle* newspaper's senior crime reporter Simon Sampson. Together they discover that the killer has friends in high places...

This is the prequel to the LAMBDA finalist *A Death in Berlin*. It explores the secret world of the 1920s, a time when your sexuality could make you a lawbreaker. When gay men and women were constantly on their guard, careful about how they presented themselves in a hostile society.

A Death At His Majesty's is the first of a series that brings together Bill and Simon and follows them as they embark on a series of sleuthing adventures.

ALSO BY DAVID C. DAWSON

A Death in Berlin

A Death in Bloomsbury

The Necessary Deaths

The Deadly Lies

The Foreign Affair

For the Love of Luke

Heroes in Love

A DEATH IN BERLIN

Berlin 1933: When the parties stop...the dying begins

The city that has been a beacon of liberation during the 1920s is about to become a city of deadly oppression. BBC foreign correspondent Simon Sampson risks his life in a bid to save thousands of gay men from the growing Nazi threat.

This is the second in the Simon Sampson mystery series. The first, A Death in Bloomsbury, was hailed as 'a good old-fashioned John Buchan-esque mystery reworked for the twenty-first century'.

Simon moves to Berlin where he meets up with British author Christopher Isherwood and his lover Heinz. He's also reunited with his banter-partner Florence Miles, better known to her friends as Bill. She's recruited him into the British intelligence services and he's got the task of hunting down communist spies.

But when Simon is ordered to spy on an old college friend, his loyalties are brought into question. Who are his real enemies? And how much can he trust his masters?

<u>Available on Amazon</u>

A DEATH IN BLOOMSBURY

Everyone has secrets... but some are fatal.

1932, London. Late one December night Simon Sampson stumbles across the body of a woman in an alleyway. Her death is linked to a plot by right-wing extremists to assassinate the King on Christmas Day. Simon resolves to do his patriotic duty and unmask the traitors.

But Simon Sampson lives a double life. Not only is he a highly respected BBC radio announcer, but he's also a man who loves men, and as such must live a secret life. His investigation risks revealing his other life and with that imprisonment under Britain's draconian homophobic laws of the time. He faces a stark choice: his loyalty to the King or his freedom.

This is the first in a new series from award-winning author David C. Dawson. A richly atmospheric novel set in the shadowy world of 1930s London, where secrets are commonplace, and no one is quite who they seem.

Available on Amazon

THE NECESSARY DEATHS

The Delingpole Mysteries: Book One

A young man. Unconscious in a hospital bed. His life is in the balance from a drugs overdose.

Attempted suicide or attempted murder?

British lawyer Dominic Delingpole investigates, with the help of his larger than life partner Jonathan McFadden.

Dominic and Jonathan uncover a conspiracy reaches into the highest levels of government and powerful corporations.

Three people are murdered, and Dominic and Jonathan struggle for their very survival in this gripping thriller.

Award winner in the 2017 FAPA President's Awards for Adult Suspense and Thrillers.

Available on Amazon

THE DEADLY LIES

The Delingpole Mysteries: Book Two

A man is murdered, and takes a deadly secret to his grave.

Is it true the murdered man is Dominic Delingpole's former lover? And were they still seeing each other just before his recent wedding to husband Jonathan?

Or are these simply lies?

This is more than a story of deceit between husbands. A man's death plunges Dominic and Jonathan into a world of international espionage, which puts their lives at risk.

What is the ruthless Charter Ninety-Nine group? Why is it chasing them across Europe and the US?

Dominic and Jonathan are forced to test their relation- ship to its limit. What deadly lies must they both confront? And if they stay alive, will their relationship remain intact?

Available on Amazon

THE FOREIGN AFFAIR

The Delingpole Mysteries: Book Three

There's a murderer stalking the gay bars of Berlin.

It's September. The time of Folsom Europe. Berlin's annual festival for gay men in leather.

And the city's become a dangerous place for them.

British lawyer, and part-time sleuth Dominic Delingpole is in town.

He discovers the attacks are linked to a sinister, Russian-backed experiment.

Dominic teams up with German lawyer Johann Hartmann, a man with the seductive charm and good looks of Dominic's late husband.

But whose side is Hartmann really on?

<u>Available on Amazon</u>

FOR THE LOVE OF LUKE

A handsome naked man. Unconscious on a bathroom floor.

He's lost his memory, and someone's out to kill him. Who is the mysterious Luke?

British TV anchor and journalist Rupert Pendley-Evans doesn't do long-term relationships. Nor does he do waifs and strays. But Luke is different. Luke is a talented American artist with a dark secret in his life.

When Rupert discovers Luke, he's intrigued, and before he can stop himself, he's in love. The aristocratic Rupert is an ambitious TV reporter with a nose for a story and a talent for uncovering the truth. As he falls deeper in love with Luke, he discovers the reason for Luke's amnesia. And the explanation puts them both in mortal danger.

Available on Amazon

HEROES IN LOVE

Not every hero wears a uniform

Can love last a lifetime?

Billy and Daniel never intended to be matchmakers.

After all, they're only at the start of their own love story.

But Billy uncovers a failed love affair that lasted over fifty years until it fell apart.

He and Daniel see their own fledgling relationship through the lens of the now estranged couple.

They vow to reunite the elderly lovers.

But as they set about their task, the pressures of modern life threaten to tear them apart.

Available on Amazon

ABOUT THE AUTHOR

David C. Dawson is an award-winning author, journalist and documentary maker, and lives in London and Oxford.

His debut novel *The Necessary Deaths* won Bronze for Best Mystery & Suspense in the FAPA awards.

A Death in Berlin was shortlisted for a LAMMY.

As a journalist he's travelled extensively, filming in nearly every continent of the world. He's lived in London, Geneva and San Francisco, but he now prefers the tranquillity of the Oxfordshire countryside.

In his spare time, David tours Europe with his boyfriend, and sings with the London Gay Men's Chorus.